Best Science Fiction Stories
of James Blish

Best Science Fiction Stories
of James Blish

(*Revised Edition*)

FABER AND FABER LTD

3 Queen Square

London

SF

First published in 1955
This revised edition 1973
by Faber and Faber Limited
3 Queen Square London W.C.1
Printed in Great Britain by
Straker Brothers Ltd Whitstable
All rights reserved

ISBN 0 571 04782 3

© *This collection by James Blish*
1965 and 1973

To my
JUDY
who somehow shared
these images of sleep
when we were all children

with all of love

Contents

A Preface to Tomorrow

Short stories of any kind are like tattoos: though they are on public display, they come into being to identify the self to the self. The commonest and hence the most stereotyped were undertaken to prove that the subject/object is grown up, with a flourish of brightly coloured but non-functional women, guns and other machinery. Another kind attempts to seal an identification with some stronger and more stable entity—Mother, Mamie, Semper Fidelis or Free Enterprise; or make real some pigeon-hole into which the personality is trying to cram itself—Lover, Killer, Mighty Hunter.

The most interesting kinds, however, are those cryptic symbols which the mentally ill inflict upon themselves. Here the vision of the outside world which the story or tattoo tries to make real is almost as private as the psyche which so stigmatizes itself. Only the necessity to adopt some sort of artistic convention, and to limit the message to something less than the whole of the mystery, makes the end-product even partially intelligible—and, to some part of the audience, holds out the hope that the mystery might be solved.

There is at least a little of the private vision in every work of fiction, but it is in fantasy that the distance between the real world —that is, the agreed-upon world, the consensus we call reality— and the private vision becomes marked and disturbing. The science-fiction writer chooses, to symbolize *his* real world, the trappings of science and technology, and in so far as the reader is unfamiliar with these, so will the story seem *outré* to him. It is commonplace for outsiders to ask science-fiction writers, "Where do you get those crazy ideas?" and to regard the habitual readers of science fiction also as rather far off the common ground. Yet it is not really the ideas that are "crazy" but the trappings; not the assumptions, but the scenery. Instead of Main Street—in itself only a symbol—we are given Mars, or the future.

The reason for this choice is put succinctly by Brian Aldiss:

"I am a surrealist at heart; that is, I'm none too sure whether the reality of the world agrees with its appearance. Only in sf, or near sf, can you express this feeling in words."

Of course, this is not entirely true; neither Kafka nor Beckford had any difficulty in expressing the same feeling in quite different trappings, in sporting quite different tattoos. But for any writer who knows how surrealistic are the assumptions of our modern metaphysics, the science-tattoo is not only attractive but compelling.

It is not even essential that the symbols be used correctly, although most conscientious science-fiction writers try to get them right in order to lure the reader into the necessary suspension of disbelief. There is no such place as Ray Bradbury's Mars—to use the most frequently cited complaint—but his readers have justly brushed the complaint aside, recognizing the feeling as authentic even though the facts are not. This is probably what Mr. Aldiss means by "near-sf", as it is what I mean by fantasy. The essential difference lies only in how close to the consensus the writer wants his private tattoo to appear.

The absolutely essential honesty, however, must lie where it has to lie in all fiction: honesty to the assumptions, not to the trappings. As Theodore Sturgeon has said:

"A good science-fiction story is a story about human beings, with a human problem, and a human solution, which would not have happened at all without its science content."

This is a laudable and workable rule of thumb, it seems to me, as long as the writer is aware that the "science content" is only another form of tattoo design, differing in detail but not in nature from those adopted by the writers of all other kinds of fiction.

I wish I could say that I have been aware of it since I began writing (or rather, publishing) science fiction in 1940, but of course

A PREFACE TO TOMORROW

the conclusion is a recent one, and rather hard come by. A collection of short stories, however, seems like a proper place for hindsight. In this volume, with the active collusion of that most valuable of editors Charles Monteith, I have assembled those few stories of mine which came closest in my own eyes to satisfying all these strictures. Even now, my tattoos and the real world (has anyone seen it lately?) do not seem to make a very good fit, but there is still no excitement like trying.

JAMES BLISH

New York
1964

POSTSCRIPT

In the eight years since the first edition of this collection was assembled, most of my work has consisted of novels and screenplays, plus a number of critical pieces for literary quarterlies; but inevitably, a number of new short stories have piled up along the way. For this edition, I have dropped my 22-year-old werewolf story *There Shall Be No Darkness* in favor of a novelet, *We All Die Naked*, which I think has better characters and a lot more emotional bite than the novella it displaces. For once, my readers agreed with me; the story was short-listed for a Hugo award. Since it is shorter than the werewolf story, I was also enabled to add another story, *How Beautiful With Banners*, chosen from some other recent ones of about the same length because I love it.

JAMES BLISH

Harpsden (Henley)
Oxon., 1972

To my considerable bafflement, this is the most popular story I have ever written. Many readers know nothing else of mine, and many who don't know my name, much less anything else I've turned out, speak of the piece with affection and with an amazing memory for its often quite esoteric details. I set out to do no more than write about what it might really be like to live in the microcosm, where such forces as surface tension are all-important and such forces as gravity negligible; but somewhere along the line I seem to have touched a nerve more mythological than molecular. I wish I knew how, for if I did, I'd do it again.

Surface Tension

Dr. Chatvieux took a long time over the microscope, leaving la Ventura with nothing to do but look at the dead landscape of Hydrot. Waterscape, he thought, would be a better word. From space, the new world had shown only one small, triangular continent, set amid endless ocean; and even the continent was mostly swamp.

The wreck of the seed-ship lay broken squarely across the one real spur of rock which Hydrot seemed to possess, which reared a magnificent twenty-one feet above sea-level. From this eminence, la Ventura could see forty miles to the horizon across a flat bed of mud. The red light of the star Tau Ceti, glinting upon thousands of small lakes, pools, ponds and puddles, made the watery plain look like a mosaic of onyx and ruby.

"If I were a religious man," the pilot said suddenly, "I'd call this a plain case of divine vengeance."

Chatvieux said: "Hmn?"

"It's as if we'd been struck down for—is it *hubris*, arrogant pride?"

"Well, is it?" Chatvieux said, looking up at last. "I don't feel exactly swollen with pride. Do you?"

"I'm not exactly proud of my piloting," la Ventura admitted.

"But that isn't quite what I meant. I was thinking about why we came here in the first place. It takes a lot of arrogance to think that you can scatter men, or at least things very much like men, all over the face of the galaxy. It takes even more pride to do the job—to pack up all the equipment and move from planet to planet and actually make men, make them suitable for every place you touch."

"I suppose it does," Chatvieux said. "But we're only one of several hundred seed-ships in this limb of the galaxy, so I doubt that the gods picked us out as special sinners." He smiled dryly. "If they had, maybe they'd have left us our ultraphone, so the Colonization Council could hear about our cropper. Besides, Paul, we try to produce men adapted to Earthlike planets, nothing more than that. We've sense enough to know that we can't adapt men to a planet like Jupiter, or to a sun, like Tau Ceti."

"Anyhow, we're here," la Ventura said grimly. "And we aren't going to get off. Phil tells me that we don't even have our germ-cell bank any more, so we can't seed this place in the usual way. We've been thrown on to a dead world and dared to adapt to it. What are the panatropes to do with our carcasses—provide built-in water-wings?"

"No," Chatvieux said calmly. "You and I and all the rest of us are going to die, Paul. Pantropic techniques don't work on the body; that was fixed for you for life when you were conceived. To attempt to rebuild it for you would only maim you. The panatropes affect only the genes, the inheritance-carrying factors. We can't give you built-in waterwings, any more than we can give you a new set of brains. I think we'll be able to populate this world with men, but we won't live to see it."

The pilot thought about it, a lump of cold blubber collecting in his stomach. "How long do you give us?"

"Who knows? A month, perhaps."

The bulkhead leading to the wrecked section of the ship was pushed back, admitting salt, muggy air, heavy with carbon dioxide. Philip Strasvogel, the communications officer, came in, tracking mud. Like la Ventura, he was now a man without a function, and it appeared to bother him. He was not well equipped for introspection, and with his ultraphone totally smashed, unresponsive to his perpetually darting hands, he had been thrown back into his own mind, whose resources were few. Only the tasks Chatvieux had set him to had prevented him from setting like a gelling colloid into a permanent sulk.

He unbuckled from around his waist a canvas belt, into the loops of which plastic vials were stuffed like cartridges. "More samples, Doc," he said. "All alike—water, very wet. I have some quicksand in one boot, too. Find anything?"

"A good deal, Phil. Thanks. Are the others around?"

Strasvogel poked his head out and hallooed. Other voices rang out over the mudflats. Minutes later, the rest of the survivors of the crash were crowding into the panatrope deck: Saltonstall, Chatvieux's senior assistant, a perpetually sanguine, perpetually youthful technician willing to try anything once, including dying; Eunice Wagner, behind whose placid face rested the brains of the expedition's only remaining ecologist; Eleftherios Venezuelos, the always-silent delegate from the Colonization Council; and Joan Heath, a midshipman whose duties, like la Ventura's and Phil's, were now without meaning, but whose bright head and tall, deceptively indolent body shone to the pilot's eyes brighter than the home sun.

Five men and two women—to colonize a planet on which "standing room" meant treading water.

They came in quietly and found seats or resting-places on the deck, on the edges of tables, in corners. Joan Heath went to stand beside la Ventura. They did not look at each other, but the warmth of her shoulder beside his was all that he needed. Nothing was as bad as it seemed.

Venezuelos said, "What's the verdict, Dr. Chatvieux?"

"This place isn't dead," Chatvieux said. "There's life in the sea and in the fresh water, both. On the animal side of the ledger, evolution seems to have stopped with the crustacea; the most advanced form I've found is a tiny crayfish, from one of the local rivulets, and it doesn't seem to be well distributed. The ponds and puddles are well stocked with small metazoans of lower orders, right up to the rotifers—including a castle-building rotifer like Earth's *Floscularidae*. In addition, there's a wonderfully variegated protozoan population, with a dominant ciliate type much like *Para-*

moecium, plus various Sarcodines, the usual spread of phytoflagel-lates, and even a phosphorescent species I wouldn't have expected to see anywhere but in salt water. As for the plants, they run from simple blue-green algae to quite advanced thallus-producing types —though none of them, of course, can live out of the water."

"The sea is about the same," Eunice said. "I've found some of the larger simple metazoans—jellyfish and so on—and some *Pali-nuridae* almost as big as lobsters. But it's normal to find salt-water species running larger than fresh-water. And there's the usual plankton and nanno-plankton population."

"In short," Chatvieux said, "we'll survive if we fight."

"Wait a minute," la Ventura said. "You've just finished telling me that we wouldn't survive. And you were talking about us, the seven of us here, not about the genus Man, because we don't have our germ-cell banks any more."

"We don't have the banks. But we ourselves can contribute germ-cells, Paul. I'll get to that in a moment." Chatvieux turned to Saltonstall. "Martin, what would you think of taking to the sea? We came out of it once."

"No good," Saltonstall said immediately. "*I* like the idea, but I don't think this planet ever heard of Swinburne, or Homer either. Looking at it as a colonization problem alone, as if we weren't involved in it ourselves, I wouldn't give you an Oc dollar for *epi oinopa ponton.* The evolutionary pressure there is too high, the competition from other species is prohibitive; seeding the sea should be the last thing we attempt. The colonists wouldn't learn a thing before they'd be gobbled up."

"Why?" la Ventura said. Once more, the death in his stomach was becoming hard to placate.

"Eunice, do your sea-going Coelenterates include anything like the Portuguese man-of-war?"

The ecologist nodded.

"There's your answer, Paul," Saltonstall said. "The sea is out. It's got to be fresh water, where the competition is less formidable and there are more places to hide."

"We can't compete with a jellyfish?" la Ventura asked.

"No, Paul," Chatvieux said. "Not with one that formidable. The panatropes make adaptations, not gods. They take human germ-cells—in this case, our own, since our bank was wiped out in the crash—and modify them genetically towards those of creatures who can live in any reasonable environment. The result will be manlike, and intelligent. It usually shows the donors' personality patterns, too, since the modifications are usually made in the morphology, not mind, of the resulting individual.

"*But we can't transmit memory*. The adapted man is worse than a child in his new environment. He has no history, no techniques, no precedents, not even a language. In the usual colonization project, the seeding teams more or less take him through elementary school before they leave the planet to him, but we won't survive long enough to give such instruction. We'll have to design our colonists with plenty of built-in protections and locate them in the most favourable environment possible, so that some of them will survive learning by experience alone."

The pilot thought about it, but nothing occurred to him which did not make the disaster seem realer and more intimate with each passing second. Joan Heath moved slightly closer to him. "One of the new creatures can have my personality pattern, but it won't be able to remember being me. Is that right?"

"That's right. In the present situation we'll probably make our colonists haploid, so that some of them, perhaps many, will have a heredity traceable to you alone. There may be just the faintest of residuums of identity—pantropy's given us some data to support the old Jungian notion of ancestral memory. But we're all going to die on Hydrot, Paul, as self-conscious persons. There's no avoiding that. Somewhere we'll leave behind people who behave as we would, think and feel as we would, but who won't remember us—or the Earth."

The pilot said nothing more.

"Saltonstall, what do you recommend as a form?"

The pantropist pulled reflectively at his nose. "Webbed extremities, of course, with thumbs and big toes heavy and thornlike for defence until the creature has had a chance to learn. Smaller external ears, and the eardrum larger and closer to the outer end of the ear-canal. We're going to have to reorganize the water-conservation system, I think; the glomerular kidney is perfectly suitable for living in fresh water, but the business of living immersed in fresh water, inside and out, for a creature with a salty inside means that the osmotic pressure inside is going to be higher than outside, so that the kidneys are going to have to be pumping virtually all the time. Under the circumstances we'd best step up production of urine, and that means the antidiuretic function of the pituitary gland is going to have to be abrogated."

"What about respiration?"

"Hmm," Saltonstall said. "I suppose book-lungs, like some of the arachnids have. They can be supplied by intercostal spiracles. They're gradually adaptable to atmosphere-breathing, if our colonist ever decides to come out of the water. Just to provide for that possibility, I'd suggest retaining the nose, maintaining the nasal cavity as a part of the otological system, but cutting off the cavity from the larynx with a membrane of cells that are supplied with oxygen by direct irrigation, rather than by the respiratory system. Such a membrane wouldn't survive for many generations, once the creature took to living out of the water even for part of its lifetime; it'd go through two or three generations as an amphibian, and then one day it'd suddenly find itself breathing through its larynx again.

"Also, Dr. Chatvieux, I'd suggest that we have it adopt sporulation. As an aquatic animal, our colonist is going to have an indefinite life-span, but we'll have to give it a breeding cycle of about six weeks to keep up its numbers during the learning period; so there'll have to be a definite break of some duration in its active year. Otherwise it'll hit overpopulation before it's learned to cope with it."

"Also, it'd be better if our colonists could winter over inside a good, hard shell," Eunice Wagner added in agreement. "So sporulation's the obvious answer. Many other microscopic creatures have it."

"Microscopic?" Phil said incredulously.

"Certainly," Chatvieux said, amused. "We can't very well crowd a six-foot man into a two-foot puddle. But that raises a question. We'll have tough competition from the rotifers, and some of them aren't strictly microscopic; for that matter even some of the protozoa can be seen with the naked eye, just barely, with dark-field illumination. I don't think your average colonist should run much under 250 microns. Give them a chance to slug it out."

"I was thinking of making them twice that big."

"Then they'd be the biggest animals in their environment," Eunice Wagner pointed out, "and won't ever develop any skills. Besides, if you make them about rotifer size, it will give them an incentive for pushing out the castle-building rotifers, and occupying the castles."

Chatvieux nodded. "All right, let's get started. While the panatropes are being calibrated, the rest of us can put our heads together on leaving a record for these people. We'll micro-engrave the record on a set of corrosion-proof metal leaves, of a size our colonists can handle conveniently. We can tell them, very simply, what happened, and plant a few suggestions that there's more to the universe than their puddles. Some day they may puzzle it out."

"Question," Eunice Wagner said. "Are we going to tell them they're microscopic? I'm opposed to it. It may saddle their entire early history with a gods-and-demons mythology that they'd be better off without."

"Yes, we are," Chatvieux said; and la Ventura could tell by the change in the tone of his voice that he was speaking now as their senior on the expedition. "These people will be of the race of men, Eunice. We want them to win their way back into the community of men. They are not toys, to be protected from the truth for ever in a fresh-water womb."

"Besides," Saltonstall observed, "they won't get the record translated at any time in their early history. They'll have to develop a written language of their own, and it will be impossible for us to leave them any sort of Rosetta Stone or other key. By the time they can decipher the truth, they should be ready for it."

"I'll make that official," Venezuelos said unexpectedly.

And then, essentially, it was all over. They contributed the cells that the panatropes would need. Privately, la Ventura and Joan Heath went to Chatvieux and asked to contribute jointly; but the scientist said that the microscopic men were to be haploid, in order to give them a minute cellular structure, with nuclei as small as

19

Earthly rickettsiae, and therefore each person had to give germ-cells individually—there would be no use for zygotes. So even that consolation was denied them: in death they would have no children, but be instead as alone as ever.

They helped, as far as they could, in the text of the message which was to go on the metal leaves. They had their personality patterns recorded. They went through the motions. Already they were beginning to be hungry, but there was nothing on Hydrot big enough to eat.

After la Ventura had set his control board to rights—a useless gesture, but a habit he had been taught to respect, and which in an obscure way made things a little easier to bear—he was out of it. He sat by himself at the far end of the rock ledge, watching Tau Ceti go redly down.

After a while Joan Heath came silently up behind him, and sat down too. He took her hand. The glare of the red sun was almost extinguished now, and together they watched it go, with la Ventura, at least, wondering sombrely which nameless puddle was to be his Lethe.

He never found out, of course. None of them did.

Old Shar set down the thick, ragged-edged metal plate at last, and gazed instead out the window of the castle, apparently resting his eyes on the glowing green-gold obscurity of the summer waters. In the soft fluorescence which played down upon him, from the Noc dozing impassively in the groined vault of the chamber, Lavon could see that he was in fact a young man. His face was so delicately formed as to suggest that it had not been many seasons since he had first emerged from his spore.

But of course there had been no real reason to have expected an old man. All the Shars had been referred to traditionally as "old" Shar. The reason, like the reasons for everything else, had been forgotten, but the custom had persisted. The adjective at least gave weight and dignity to the office—that of the centre of wisdom of all the people, as each Lavon had been the centre of authority.

The present Shar belonged to the generation XVI, and hence

would have to be at least two seasons younger than Lavon himself. If he was old, it was only in knowledge.

"Lavon, I'm going to have to be honest with you," Shar said at last, still looking out of the tall, irregular window. "You've come to me at your maturity for the secrets on the metal plates, just as your predecessors did to mine. I can give some of them to you—but for the most part, I don't know what they mean."

"After so many generations?" Lavon asked, surprised. "Wasn't it Shar III who first found out how to read them?"

The young man turned and looked at Lavon with eyes made dark and wide by the depths into which they had been staring. "I can read what's on the plates, but most of it seems to make no sense. Worst of all, the plates are incomplete. You didn't know that? They are. One of them was lost in a battle during the final war with the Eaters, while these castles were still in their hands."

"What am I here for, then?" Lavon said. "Isn't there anything of value on the remaining plates? Do they really contain 'the wisdom of the Creators', or is *that* myth?"

"No. No, it's true," Shar said slowly, "as far as it goes."

He paused, and both men turned and gazed at the ghostly creature which had appeared suddenly outside the window. Then Shar said gravely, "Come in, Para."

The slipper-shaped organism, nearly transparent except for the thousands of black-and-silver granules and frothy bubbles which packed its interior, glided into the chamber and hovered, with a muted whirring of cilia. For a moment it remained silent, probably speaking telepathically to the Noc floating in the vault, after the ceremonious fashion of all the protos. No human had ever intercepted one of these colloquies, but there was no doubt about their reality; humans had used protos for long-range communication for generations.

Then the Para's cilia buzzed once more. Each separate hair-like process vibrated at an independent, changing rate; the resulting sound waves spread through the water, intermodulating, reinforcing or cancelling each other. The aggregate wave-front, by the time it reached human ears, was eerie but recognizable human speech.

"We are arrived, according to the custom."

"And welcome," said Shar. "Lavon, let's leave this matter of the plates for a while, until you hear what Para has to say; that's a part of the knowledge Lavons must have as they come into their office, and it comes before the plates. I can give you some hints of what we are. First Para has to tell you something about what we aren't."

Lavon nodded, willingly enough, and watched the proto as it settled gently to the surface of the hewn table at which Shar had been sitting. There was in the entity such a perfection and economy of organization, such a grace and surety of movement, that he could hardly believe in his own new-won maturity. Para, like all the protos, made him feel unfinished.

"We know that in this universe there is logically no place for man," the gleaming, now immobile cylinder upon the table droned abruptly. "Our memory is the common property of all our races. It reaches back to a time when there were no such creatures as men here, nor any even remotely like men. It remembers also that once upon a day there were men here, suddenly, and in some numbers. Their spores littered the bottom; we found the spores only a short time after our season's Awakening, and inside them we saw the forms of men, slumbering.

"Then men shattered their spores and emerged. At first they seemed helpless, and the Eaters devoured them by scores, as in those days they devoured anything that moved. But that soon ended. Men were intelligent, active. And they were gifted with a trait, a character, possessed by no other creature in this world. Not even the savage Eaters had it. Men organized us to exterminate the Eaters, and therein lay the difference. Men had initiative. We have the word now, which you gave us, and we apply it, but we still do not know what the thing is that it labels."

"You fought beside us," Lavon said.

"Gladly. We would never have thought of that war by ourselves, but it was good and brought good. Yet we wondered. We saw that men were poor swimmers, poor walkers, poor crawlers, poor climbers. We saw that men were formed to make and use tools, a concept we still do not understand, for so wonderful a gift is largely wasted in this universe, and there is no other. What good are tool-useful members such as the hands of men? We do not know. It

22

seems plain that so radical a thing should lead to a much greater rulership over the world than has, in fact, proven to be possible for men."

Lavon's head was spinning. "Para, I had no notion that you people were philosophers."

"The protos are old," Shar said. He had again turned to look out the window, his hands locked behind his back. "They aren't philosophers, Lavon, but they are remorseless logicians. Listen to Para."

"To this reasoning there could be but one outcome," the Para said. "Our strange ally, Man, was like nothing else in this universe. He was and is unfitted for it. He does not belong here; he has been—adopted. This drives us to think that there are other universes besides this one, but where these universes might lie, and what their properties might be, it is impossible to imagine. We have no imagination, as men know."

Was the creature being ironic? Lavon could not tell. He said slowly: "Other universes? How could that be true?"

"We do not know," the Para's uninflected voice hummed.

Shar had resumed sitting on the window-sill, clasping his knees, watching the come and go of dim shapes in the lighted gulf. "It is quite true," he said. "What is written on the plates makes it plain. I'll tell you what they say.

"*We were made*, Lavon. We were made by men who were not as we are, but men who were our ancestors all the same. They were caught in some disaster, and they made us, and put us here in our universe—so that, even though they had to die, the race of men would live."

Lavon surged up from the woven spyrogyra mat upon which he had been sitting. "You must think I'm a fool!"

"No. You're our Lavon; you have a right to know the facts. Make what you like of them." Shar swung his webbed toes back into the chamber. "What I've told you may be hard to believe, but it seems to be so; what Para says backs it up. Our unfitness to live here is self-evident.

"The past four Shars discovered that we won't get any farther in our studies until we learn how to control heat. We've produced enough heat chemically to show that even the water around us changes when the temperature gets high enough. But there we're stopped."

"Why?"

"Because heat produced in open water is carried off as rapidly as it's produced. Once we tried to enclose that heat, and we blew up a whole tube of the castle and killed everything in range; the shock was terrible. We measured the pressures that were involved in that explosion, and we discovered that no substance we know could have resisted them. Theory suggests some stronger substances—*but we need heat to form them!*

"Take our chemistry. We live in water. Everything seems to dissolve in water, to some extent. How do we confine a chemical test to the crucible we put it in? How do we maintain a solution at one dilution? I don't know. Every avenue leads me to the same stone door. We're thinking creatures, Lavon, but there's something drastically wrong in the way we think about this universe we live in. It just doesn't seem to lead to results."

Lavon pushed back his floating hair futilely. "Maybe you're thinking about the wrong results. We've had no trouble with warfare, or crops, or practical things like that. If we can't create much heat, well, most of us won't miss it; we don't need any. What's the other universe supposed to be like, the one our ancestors lived in? Is it any better than this one?"

"I don't know," Shar admitted. "It was so different that it's hard to compare the two. The metal plates tell a story about men who were travelling from one place to another in a container that moved by itself. The only analogy I can think of is the shallops of diatom shells that our youngsters use to sled along the thermocline; but evidently what's meant is something much bigger.

"I picture a huge shallop, closed on all sides, big enough to hold many people—maybe twenty or thirty. It had to travel for generations through some kind of space where there wasn't any water to breathe, so that the people had to carry their own water and renew it constantly. There were no seasons; no ice formed on the sky, because there wasn't any sky in a closed shallop.

"Then the shallop was wrecked somehow. The people in it knew

24

they were going to die. They made us, and put us here, as if we were their children. Because they had to die, they wrote their story on the plates, to tell us what had happened. I suppose we'd understand it better if we had the plate Shar III lost during the war, but we don't."

"The whole thing sounds like a parable," Lavon said, shrugging. "Or a song. I can see why you don't understand it. What I can't see is why you bother to try."

"Because of the plates," Shar said. "You've handled them yourself now, so you know that we've nothing like them. We have crude, impure metals we've hammered out, metals that last for a while and then decay. But the plates shine on, generation after generation. They don't change; our hammers and our graving tools break against them; the little heat we can generate leaves them unharmed. Those plates weren't formed in our universe—and that one fact makes every word on them important to me. Someone went to a great deal of trouble to make those plates indestructible, and to give them to us. Someone to whom the word 'stars' was important enough to be worth fourteen repetitions, despite the fact that the word doesn't seem to mean anything."

Lavon stood up once more.

"All these extra universes and huge shallops and meaningless words—I can't say that they don't exist, but I don't see what difference it makes," he said. "The Shars of a few generations ago spent their whole lives breeding better algae crops for us, and showing us how to cultivate them, instead of living haphazardly on bacteria. Farther back, the Shars devised war engines, and war plans. All that was work worth doing. The Lavons of those days evidently got along without the metal plates and their puzzles, and saw to it that the Shars did, too. Well, as far as I'm concerned, you're welcome to the plates, if you like them better than crop improvement—but I think they ought to be thrown away."

"All right," Shar said, shrugging. "If you don't want them, that ends the traditional interview. We'll go our——"

There was a rising drone from the table-top. The Para was lifting itself, waves of motion passing over its cilia, like the waves which went silently across the fruiting stalks of the fields of delicate fungi with which the bottom was planted. It had been so silent that Lavon had forgotten it; he could tell that Shar had, too.

"This is a great decision," the waves of sound washing from the creature throbbed. "Every proto has heard it, and agrees with it. We have been afraid of these metal plates for a long time, afraid that men would learn to understand them and to follow what they say to some secret place, leaving the protos. Now we are not afraid."

"There wasn't anything to be afraid of," Lavon said indulgently.

"No Lavon before you had ever said so," the Para said. "We are glad. We will throw the plates away."

With that, the shining creature swooped towards the embrasure. With it, it bore away the remaining plates, which had been resting under it on the table-top, suspended delicately in the curved tips of its supple ventral cilia. Inside its pellucid body, vacuoles swelled to increase its buoyancy and enable it to carry the heavy weight.

With a cry, Shar plunged towards the window.

"Stop, Para!"

But Para was already gone, so swiftly that it had not even heard the call. Shar twisted his body and brought up on one shoulder against the tower wall. He said nothing. His face was enough. Lavon could not look into it for more than an instant.

The shadows of the two men began to move slowly along the uneven cobbled floor. The Noc descended towards them from the vault, its single thick tentacle stirring the water, its internal light flaring and fading irregularly. It, too, drifted through the window after its cousin, and sank slowly away towards the bottom. Gently its living glow dimmed, flickered in the depths, and winked out.

For many days, Lavon was able to avoid thinking much about the loss. There was already a great deal of work to be done. Maintenance of the castles, which had been built by the now-extinct Eaters rather than by human hands, was a never-ending task. The thousand dichotomously branching wings tended to crumble with time, especially at their bases where they sprouted from one another, and no Shar had yet come forward with a mortar as good as the rotifer-spittle which had once held them together. In addition, the breaking through of windows and the construction of chambers in the early days had been haphazard and often unsound. The instinctive architecture of the Eaters, after all, had not been meant to meet the needs of human occupants.

And then there were the crops. Men no longer fed precariously upon passing bacteria snatched to the mouth; now there were the drifting mats of specific water-fungi and algae, and the mycelia on the bottom, rich and nourishing, which had been bred by five generations of Shars. These had to be tended constantly to keep the strains pure, and to keep the older and less intelligent species of the protos from grazing on them. In this latter task, to be sure, the more intricate and far-seeing proto types co-operated, but men were needed to supervise.

There had been a time, after the war with the Eaters, when it had been customary to prey upon the slow-moving and stupid diatoms, whose exquisite and fragile glass shells were so easily burst, and who were unable to learn that a friendly voice did not necessarily mean a friend. There were still people who would crack open a diatom when no one else was looking, but they were regarded as barbarians, to the puzzlement of the protos. The blurred and simple-minded speech of the gorgeously engraved plants had brought them into the category of pets—a concept which the protos were unable to grasp, especially since men admitted diatoms on the half-frustrule were delicious.

Lavon had had to agree, very early, that the distinction was tiny. After all, humans did eat the desmids, which differed from the diatoms only in three particulars: their shells were flexible, they could not move (and for that matter neither could all but a few groups of diatoms), and they did not speak. Yet to Lavon, as to most men, there did seem to be some kind of distinction, whether the protos could see it or not, and that was that. Under the circumstance he felt that it was a part of his duty, as the hereditary leader of men, to protect the diatoms from the few who poached on them, in defiance of custom, in the high levels of the sunlit sky.

Yet Lavon found it impossible to keep himself busy enough to forget that moment when the last clues to Man's origin and destination had been lifted, on authority of his own careless exaggeration, and borne away.

It might be possible to ask Para for the return of the plates, explain that a mistake had been made. The protos were creatures of implacable logic, but they respected Man, were used to illogic in Man, and might reverse their decision if pressed—

We are sorry. The plates were carried over the bar and released in the gulf. We will have the bottom there searched, but . . .

With a sick feeling he could not repress, Lavon knew that that would be the answer, or something very like it. When the protos decided something was worthless, they did not hide it in some chamber like old women. They threw it away—efficiently.

Yet despite the tormenting of his conscience, Lavon was nearly convinced that the plates were well lost. What had they ever done for Man, except to provide Shars with useless things to think about in the late seasons of their lives? What the Shars themselves had done to benefit Man, here, in the water, in the world, in the universe, had been done by direct experimentation. No bit of useful knowledge had ever come from the plates. There had never been anything in the plates but things best left unthought. The protos were right.

Lavon shifted his position on the plant frond, where he had been sitting in order to overlook the harvesting of an experimental crop of blue-green, oil-rich algae drifting in a clotted mass close to the top of the sky, and scratched his back gently against the coarse bole. The protos were seldom wrong, after all. Their lack of creativity, their inability to think an original thought, was a gift as well as a limitation. It allowed them to see and feel things at all times as they were—not as they hoped they might be, for they had no ability to hope, either.

"La-von! Laa-vah-on!"

The long halloo came floating up from the sleepy depths. Propping one hand against the top of the frond, Lavon bent and looked down. One of the harvesters was looking up at him, holding loosely the adze with which he had been splitting free from the raft the glutinous tetrads of the algae.

"I'm up here. What's the matter?"

"We have the ripened quadrant cut free. Shall we tow it away?"

"Tow it away," Lavon said, with a lazy gesture. He leaned back

28

again. At the same instant, a brilliant reddish glory burst into being above him, and cast itself down towards the depths like mesh after mesh of the finest drawn gold. The great light which lived above the sky during the day, brightening or dimming according to some pattern no Shar ever had fathomed, was blooming again.

Few men, caught in the warm glow of that light, could resist looking up at it—especially when the top of the sky itself wrinkled and smiled just a moment's climb or swim away. Yet, as always, Lavon's bemused upward look gave him back nothing but his own distorted, bobbling reflection, and a reflection of the plant on which he rested. Here was the upper limit, the third of the three surfaces of the universe.

The first surface was the bottom, where the water ended.

The second surface was the thermocline, the invisible division between the colder waters of the bottom and the warm, light waters of the sky. During the height of the warm weather, the thermocline was so definite a division as to make for good sledding and for chilly passage. A real interface formed between the cold, denser bottom waters and the warm reaches above, and maintained itself almost for the whole of the warm season.

The third surface was the sky. One could no more pass through that surface than one could penetrate the bottom, nor was there any better reason to try. There the universe ended. The light which played over it daily, waxing and waning as it chose, seemed one of its properties.

Towards the end of the season, the water gradually became colder and more difficult to breathe, while at the same time the light grew duller and stayed for shorter periods between darknesses. Slow currents started to move. The high waters turned chill and started to fall. The bottom mud stirred and smoked away, carrying with it the spores of the fields of fungi. The thermocline tossed, became choppy, and melted away. The sky began to fog with particles of soft silt carried up from the bottom, the walls, the corners of the universe. Before very long, the whole world was cold, flocculent with dying creatures.

Then the protos encysted; the bacteria, even most of the plants— and, not long afterwards, men, too—curled up in their oil-filled amber shells. The world died until the first current of warm water broke the winter silence.

"La-von!"

Just after the long call, a shining bubble rose past Lavon. He reached out and poked it, but it bounded away from his sharp thumb. The gas bubbles which rose from the bottom in late summer were almost invulnerable—and when some especially hard blow or edge did penetrate them, they broke into smaller bubbles which nothing could touch, leaving behind a remarkably bad smell.

Gas. There was no water inside a bubble. A man who got inside a bubble would have nothing to breathe.

But, of course, it was impossible to enter a bubble. The surface tension was too strong. As strong as Shar's metal plates. As strong as the top of the sky.

As strong as the top of the sky. And above that—once the bubble was broken—a world of gas instead of water? Were all worlds bubbles of water drifting in gas?

If it were so, travel between them would be out of the question, since it would be impossible to pierce the sky to begin with. Nor did the infant cosmography include any provisions for bottoms for the worlds.

And yet some of the local creatures did burrow *into* the bottom, quite deeply, seeking something in those depths which was beyond the reach of Man. Even the surface of the ooze, in high summer, crawled with tiny creatures for which mud was a natural medium. Man, too, passed freely between the two countries of water which were divided by the thermocline, though many of the creatures with which he lived could not pass that line at all, once it had established itself.

And if the new universe of which Shar had spoken existed at all, it had to exist beyond the sky, where the light was. Why could not the sky be passed, after all? The fact that bubbles could sometimes be broken showed that the surface skin that formed between water and gas wasn't completely invulnerable. Had it ever been tried?

Lavon did not suppose that one man could butt his way through the top of the sky, any more than he could burrow into the bottom, but there might be ways around the difficulty. Here at his back, for instance, was a plant which gave every appearance of continuing beyond the sky.

It had always been assumed that the plants died where they touched the sky. For the most part, they did, for frequently the dead extension could be seen, leached and yellow, the boxes of its component cells empty, floating embedded in the perfect mirror. But some were simply chopped off, like the one which sheltered him now. Perhaps that was only an illusion, and instead it soared indefinitely into some other place—some place where men might once have been born, and might still live . . .

The plates were gone. There was only one other way to find out.

Determinedly, Lavon began to climb towards the wavering mirror of the sky. His thorn-thumbed feet trampled obliviously upon the clustered sheathes of fragile stippled diatoms. The tulip-heads of Vortae, placid and murmurous cousins of Para, retracted startledly out of his way upon coiling stalks, to make silly gossip behind him.

Lavon did not hear them. He continued to climb doggedly towards the light, his fingers and toes gripping the plant-bole.

"Lavon! Where are you going? Lavon!"

He leaned out and looked down. The man with the adze, a doll-like figure, was beckoning to him from a patch of blue-green retreating over a violet abyss. Dizzily he looked away, clinging to the bole; he had never been so high before. He had, of course, nothing to fear from falling, but the fear was in his heritage. Then he began to climb again.

After a while, he touched the sky with one hand. He stopped to breathe. Curious bacteria gathered about the base of his thumb where blood from a small cut was fogging away, scattered at his gesture, and wriggled mindlessly back towards the dull red lure.

He waited until he no longer felt winded, and resumed climbing. The sky pressed down against the top of his head, against the back of his neck, against his shoulders. It seemed to give slightly, with a tough, frictionless elasticity. The water here was intensely bright, and quite colourless. He climbed another step, driving his shoulders against that enormous weight.

He might as well have tried to penetrate a cliff.

Again he had to rest. While he panted, he made a curious discovery. All around the bole of the water plant, the steel surface of the sky curved upwards, making a kind of sheathe. He found that he would insert his hand into it—there was almost enough space to admit his head as well. Clinging closely to the bole, he looked up into the inside of the sheathe, probing it with his injured hand. The glare was blinding.

There was a kind of soundless explosion. His whole wrist was suddenly encircled in an intense, impersonal grip, as if it were being cut in two. In blind astonishment, he lunged upwards.

The ring of pain travelled smoothly down his upflung arm as he rose, was suddenly around his shoulders and chest. Another lunge and his knees were being squeezed in the circular vise. Another—

Something was horribly wrong. He clung to the bole and tried to gasp, but there was—nothing to breathe.

The water came streaming out of his body, from his mouth, his nostrils, the spiracles in his sides, spurting in tangible jets. An intense and fiery itching crawled over the surface of his body. At each spasm, long knives ran into him, and from a great distance he heard more water being expelled from his book-lungs in an obscene, frothy sputtering. Inside his head, a patch of fire began to eat away at the floor of his nasal cavity.

Lavon was drowning.

With a final convulsion, he kicked himself away from the splintery bole, and fell. A hard impact shook him; and then the water, which had clung to him so tightly when he had first attempted to leave it, took him back with cold violence.

Sprawling and tumbling grotesquely, he drifted, down and down and down, towards the bottom.

For many days, Lavon lay curled insensibly in his spore, as if in the winter sleep. The shock of cold which he had felt on re-entering his native universe had been taken by his body as a sign of coming winter, as it had taken the oxygen-starvation of his brief sojourn above the sky. The spore-forming glands had at once begun to function.

Had it not been for this, Lavon would surely have died. The danger of drowning disappeared even as he fell, as the air bubbled out of his lungs and readmitted the life-giving water. But for acute dessication and third-degree sunburn, the sunken universe knew no remedy. The healing amnionic fluid generated by the spore-forming glands, after the transparent amber sphere had enclosed him, offered Lavon his only chance.

The brown sphere was spotted after some days by a prowling amoeba, quiescent in the eternal winter of the bottom. Down there the temperature was always an even $4°$, no matter what the season, but it was unheard of that a spore should be found there while the high epilimnion was still warm and rich in oxygen.

Within an hour, the spore was surrounded by scores of astonished protos, jostling each other to bump their blunt eyeless prows against the shell. Another hour later, a squad of worried men came plunging from the castles far above to press their own noses against the transparent wall. Then swift orders were given.

Four Para grouped themselves about the amber sphere, and there was a subdued explosion as the trichocysts which lay embedded at the bases of their cilia, just under the pellicle, burst and cast fine lines of a quickly solidifying liquid into the water. The four Paras thrummed and lifted, tugging.

Lavon's spore swayed gently in the mud and then rose slowly, entangled in the web. Nearby, a Noc cast a cold pulsating glow over the operation—not for the Paras, who did not need the light, but for the baffled knot of men. The sleeping figure of Lavon, head bowed, knees drawn up to its chest, revolved with an absurd solemnity inside the shell as it was moved.

"Take him to Shar, Para."

The young Shar justified, by minding his own business, the traditional wisdom with which his hereditary office had invested him. He observed at once that there was nothing he could do for the encysted Lavon which would not be classifiable as simple meddling.

He had the sphere deposited in a high tower room of his castle, where there was plenty of light and the water was warm, which should suggest to the estivating form that spring was again on the way. Beyond that, he simply sat and watched, and kept his speculations to himself.

Inside the spore, Lavon's body seemed rapidly to be shedding its skin, in long strips and patches. Gradually, his curious shrunkenness disappeared. His withered arms and legs and sunken abdomen filled out again.

The days went by while Shar watched. Finally he could discern no more changes, and, on a hunch, had the spore taken up to the top of the tower, into the direct daylight.

An hour later, Lavon moved in his amber prison.

He uncurled and stretched, turned blank eyes up towards the light. His expression was that of a man who had not yet awakened from a ferocious nightmare. His whole body shone with a strange pink newness.

Shar knocked gently on the walls of the spore. Lavon turned his blind face towards the sound, life coming into his eyes. He smiled tentatively and braced his hands and feet against the inner wall of the shell.

The whole sphere fell abruptly to pieces with a sharp crackling. The amnionic fluid dissipated around him and Shar, carrying away with it the suggestive odour of a bitter struggle against death.

Lavon stood among the shards and looked at Shar silently. At last he said:

"Shar—I've been above the sky."

"I know," Shar said gently.

Again Lavon was silent. Shar said, "Don't be humble, Lavon. You've done an epoch-making thing. It nearly cost you your life. You must tell me the rest—all of it."

"The rest?"

"You taught me a lot while you slept. Or are you still opposed to 'useless' knowledge?"

Lavon could say nothing. He no longer could tell what he knew from what he wanted to know. He had only one question left, but he could not utter it. He could only look dumbly into Shar's delicate face.

"You have answered me," Shar said, even more gently than

34

before. "Come, my friend; join me at my table. We will plan our journey to the stars."

There were five of them around Shar's big table: Shar himself, Lavon, and the three assistants assigned by custom to the Shars from the families Than, Tanol and Stravol. The duties of these three men—or, sometimes, women—under many previous Shars had been simple and onerous: to put into effect in the field the genetic changes in the food crops which the Shar himself had worked out in laboratory tanks and flats. Under other Shars more interested in metal-working or in chemistry, they had been smudged men—diggers, rock-splitters, fashioners and cleaners of apparatus.

Under Shar XVI, however, the three assistants had been more envied than usual among the rest of Lavon's people, for they seemed to do very little work of any kind. They spent long hours of every day and evening talking with Shar in his chambers, pouring over records, making mysterious scratch-marks on slate, or just looking at simple things about which there was no obvious mystery. Sometimes they actually worked with Shar in his laboratory, but mostly they just sat.

Shar XVI had, as a matter of fact, discovered certain rudimentary rules of inquiry which, as he explained it to Lavon, he had recognized as tools of enormous power. He had become more interested in passing these on to future workers than in the seductions of any specific experiment, the journey to the stars perhaps excepted. The Than, Tanol and Stravol of his generation were having scientific method pounded into their heads, a procedure they maintained was sometimes more painful than heaving a thousand rocks.

That they were the first of Lavon's people to be taxed with the problem of constructing a spaceship was, therefore, inevitable. The results lay on the table: three models, made of diatom-glass, strands of algae, flexible bits of cellulose, flakes of stonewort, slivers of wood, and organic glues collected from the secretions of a score of different plants and animals.

Lavon picked up the nearest one, a fragile spherical construction inside which little beads of dark-brown lava—actually bricks of rotifer-spittle painfully chipped free from the wall of an unused castle—moved freely back and forth in a kind of ball-bearing race. "Now whose is this one?" he said, turning the sphere curiously to and fro.

"That's mine," Tanol said. "Frankly I don't think it comes anywhere near meeting all the requirements. It's just the only design I could arrive at that I think we could build with the materials and knowledge we have."

"But how does it work?"

"Hand it here a moment, Lavon. This bladder you see inside at the centre, with the hollow spyrogyra straws leading out from it to the skin of the ship, is a buoyancy tank. The idea is that we trap ourselves a big gas-bubble as it rises from the bottom and install it in the tank. Probably we'll have to do that piecemeal. Then the ship rises to the sky on the buoyancy of the bubble. The little paddles, here along these two bands on the outside, rotate when the crew—that's these bricks you hear shaking around inside—walks a treadmill that runs around the inside of the hull; they paddle us over to the edge of the sky. Then we pull the paddles in—they fold over into slots, like this—and, still by weight-transfer from the inside, roll ourselves up the slope until we're out in space. When we hit another world and enter the water again, we let the gas out of the tank gradually through the exhaust tubes represented by these straws, and sink down to a landing at a controlled rate."

"Very ingenious," Shar said thoughtfully. "But I can foresee some difficulties. For one thing, the design lacks stability."

"Yes, it does," Tanol agreed. "And keeping it in motion is going to require a lot of footwork. On the other hand, the biggest expenditure of energy involved in the whole trip is going to be getting the machine up to the sky in the first place, and with this design that's taken care of—as a matter of fact, once the bubble's installed, we'll have to keep the ship tied down until we're ready to go."

"How about letting the gas out?" Lavon said. "Will it go out through those little tubes when we want it to? Won't it just cling to the walls of the tank instead? The skin between water and gas is pretty difficult to deform—to that I can testify."

Tanol frowned. "That I don't know. Don't forget that the tubes

36

will be large in the real ship, not just straws as they are in the model."

"Bigger than a man's body?" Than said.

"No, hardly. Maybe as big, though, as a man's head."

"Won't work," Than said tersely. "I tried it. You can't lead a bubble through a pipe that small. As Lavon said, it clings to the inside of the tube and won't be budged. If we build this ship, we'll just have to abandon it once we hit our new world."

"That's out of the question," Lavon said at once. "Putting aside for the moment the waste involved, we may have to use the ship again in a hurry. Who knows what the new world will be like? We're going to have to be able to leave it again if it is impossible to live in."

"Which is your model, Than?" Shar said.

"This one. With this design, we do the trip the hard way—crawl along the bottom until it meets the sky, crawl until we hit the next world, and crawl wherever we're going when we get there. No aquabatics. She's treadmill-powered, like Tanol's, but not necessarily man-powered; I've been thinking a bit about using diatoms. She steers by varying the power on one side or the other; also we can hitch a pair of thongs to opposite ends of the rear axle and swivel her that way, but that would be slower and considerably less precise."

Shar looked closely at the tube-shaped model and pushed it experimentally along the table a little way. "I like that," he said presently. "It sits still when you want it to. With Than's spherical ship, we'd be at the mercy of any stray current at home or in the new world—and for all I know there may be currents of some sort in space, too, gas currents perhaps. Lavon, what do you think?"

"How would we build it?" Lavon said. "It's round in cross-section. That's all very well for a model, but how do you make a really big tube of that shape that won't fall in on itself?"

"Look inside, through the front window," Than said. "You'll see beams that cross at the centre, at right angles to the long axis. They hold the walls braced."

"That consumes a lot of space," Stravol objected. By far the quietest and most introspective of the three assistants, he had not spoken until now since the beginning of the conference. "You've pretty well got to have free passage back and forth inside the ship. How are we going to keep everything operating if we have to be crawling around beams all the time?"

"All right, come up with something better," Than said, shrugging.

"That's easy. We bend hoops."

"Hoops!" Tanol said. "On *that* scale? You'd have to soak your wood in mud for a year before it would be flexible enough, and then it wouldn't have the strength you'd need."

"No, you wouldn't," Stravol said. "I didn't build a ship-model, I just made drawings, and my ship isn't as good as Than's by a long distance. But my design for the ship is also tubular, so I did build a model of a hoop-bending machine—that's it on the table. You lock one end of your beam down in a heavy vise, like so, leaving the butt sticking out the other side. Then you tie up the other end with a heavy line, around this notch. Then you run your rope around a windlass, and five or six men wind up the windlass, like so. That pulls down the free end of the beam until the notch engages with this key-slot, which you've pre-cut at the other end. Then you unlock the vise, and there's your hoop; for safety you might drive a peg through the joint to keep the thing from springing open unexpectedly."

"Wouldn't the beam you were using break after it had bent a certain distance?" Lavon asked.

"Stock timber certainly would," Stravol said. "But for this trick you use *green* wood, not seasoned. Otherwise you'd have to soften your beam to uselessness, as Tanol says. But live wood will flex enough to make a good, strong, single-unit hoop—or if it doesn't, Shar, the little rituals with numbers that you've been teaching us don't mean anything after all!"

Shar smiled. "You can easily make a mistake in using numbers," he said.

"I checked everything."

"I'm sure of it. And I think it's well worth a trial. Anything else to offer?"

"Well," Stravol said, "I've got a kind of live ventilating system

I think should be useful. Otherwise, as I said, Than's ship strikes me as the type we should build; my own's hopelessly cumbersome."

"I have to agree," Tanol said regretfully. "But I'd like to try putting together a lighter-than-water ship sometime, maybe just for local travel. If the new world is bigger than ours, it might not be possible to swim everywhere you might want to go there."

"That never occurred to me," Lavon exclaimed. "Suppose the new world *is* twice, three times, eight times as big as ours? Shar, is there any reason why that couldn't be?"

"None that I know of. The history plates certainly seem to take all kinds of enormous distances practically for granted. All right, let's make up a composite design from what we have here. Tanol, you're the best draughtsman among us, suppose you draw it up. Lavon, what about labour?"

"I've a plan ready," Lavon said. "As I see it, the people who work on the ship are going to have to be on the job full-time. Building the vessel isn't going to be an overnight task, or even one that we can finish in a single season, so we can't count on using a rotating force. Besides, this is technical work; once a man learns how to do a particular task, it would be wasteful to send him back to tending fungi just because somebody else has some time on his hands.

"So I've set up a basic force involving the two or three most intelligent hand-workers from each of the various trades. Those people I can withdraw from their regular work without upsetting the way we run our usual concerns, or noticeably increasing the burden on the others in a given trade. They will do the skilled labour, and stick with the ship until it's done. Some of them will make up the crew, too. For heavy, unskilled jobs, we can call on the various seasonal pools of idle people without disrupting our ordinary life."

"Good," Shar said. He leaned forward and rested linked hands on the edge of the table—although, because of the webbing between his fingers, he could link no more than the finger-tips. "We've really made remarkable progress. I didn't expect that we'd have matters advanced a tenth as far as this by the end of this meeting.

But maybe I've overlooked something important. Has anybody any more suggestions, or any questions?"

"I've got one," Stravol said quietly.

"All right, let's hear it."

"*Where are we going?*"

There was quite a long silence. Finally Shar said: "Stravol, I can't answer that yet. I could say that we're going to the stars, but since we still have no idea what a star is, that answer wouldn't do you much good. We're going to make this trip because we've found that some of the fantastic things that the history plates say are really so. We know now that the sky can be passed, and that beyond the sky there's a region where there's no water to breathe, the region our ancients called 'space'. Both of these ideas always seemed to be against common sense, but nevertheless we've found that they're true.

"The history plates also say that there are other worlds than ours, and actually that's an easier idea to accept, once you've found out that the other two are so. As for the stars—well, we just don't know yet, we haven't any information at all that would allow us to read the history plates on that subject with new eyes, and there's no point in making wild guesses unless we can test the guesses. The stars are in space, and presumably, once we're out in space, we'll see them and the meaning of the word will become clear. At least we can confidently expect to see some clues—look at all the information we got from Lavon's trip of a few seconds above the sky!

"But in the meantime, there's no point in our speculating in a bubble. We think there are other worlds somewhere, and we're devising means to make the trip. The other questions, the pendant ones, just have to be put aside for now. We'll answer them eventually—there's no doubt in my mind about that. But it may take a long time."

Stravol grinned ruefully. "I expected no more. In a way, I think the whole project is crazy. But I'm in it right out to the end, all the same."

Shar and Lavon grinned back. All of them had the fever, and Lavon suspected that their whole enclosed universe would share it with them before long. He said:

"Then let's not waste a minute. There's a huge mass of detail to be worked out still, and after that, all the hard work will just have begun. Let's get moving!"

The five men arose and looked at each other. Their expressions varied, but in all their eyes there was in addition the same mixture of awe and ambition: the composite face of the shipwright and of the astronaut.

Then they went out, severally, to begin their voyages.

It was two winter sleeps after Lavon's disastrous climb beyond the sky that all work on the spaceship stopped. By then, Lavon knew that he had hardened and weathered into that temporarily ageless state a man enters after he has just reached his prime; and he knew also that there were wrinkles engraved on his brow, to stay and to deepen.

"Old" Shar, too, had changed, his features losing some of their delicacy as he came into his maturity. Though the wedge-shaped bony structure of his face would give him a withdrawn and poetic look for as long as he lived, participation in the plan had given his expression a kind of executive overlay, which at best gave it a mask-like rigidity, and at worst coarsened it somehow.

Yet despite the bleeding away of the years, the spaceship was still only a hulk. It lay upon a platform built above the tumbled boulders of the sandbar which stretched out from one wall of the world. It was an immense hull of pegged wood, broken by regularly spaced gaps through which the raw beams of the skeleton could be seen.

Work upon it had progressed fairly rapidly at first, for it was not hard to visualize what kind of vehicle would be needed to crawl through empty space without losing its water; Than and his colleagues had done that job well. It had been recognized, too, that the sheer size of the machine would enforce a long period of construction, perhaps as long as two full seasons; but neither Shar and his assistants nor Lavon had anticipated any serious snag.

For that matter, part of the vehicle's apparent incompleteness was an illusion. About a third of its fittings were to consist of living creatures, which could not be expected to install themselves in the vessel much before the actual take-off.

Yet time and time again, work on the ship had had to be halted for long periods. Several times whole sections needed to be ripped out, as it became more and more evident that hardly a single normal, understandable concept could be applied to the problem of space travel.

The lack of the history plates, which the Para steadfastly refused to deliver up, was a double handicap. Immediately upon their loss, Shar had set himself to reproduce them from memory; but unlike the more religious of his ancestors he had never regarded them as holy writ, and hence had never set himself to memorizing them word by word. Even before the theft, he had accumulated a set of variant translations of passages presenting specific experimental problems, which were stored in his library, carved in wood. But most of these translations tended to contradict each other, and none of them related to spaceship construction, upon which the original had been vague in any case.

No duplicates of the cryptic characters of the original had ever been made, for the simple reason that there was nothing in the sunken universe capable of destroying the originals, nor of duplicating their apparently changeless permanence. Shar remarked too late that through simple caution they should have made a number of verbatim temporary records—but after generations of green-gold peace, simple caution no longer covers preparation against catastrophe. (Nor, for that matter, did a culture which had to dig each letter of its simple alphabet into pulpy waterlogged wood with a flake of stonewort encourage the keeping of records in triplicate.)

As a result, Shar's imperfect memory of the contents of the history plates, plus the constant and millenial doubt as to the accuracy of the various translations, proved finally to be the worst obstacle to progress on the spaceship itself.

"Men must paddle before they can swim," Lavon observed belatedly, and Shar was forced to agree with him.

Obviously, whatever the ancients had known about spaceship construction, very little of that knowledge was usable to a people still trying to build its first spaceship from scratch. In retrospect, it was not surprising that the great hulk still rested incomplete upon its platform above the sand boulders, exuding a musty odour of wood steadily losing its strength, two generations after its flat bottom had been laid down.

The fat-faced young man who headed the strike delegation to Shar's chambers was Phil XX, a man two generations younger than Shar, four younger than Lavon. There were crow's-feet at the corners of his eyes, which made him look both like a querulous old man and like an infant spoiled in the spore.

"We're calling a halt to this crazy project," he said bluntly. "We've slaved away our youth on it, but now that we're our own masters, it's over, that's all. Over."

"Nobody's compelled you," Lavon said angrily.

"Society does; our parents do," a gaunt member of the delegation said. "But now we're going to start living in the real world. Everybody these days knows that there's no other world but this one. You oldsters can hang on to your superstitions if you like. We don't intend to."

Baffled, Lavon looked over at Shar. The scientist smiled and said, "Let them go, Lavon. We have no use for the faint-hearted."

The fat-faced young man flushed. "You can't insult us into going back to work. We're through. Build your own ship to noplace!"

"All right," Lavon said evenly. "Go on, beat it. Don't stand around here orating about it. You've made your decision and we're not interested in your self-justifications. Good-bye."

The fat-faced young man evidently still had quite a bit of heroism to dramatize which Lavon's dismissal had short-circuited. An examination of Lavon's stony face, however, seemed to convince him that he had to take his victory as he found it. He and the delegation trailed ingloriously out the archway.

"Now what?" Lavon asked when they had gone. "I must admit, Shar, that I would have tried to persuade them. We do need the workers, after all."

"Not as much as they need us," Shar said tranquilly. "I know all those young men. I think they'll be astonished at the runty crops their fields will produce next season, after they have to breed them without my advice. Now, how many volunteers have you got for the crew of the ship?"

"Hundreds. Every youngster of the generation after Phil's wants

43

to go along. Phil's wrong about that segment of the populace, at least. The project catches the imagination of the very young."

"Did you give them any encouragement?"

"Sure," Lavon said. "I told them we'd call on them if they were chosen. But you can't take that seriously! We'd do badly to displace our picked group of specialists with youths who have enthusiasm and nothing else."

"That's not what I had in mind, Lavon. Didn't I see a Noc in these chambers somewhere? Oh, there he is, asleep in the dome. Noc!"

The creature stirred its tentacle lazily.

"Noc, I've a message," Shar called. "The protos are to tell all men that those who wish to go to the next world with the spaceship must come to the staging area right away. Say that we can't promise to take everyone, but that only those who help us to build the ship will be considered at all."

The Noc curled its tentacle again, and appeared to go back to sleep.

Lavon turned from the arrangement of speaking-tube megaphones which was his control board and looked at the Para. "One last try," he said. "Will you give us back the history plates?"

"No, Lavon. We have never denied you anything before, but this we must."

"You're going with us though, Para. Unless you give us back the knowledge we need, you'll lose your life if we lose ours."

"What is one Para?" the creature said. "We are all alike. This cell will die; but the protos need to know how you fare on this journey. We believe you should make it without the plates, for in no other way can we assess the real importance of the plates."

"Then you admit you still have them. What if you can't communicate with your fellows once we're out in space? How do you know that water isn't essential to your telepathy?"

The proto was silent. Lavon stared at it a moment, then turned deliberately back to the speaking-tubes. "Everyone hang on," he said. He felt shaky. "We're about to start. Stravol, is the ship sealed?"

"As far as I can tell, Lavon."

Lavon shifted to another megaphone. He took a deep breath. Already the water seemed stifling, although the ship hadn't moved.

"Ready with one-quarter power. . . . One, two, three, *go*."

The whole ship jerked and settled back into place again. The raphe diatoms along the under-hull settled into their niches, their jelly treads turning against broad endless belts of crude nematode leather. Wooden gears creaked, stepping up the slow power of the creatures, transmitting it to the sixteen axles of the ship's wheels.

The ship rocked and began to roll slowly along the sandbar. Lavon looked tensely through the mica port. The world flowed painfully past him. The ship canted and began to climb the slope. Behind him, he could feel the electric silence of Shar, Para, and the two alternate pilots, Than and Stravol, as if their gaze were stabbing directly through his body and on out the port. The world looked different, now that he was leaving it. How had he missed all this beauty before?

The slapping of the endless belts and the squeaking and groaning of the gears and axles grew louder as the slope steepened. The ship continued to climb, lurching. Around it, squadrons of men and protos dipped and wheeled, escorting it towards the sky.

Gradually the sky lowered and pressed down towards the top of the ship.

"A little more work from your diatoms, Tanol," Lavon said. "Boulder ahead." The ship swung ponderously. "All right, slow them up again. Give us a shove from your side, Tol—no, that's too much—there, that's it. Back to normal; you're still turning us! Tanol, give us one burst to line us up again. Good. All right, steady drive on all sides. It shouldn't be long now."

"How can you think in webs like that?" the Para wondered behind him.

"I just do, that's all. It's the way men think. Overseers, a little more thrust now; the grade's getting steeper."

The gears groaned. The ship nosed up. The sky brightened in Lavon's face. Despite himself, he began to be frightened. His lungs seemed to burn, and in his mind he felt his long fall through nothingness towards the chill slap of the water as if he were ex-

45

periencing it for the first time. His skin itched and burned. Could he go up *there* again? Up there into the burning void, the great gasping agony where no life should go?

The sandbar began to level out and the going became a little easier. Up here, the sky was so close that the lumbering motion of the huge ship disturbed it. Shadows of wavelets ran across the sand. Silently, the thick-barrelled bands of blue-green algae drank in the light and converted it to oxygen, writhing in their slow mindless dance just under the long mica skylight which ran along the spine of the ship. In the hold, beneath the latticed corridor and cabin floors, whirring Vortae kept the ship's water in motion, fuelling themselves upon drifting organic particles.

One by one, the figures wheeling about the ship outside waved arms or cilia and fell back, coasting down the slope of the sandbar towards the familiar world, dwindling and disappearing. There was at last only one single Euglena, half-plant cousin of the protos, forging along beside the spaceship into the marches of the shallows. It loved the light, but finally it, too, was driven away into deeper, cooler waters, its single whiplike tentacle undulating placidly as it went. It was not very bright, but Lavon felt deserted when it left.

Where they were going, though, none could follow.

Now the sky was nothing but a thin, resistant skin of water coating the top of the ship. The vessel slowed, and when Lavon called for more power, it began to dig itself in among the sand-grains and boulders.

"That's not going to work," Shar said tensely. "I think we'd better step down the gear-ratio, Lavon, so you can apply stress more slowly."

"All right," Lavon agreed. "Full stop, everybody. Shar, will you supervise gear-changing, please?"

Insane brilliance of empty space looked Lavon full in the face just beyond his big mica bull's-eye. It was maddening to be forced to stop here upon the threshold of infinity; and it was dangerous, too. Lavon could feel building in him the old fear of the outside. A few moments more of inaction, he knew with a gathering coldness at the pit of his stomach, and he would be unable to go through with it.

Surely, he thought, there must be a better way to change gear-ratios than the traditional one, which involved dismantling almost the entire gear-box. Why couldn't a number of gears of different sizes be carried on the same shaft, not necessarily all in action all at once, but awaiting use simply by shoving the axle back and forth longitudinally in its sockets? It would still be clumsy, but it could be worked on orders from the bridge and would not involve shutting down the entire machine—and throwing the new pilot into a blue-green funk.

Shar came lunging up through the trap and swam himself to a stop.

"All set," he said. "The big reduction gears aren't taking the strain too well, though."

"Splintering?"

"Yes. I'd go it slow at first."

Lavon nodded mutely. Without allowing himself to stop, even for a moment, to consider the consequences of his words, he called: "Half power."

The ship hunched itself down again and began to move, very slowly indeed, but more smoothly than before. Overhead, the sky thinned to complete transparency. The great light came blasting in. Behind Lavon there was an uneasy stir. The whiteness grew at the front ports.

Again the ship slowed, straining against the blinding barrier. Lavon swallowed and called for more power. The ship groaned like something about to die. It was now almost at a standstill.

"More power," Lavon ground out.

Once more, with infinite slowness, the ship began to move. Gently, it tilted upwards.

Then it lunged forward and every board and beam in it began to squall.

"Lavon! Lavon!"

Lavon started sharply at the shout. The voice was coming at him from one of the megaphones, the one marked for the port at the rear of the ship.

"Lavon!"

"What is it? Stop your damn yelling."

"I can see the top of the sky! From the *other* side, from the top side! It's like a big flat sheet of metal. We're going away from it. We're above the sky, Lavon, we're above the sky!"

Another violent start swung Lavon around towards the forward port. On the outside of the mica, the water was evaporating with shocking swiftness, taking with it strange distortions and patterns made of rainbows.

Lavon saw Space.

It was at first like a deserted and cruelly dry version of the bottom. There were enormous boulders, great cliffs, tumbled, split, riven, jagged rocks going up and away in all directions, as if scattered at random by some giant.

But it had a sky of its own—a deep blue dome so far away that he could not believe in, let alone compute, what its distance might be. And in this dome was a ball of reddish fire that seared his eyeballs.

The wilderness of rock was still a long way away from the ship, which now seemed to be resting upon a level, glistening plain. Beneath the surface-shine, the plain seemed to be made of sand, nothing but familiar sand, the same substance which had heaped up to form a bar in Lavon's own universe, the bar along which the ship had climbed. But the glassy, colourful skin over it—

Suddenly Lavon became conscious of another shout from the megaphone banks. He shook his head savagely and asked, "What is it now?"

"Lavon, this is Tol. What have you gotten us into? The belts are locked. The diatoms can't move them. They aren't faking, either; we've rapped them hard enough to make them think we were trying to break their shells, but they still can't give us more power."

"Leave them alone," Lavon snapped. "They can't fake; they haven't enough intelligence. If they say they can't give you more power, they can't."

"Well, then, you get us out of it," Tol's voice said frightenedly.

Shar came forward to Lavon's elbow. "We're on a space-water interface, where the surface tension is very high," he said softly.

48

"This is why I insisted on our building the ship so that we could lift the wheels off the ground whenever necessary. For a long while I couldn't understand the reference of the history plates to 'retractable landing gear', but it finally occurred to me that the tension along a space-water interface—or, to be more exact, a space-mud interface—would hold any large object pretty tightly. If you order the wheels pulled up now, I think we'll make better progress for a while on the belly-treads."

"Good enough," Lavon said. "Hello below—up landing gear. Evidently the ancients knew their business after all, Shar."

Quite a few minutes later—for shifting power to the belly-treads involved another setting of the gear box—the ship was crawling along the shore towards the tumbled rock. Anxiously, Lavon scanned the jagged, threatening wall for a break. There was a sort of rivulet off towards the left which might offer a route, though a dubious one, to the next world. After some thought, Lavon ordered his ship turned towards it.

"Do you suppose that thing in the sky is a 'star'?" he asked. "But there were supposed to be lots of them. Only one is up there—and one's plenty for *my* taste."

"I don't know," Shar admitted. "But I'm beginning to get a picture of the way the universe is made, I think. Evidently our world is a sort of cup in the bottom of this huge one. This one has a sky of its own; perhaps it, too, is only a cup in the bottom of a still huger world, and so on and on without end. It's a hard concept to grasp, I'll admit. Maybe it would be more sensible to assume that all the worlds are cups in this one common surface, and that the great light shines on them all impartially."

"Then what makes it seem to go out every night, and dim even in the day during winter?" Lavon demanded.

"Perhaps it travels in circles, over first one world, then another. How could I know yet?"

"Well, if you're right, it means that all we have to do is crawl along here for a while, until we hit the top of the sky of another world," Lavon said. "Then we dive in. Somehow it seems too simple, after all our preparations."

Shar chuckled, but the sound did not suggest that he had discovered anything funny. "Simple? Have you noticed the temperature yet?"

Lavon had noticed it, just beneath the surface of awareness, but at Shar's remark he realized that he was gradually being stifled. The oxygen content of the water, luckily, had not dropped, but the temperature suggested the shallows in the last and worst part of autumn. It was like trying to breathe soup.

"Than, give us more action from the Vortae," Lavon said. "This is going to be unbearable unless we get more circulation."

There was a reply from Than, but it came to Lavon's ears only as a mumble. It was all he could do now to keep his attention on the business of steering the ship.

The cut or defile in the scattered razor-edged rocks was a little closer, but there still seemed to be many miles of rough desert to cross. After a while the ship settled into a steady, painfully slow crawling, with less pitching and jerking than before, but also with less progress. Under it, there was now a sliding, grinding sound, rasping against the hull of the ship itself, as if it were treadmilling over some coarse lubricant the particles of which were each as big as a man's head.

Finally Shar said, "Lavon, we'll have to stop again. The sand this far up is dry, and we're wasting energy using the treads."

"Are you sure we can take it?" Lavon asked, gasping for breath. "At least we are moving. If we stop to lower the wheels and change gears again, we'll boil."

"We'll boil if we don't," Shar said calmly. "Some of our algae are dead already and the rest are withering. That's a pretty good sign that we can't take much more. I don't think we'll make it into the shadows, unless we do change over and put on some speed."

There was a gulping sound from one of the mechanics. "We ought to turn back," he said raggedly. "We were never meant to be out here in the first place. We were made for the water, not for this hell."

"We'll stop," Lavon said, "but we're not turning back. That's final."

The words made a brave sound, but the man had upset Lavon

more than he dared to admit, even to himself. "Shar," he said, "make it fast, will you?"

The scientist nodded and dived below.

The minutes stretched out. The great red gold globe in the sky blazed and blazed. It had moved down the sky, far down, so that the light was pouring into the ship directly in Lavon's face, illuminating every floating particle, its rays like long milky streamers. The currents of water passing Lavon's cheek were almost hot.

How could they dare go directly forward into that inferno? The land directly under the "star" must be even hotter than it was here!

"Lavon! Look at Para!"

Lavon forced himself to turn and look at his proto ally. The great slipper had settled to the deck, where it was lying with only a feeble pulsation of its cilia. Inside, its vacuoles were beginning to swell, to become bloated, pear-shaped bubbles, crowding the granulated protoplasm, pressing upon the dark nuclei.

"Is . . . is he dying?"

"This cell is dying," Para said, as coldly as always. "But go on—go on. There is much to learn, and you may live, even though we do not. Go on."

"You're—for us now?" Lavon whispered.

"We have always been for you. Push your folly to the uttermost. We will benefit in the end, and so will Man."

The whisper died away. Lavon called the creature again, but it did not respond.

There was a wooden clashing from below, and then Shar's voice came tinnily from one of the megaphones. "Lavon, go ahead! The diatoms are dying, too, and then we'll be without power. Make it as quickly and directly as you can."

Grimly, Lavon leaned forward. "The 'star' is directly over the land we're approaching."

"It is? It may go lower still and the shadows will get longer. That's our only hope."

Lavon had not thought of that. He rasped into the banked megaphones. Once more, the ship began to move, a little faster now, but still seemingly at a crawl. The thirty-two wheels rumbled.

It got hotter.

Steadily, with a perceptible motion, the "star" sank in Lavon's face. Suddenly a new terror struck him. Suppose it should continue to go down until it was gone entirely? Blasting though it was now, it was the only source of heat. Would not space become bitter cold on the instant—and the ship an expanding, bursting block of ice?

The shadows lengthened menacingly, stretching across the desert towards the forward-rolling vessel. There was no talking in the cabin, just the sound of ragged breathing and the creaking of the machinery.

Then the jagged horizon seemed to rush upon them. Stony teeth cut into the lower rim of the ball of fire, devoured it swiftly. It was gone.

They were in the lee of the cliffs.

Lavon ordered the ship turned to parallel the rock-line; it responded heavily, sluggishly. Far above, the sky deepened steadily, from blue to indigo.

Shar came silently up through the trap and stood beside Lavon, studying that deepening colour and the lengthening of the shadows down the beach towards their world. He said nothing, but Lavon was sure that the same chilling thought was in his mind.

"Lavon."

Lavon jumped. Shar's voice had iron in it. "Yes?"

"We'll have to keep moving. We must make the next world, wherever it is, very shortly."

"How can we dare move when we can't see where we're going? Why not sleep it over—if the cold will let us?"

"It will let us," Shar said. "It can't get dangerously cold up here. If it did, the sky—or what we used to think of as the sky— would have frozen over every night, even in summer. But what I'm thinking about is the water. The plants will go to sleep now. In our world that wouldn't matter; the supply of oxygen there is enough to last through the night. But in this confined space, with so many creatures in it and no supply of fresh water, we will probably smother."

Shar seemed hardly to be involved at all, but spoke rather with the voice of implacable physical laws.

"Furthermore," he said, staring unseeingly out at the raw landscape, "the diatoms are plants, too. In other words, we must stay on the move for as long as we have oxygen and power—and pray that we make it."

"Shar, we had quite a few protos on board this ship once. And Para there isn't quite dead yet. If he were, the cabin would be intolerable. The ship is nearly sterile of bacteria, because all the protos have been eating them as a matter of course and there's no outside supply of them, any more than there is for oxygen. But still and all there would have been some decay."

Shar bent and tested the pellicle of the motionless Para with a probing finger. "You're right, he's still alive. What does that prove?"

"The Vortae are also alive; I can feel the water circulating. Which proves that it wasn't the heat that hurt Para. *It was the light.* Remember how badly my skin was affected after I climbed beyond the sky? Undiluted starlight is deadly. We should add that to the information from the plates."

"I still don't get the point."

"It's this. We've got three or four Noc down below. They were shielded from the light, and so must be alive. If we concentrate them in the diatom galleys, the dumb diatoms will think it's still daylight and will go on working. Or we can concentrate them up along the spine of the ship, and keep the algae putting out oxygen. So the question is: which do we need more, oxygen or power? Or can we split the difference?"

Shar actually grinned. "A brilliant piece of thinking. We may make a Shar of you yet, Lavon. No, I'd say that we can't split the difference. There's something about daylight, some quality, that the light Noc emits doesn't have. You and I can't detect it, but the green plants can, and without it they don't make oxygen. So we'll have to settle for the diatoms—for power."

"All right. Set it up that way, Shar."

Lavon brought the vessel away from the rocky lee of the cliff, out on to the smoother sand. All trace of direct light was gone now, although there was still a soft, general glow on the sky.

"Now then," Shar said thoughtfully, "I would guess that there's water over there in the canyon, if we can reach it. I'll go below again and arrange———"

Lavon gasped.

"What's the matter?"

Silently, Lavon pointed, his heart pounding.

The entire dome of indigo above them was spangled with tiny, incredibly brilliant lights. There were hundreds of them, and more and more were becoming visible as the darkness deepened. And far away, over the ultimate edge of the rocks, was a dim red globe, crescented with ghostly silver. Near the zenith was another such body, much smaller, and silvered all over. . . .

Under the two moons of Hydrot, and under the eternal stars, the two-inch wooden spaceship and its microscopic cargo toiled down the slope towards the drying little rivulet.

The ship rested on the bottom of the canyon for the rest of the night. The great square doors were thrown open to admit the raw, irradiated, life-giving water from outside—and the wriggling bacteria which were fresh food.

No other creatures approached them, either with curiosity or with predatory intent, while they slept, although Lavon had posted guards at the doors. Evidently, even up here on the very floor of space, highly organized creatures were quiescent at night.

But when the first flush of light filtered through the water, trouble threatened.

First of all, there was the bug-eyed monster. The thing was green and had two snapping claws, either one of which could have broken the ship in two like a spyrogyra straw. Its eyes were black and globular, on the ends of short columns, and its long feelers were as thick through as a plant-bole. It passed in a kicking fury of motion, however, never noticing the ship at all.

"Is that—a sample of the kind of life we can expect in the next world?" Lavon whispered. Nobody answered, for the very good reason that nobody knew.

After a while, Lavon risked moving the ship forward against the current, which was slow but heavy. Enormous writhing worms, far bigger than the nematodes of home, whipped past them. One struck the hull a heavy blow, then thrashed on obliviously.

"They don't notice us," Shar said. "We're too small. Lavon, the ancients warned us of the immensity of space, but even when you see it, it's impossible to grasp. And all those stars—can they mean what I think they mean? It's beyond thought, beyond belief!"

"The bottom's sloping," Lavon said, looking ahead intently. "The walls of the canyon are retreating, and the water's becoming rather silty. Let the stars wait, Shar; we're coming towards the entrance of our new world."

Shar subsided moodily. His vision of space had disturbed him, perhaps seriously. He took little notice of the great thing that was happening, but instead huddled worriedly over his own expanding speculations. Lavon felt the old gap between their two minds widening once more.

Now the bottom was tilting upwards again. Lavon had no experience with delta-formation, for no rivulets left his own world, and the phenomenon worried him. But his worries were swept away in wonder as the ship topped the rise and nosed over.

Ahead, the bottom sloped away again, indefinitely, into glimmering depths. A proper sky was over them once more, and Lavon could see small rafts of plankton floating placidly beneath it. Almost at once, too, he saw several of the smaller kinds of protos, a few of which were already approaching the ship—

Then the girl came darting out of the depths, her features blurred and distorted with distance and terror. At first she did not seem to see the ship at all. She came twisting and turning lithely through the water, obviously hoping only to throw herself over the mound of the delta and into the savage streamlet beyond.

Lavon was stunned. Not that there were men here—he had hoped for that, had even known somehow that men were everywhere in the universe—but at the girl's single-minded flight towards suicide.

"What——"

Then a dim buzzing began to grow in his ears, and he understood.

"Shar! Than! Stravol!" he bawled. "Break out crossbows and spears! Knock out all the windows!" He lifted a foot and kicked through the big bull's-eye port in front of him. Someone thrust a crossbow into his hand.

"Eh? What's happening?" Shar blurted.

"*Eaters!*"

The cry went through the ship like a galvanic shock. The rotifers back in Lavon's own world were virtually extinct, but everyone knew thoroughly the grim history of the long battle man and proto had waged against them.

The girl spotted the ship suddenly and paused, obviously stricken with despair at the sight of the new monster. She drifted with her own momentum, her eyes alternately fixed upon the ship and jerking back over her shoulder, towards where the buzzing snarled louder and louder in the dimness.

"Don't stop!" Lavon shouted. "This way, this way! We're friends! We'll help!"

Three great semi-transparent trumpets of smooth flesh bored over the rise, the many thick cilia of their coronas whirring greedily. Dicrans—the most predacious of the entire tribe of Eaters. They were quarrelling thickly among themselves as they moved, with the few blurred, pre-symbolic noises which made up their "language".

Carefully, Lavon wound the crossbow, brought it to his shoulder, and fired. The bolt sang away through the water. It lost momentum rapidly, and was caught by a stray current which brought it closer to the girl than to the Eater at which Lavon had aimed.

He bit his lip, lowered the weapon, wound it up again. It did not pay to underestimate the range; he would have to wait until he could fire with effect. Another bolt, cutting through the water from a side port, made him issue orders to cease firing.

The sudden irruption of the rotifers decided the girl. The motionless wooden monster was strange to her, but it had not yet menaced her—and she must have known what it would be like to have three Dicrans over her, each trying to grab away from the others the largest share. She threw herself towards the bull's-eye port. The three Eaters screamed with fury and greed and bored in after her.

She probably would not have made it, had not the dull vision of the lead Dicran made out the wooden shape of the ship at the last instant. It backed off, buzzing, and the other two sheered away to avoid colliding with it. After that they had another argument, though they could hardly have formulated what it was that they were fighting about. They were incapable of saying anything much more complicated than the equivalent of "Yaah," "Drop dead," and "You're another."

While they were still snarling at each other, Lavon pierced the nearest one all the way through with an arbalest bolt. It disintegrated promptly—rotifers are delicately organized creatures despite their ferocity—and the surviving two were at once involved in a lethal battle over the remains.

"Than, take a party out and spear me those two Eaters while they're still fighting," Lavon ordered. "Don't forget to destroy their eggs, too. I can see that this world needs a little taming."

The girl shot through the port and brought up against the far wall of the cabin, flailing in terror. Lavon tried to approach her, but from somewhere she produced a flake of stonewort chipped to a nasty point. Since she was naked, it was hard to tell where she had been hiding it, but its purpose was plain. Lavon retreated and sat down on the stool before his control board, waiting while she took in the cabin, Lavon, Shar, the other pilots, the senescent Para.

At last she said: "Are—you—the gods—from beyond the sky?"

"We're from beyond the sky, all right," Lavon said. "But we're not gods. We're human beings, just like you. Are there many humans here?"

The girl seemed to assess the situation very rapidly, savage though she was. Lavon had the odd and impossible impression that he should recognize her: a tall, deceptively relaxed, tawny young woman, someone from another world, but still . . .

She tucked the knife back into her bright, matted hair—aha, Lavon thought confusedly, that's a trick I may need to remember— and shook her head.

"We are few. The Eaters are everywhere. Soon they will have the last of us."

Her fatalism was so complete that she actually did not seem to care.

"And you've never co-operated against them? Or asked the protos to help?"

"The protos?" She shrugged. "They are as helpless as we are against the Eaters. We have no weapons which kill at a distance, like yours. And it is too late now for such weapons to do any good. We are too few, the Eaters too many."

Lavon shook his head emphatically. "You've had one weapon that counts, all along. Against it, numbers mean nothing. We'll show you how we've used it. You may be able to use it even better than we did, once you've given it a try."

The girl shrugged again. "We have dreamed of such a weapon now and then, but never found it. I do not think that what you say is true. What is this weapon?"

"Brains," Lavon said. "Not just one brain, but brains. Working together. Co-operation."

"Lavon speaks the truth," a weak voice said from the deck.

The Para stirred feebly. The girl watched it with wide eyes. The sound of the Para using human speech seemed to impress her more than the ship itself, or anything else it contained.

"The Eaters can be conquered," the thin, burring voice said. "The protos will help, as they helped in the world from which we came. The protos fought this flight through space, and deprived Man of his records; but Man made the trip without the records. The protos will never oppose Man again. I have already spoken to the protos of this world, and have told them that what Man can dream, Man can do, whether the protos wish it or not.

"Shar, your metal records are with you. They were hidden in the ship. My brothers will lead you to them.

"This organism dies now. It dies in confidence of knowledge, as an intelligent creature dies. Man has taught us this. There is nothing that knowledge . . . cannot do. With it, men . . . have crossed . . . have crossed space. . . ."

The voice whispered away. The shining slipper did not change, but something about it was gone. Lavon looked at the girl; their eyes met. He felt an unaccountable warmth.

"We have crossed space," Lavon repeated softly.

Shar's voice came to him across a great distance. The young-old man was whispering: "But—*have* we?"

Lavon was looking at the girl. He had no answer for Shar's question. It did not seem to be important.

This was an attempt to write two different kinds of stories within the same compass. At the bottom the only "science" represented is clinical psychology: the story observes successive stages in the disintegration of a paranoid schizophrenic, from the first delusions of reference to the infantile moment before he becomes lost to all human contact, and concludes with the human, humble raw material upon which the preceding stages were built. But my imaginary patient was a science fiction reader in his formative years, so his delusions take on a science-fictional coloration—and any reader who would like to think that each section of the story has an independent narrator, and that the catastrophe each one describes really happened, or may some day happen, may do so at his peril.

Testament of Andros

Beside the fire lie the ashes. There are voices in them. Listen. . . .

I

My name is Theodor Andresson. I will write my story if you wish. I was at one time Resident in Astrophysics at Krajputnii, which I may safely describe as the greatest centre of learning in the Middle East, perhaps of the entire Eastern Hemisphere. Later—until the chain of incidents which brought me to this *Zucht-Haus*—I was professor-emeritus in radio-astronomy at Calimyrna University, where I did the work leading to the discovery of the solar pulsation cycle.

I am sure that this work is not credited to me; that is of no importance. I would like it clearly understood that I am not making this record for your benefit, but for mine. Your request means nothing to me, and your pretence of interest in what I may write cannot deceive me. My erstwhile colleagues in the so-called sciences were masters of this kind of pretence; but they, too, were unable to prevent me from penetrating the masquerade at the end. How then does a simple doctor hope to succeed where the finest charlatanry has failed?

And what is allocation of credit—of what importance is priority of discovery before the inexorability of the pulsation cycle? It will work to its new conclusion without regard for your beliefs, my colleagues', or mine. Neither the pretended solicitude nor the real metal bars with which you have surrounded me will matter after that.

I proceed, therefore, to the matter at hand. My position at Calimyrna in that remote time before the cycle was discovered, befit my age (84 years) and the reputation I had achieved in my specialty. I was in excellent health, though subject occasionally to depression of spirit, readily ascribable to my being in a still-strange land and to those scars inflicted upon me in earlier times.

Despite these fits of moodiness, I had every reason to be happy. My eminence in my field afforded me the utmost satisfaction; despite poverty and persecution in youth, I had won to security. I had married Marguerita L—, in her youth and mine the toast of twelve continents, not only for her beauty but for her voice. I can still hear now the sound of her singing as I heard it for the first time—singing, on the stage of La Scala in Moscow, the rapturous quartet from the second act of Wagner's *Tristan et Messalina*.

It is quite true—I admit it immediately and calmly—that there were certain flaws in my world, even at Calimyrna. I do not mean the distractions which in old age replace, in the ordinary man, the furies of youth, but rather certain faults and fissures which I found in the world outside myself.

Even a man of my attainments expects at some time to grow old, and to find that process changing the way in which he looks at the world around him. There comes a time, however, when even the most rational of men must notice when these changes exceed the bounds of reason—when they begin to become extraordinary, even sinister. Shall I be specific? Consider, then—quite calmly—the fact that Marguerita did not herself grow old.

I passed into my eighth decade without taking more than perfunctory notice. I was deeply involved in the solar work we were then carrying on at Calimyrna. I had with me a young graduate student, a brilliant fellow of about 30, who assisted me and who made certain original contributions of his own to the study. His name, and you will recognize it, was Mario di Ferruci. Calimyrna had completed its thousand-inch radio-telescope, the largest such antenna anywhere in the world—except for the 250-foot Manchester instrument. This was at once put to work in the search for so-called radio stars—those invisible bodies, many of them doubtless nearer to Earth than the nearest visible star, which can be detected only by their emission in the radio spectrum.

Completion of the thousand-inch freed the 600-inch paraboloid antenna for my use in solar work. The smaller instrument had insufficient beam-width between half-power points for the critical stellar studies, but it was more suitable for my purpose.

I had in mind at that time a study of the disturbed sun. Hagen of the Naval Research Laboratory had already done the definitive study on the sun in its quiet state. I found myself more drawn to what goes on in the inferno of the sunspots—in the enormous, puzzling catastrophes of the solar flares—the ejection of immense radio-active clouds from the sun's interior high into its atmosphere.

It had already become clear that the radio-frequency emission from the disturbed sun was not, and could not be, thermal in origin, as in the RF emission of the quiet sun. The equivalent temperature of the disturbed sun in selected regions at times rises to billions of degrees, rendering the whole concept of thermal equivalency meaningless.

That the problem was not merely academic impressed me from the first. I have, if you will allow me the term, always had a sense of destiny, of *Schicksal*, an almost Spenglerian awareness of the pressure of fate against the retaining walls of human survival. It is not unique in me; I lay it to my Teutonic ancestry. And when I first encountered the problem of the disturbed sun, something within me felt that I had found destiny itself.

For here, just *here* was the problem in which destiny was interested, in which some fateful answer awaited the asking of the omnipotent question. I felt this from the moment when I had first opened Hagen's famous paper—NRL Report 3504—and the more deeply I became interested in the sun as an RF radiator, the more the sensation grew.

Yet how to describe it? I was 84, and this was early in 1956; in all those preceding years I had not known that the mortal frame could sustain such an emotion. Shall I call it a sensation of enormous unresolvable dread? But I felt at the same time an ecstasy beyond joy, beyond love, beyond belief; and these transports of rapture and terror did not alternate as do the moods of an insane man, but occurred simultaneously—they were one and the same emotion.

Nor did the solar flares prove themselves unworthy of such deep responses. Flares have been observed in many stars. Some of them have been major outbursts, as indeed they would have to be to be visible to us at all. That such a flare could never occur on our own sun, furthermore, could not be said with certainty, for flares are local phenomena—they expend their energy only on one side of a star, not in all directions like a nova—and we had already seen the great detonation of 29th July 1948 on our own sun, which reached an energy level 100 times the output of the quiet sun, which showed that we did not dare to set limits to what our own sun might yet do.

It was here, however, that I ran into trouble with young di Ferruci. He persistently and stubbornly refused to accept the analogy.

"It's penny-dreadful," he would say, as he had said dozens of times before. "You remind me of Dr. Richardson's stories—you know, the ones he writes for those magazines, about the sun going nova and all that. Whenever it's cloudy at Palomar he dreams up a new catastrophe."

"Richardson is no fool," I would point out. "Other suns have exploded. If he wants to postulate that it could happen to ours, he has every right to do so."

"Sure, Dr. Andresson, in a story," di Ferruci would object. "But as a serious proposition it doesn't hold water. Our sun just isn't the spectral type that goes nova; it hasn't ever even approached the critical instability percentage. It can't even produce a good flare of the Beta Centauri type."

"I don't expect it to go nova. But it's quite capable of producing a major flare, in my opinion. I expect to prove it."

di Ferruci would shrug, as he always did. "I wouldn't ride any money on you, Dr. Andresson. But I'll be more than interested in what the telescope shows—let's see what we have here right now. The thermocouple's been calibrated; shall I cut in the hot load?"

At this point—I am now reporting a particular incident, although it, too, was frequently typical of these conversations—I became aware that Marguerita was in the observatory. I swung sharply around, considerably annoyed. My wife is innocent of astronomical knowledge, and her usually ill-timed obtrusions upon our routine— although I suppose they were of the desire to "take an interest" in her husband's profession—were distracting.

Today, however, I was not only annoyed, but stunned. How had I failed to notice this before—I, who pride myself on the acuity of my observation? What stood before me was a young woman!

How shall I say how young? These things are relative. We had married when she was 36, and I was 44; a difference of eight years is virtually no difference during the middle decades, though it is enormous when both parties are young. Marguerita had been in no sense a child at the time of our marriage.

Yet now, as I was finding, a spread as small as eight years can again become enormous when the dividing-line of old age insensibly approaches. And the difference was even greater than this—for now Marguerita, as she stood looking down at our day's three-dimensional graph of solar activity, seemed no older to me than the day on which I had first met her: a woman, tall, graceful, lithe, platinum-haired, and with the sombre, smouldering, unreadable face of Eve—and yet compared to me now a child in truth.

"Good afternoon, Mrs. Andresson," di Ferruci said, smiling.

She looked up and smiled back. "Good afternoon," she said. "I see you're about to take another series of readings. Don't let me interrupt you."

"That's quite all right; thus far it's routine," di Ferruci said. I glanced sideways at him and then back to my wife. "We'd just begun to take readings to break up the monotony of the old argument."

"That's true," I said. "But it would be just as well if you didn't drop in on us unexpectedly, Marguerita. If this had been a critical stage——"

"I'm sorry," she said contritely. "I should have phoned, but I'm always afraid that the telephone will interrupt you, too. When I'm here I can hope to see whether or not you're busy—and you can see who's calling. The telephone has no eyes."

She touched the graph, delicately. This graph, I should explain, is made of fourteen curves cut out in cardboard, and assembled so that one set of seven curved pieces is at right angles to the other set. It expresses the variation in intensity of RF emanation across the surface of the sun at the 10-centimetre wavelength, where our readings commonly are taken; we make a new such model each day. It shows at a glance, by valley or peak, any deviation from the sun's normal output, thus helping us greatly in interpreting our results.

"How strange it looks today," she said. "It's always in motion, like a comber racing towards the shore. I keep expecting it to begin to break at the top."

di Ferruci stopped tinkering with the drive clock and sat down before the control desk, his blue-black helmet of hair—only a little peppered by his memories of the Inchon landing—swivelling sharply towards her. I could not see his face. "What an eerie notion," he said. "Mrs. Andresson, you and the doctor'll have me sharing your presentiments of doom any minute now."

"It isn't a question of presentiments," I said sharply. "You should be aware by now, Mario, that in the RF range the sun is a variable star. Does that mean nothing to you? Let me ask you another question: How do you explain Eta Carina?"

"What's Eta Carina?" Marguerita said.

I did not know quite how to begin answering her, but di Ferruci, who lacked my intimate knowledge of her limitations, had no such qualms.

"It's a freak—one of the worst freaks of the past ten years," he said eagerly. "It's a star that's gone nova three times. The last time was in 1952, about a hundred years before the previous explosion. Before that it had an outburst in the 1600's, and it may have blown up about A.D. 142, too. Each time it gains in brightness nearly 100,000 times—as violent a stellar catastrophe as you can find anywhere in the records." He offered the data to her like a bouquet, and before I could begin to take offence, swung back upon me again. "Surely, Doc, you don't maintain that Eta Carina is a flare star?"

"All stars are flare stars," I said, looking steadily at him. His eyes were in shadow. "More than that: all stars are novas, in the long run. Young stars like our sun are variable only in the radio spectrnm, but gradually they become more and more unstable, and begin to produce small flares. Then come the big flares, like the Beta Centauri outburst; then they go nova; and then the cycle begins again."

"Evidence?"

"Everywhere. The process goes on in little in the short-term variables, the Cepheids. Eta Carina shows how it works in a smaller, non-cluster star. The other novas we've observed simply have longer periods—they haven't had time to go nova again within recorded history. But they will."

"Well," di Ferruci said. "If that's so, Richardson's visions of our sun exploding seems almost pleasant. You see us being roasted gradually instead, in a series of hotter and hotter flares. When does the first one hit us, by your figures?"

Mario was watching me steadily. Perhaps I looked strange, for I was once again in the grip of that anamolous emotion, so impossible to describe, in which terror and ecstasy blended and fused into some whole beyond any possibility of communication. As I had stated for the first time what I saw, and saw so clearly, was ahead for us all, this deep radical emotion began to shake me as if I had stepped all unawares from the comfortable island of relative, weighable facts into some blastingly cold ocean of Absolute Truth.

"I don't know," I said. "It needs checking. But I give us six months."

Marguerita's and di Ferruci's eyes met. Then he said, "Let's check it, then. We should be able to find the instability threshold for each stage, from RR Lyrae stars right through classical Cepheids, long-periods, and irregulars to radio-variables. We already know the figure for novas. Let's dot the i's and cross the t's—and then find out where our sun stands."

"Theodor," Marguerita said. "What—what will happen if you're right?"

"Then the next flare will be immensely greater than the 1948 one. The Earth will survive it; life on Earth probably will not—certainly not human life."

Marguerita remained standing beside the model a moment longer, nursing the hand which had been touching it. Then she looked at me out of eyes too young for me to read, and left the observatory.

With a hasty word to di Ferruci, I followed her, berating myself as I went. Suspecting as I did the shortness of the span left to us, I had not planned to utter a word about what was to be in store for us in her presence; that had been one of the reasons why I had objected to her visits to the observatory. There had simply been no reason to cloud our last months together with the shadow of a fate she could not understand.

But when I reached the top of the granite steps leading down to the road, she was gone—nor could I see either her figure or any sign of a car on the road which led down the mountain. She had vanished as completely as if she had never existed.

Needless to say, I was disturbed. There are cabins in the woods, only a short distance away from the observatory proper, which are used by staff members as temporary residences; we had never made use of them—radio-astronomy being an art which can be carried on by day better than by night—but nevertheless I checked them systematically. It was inconceivable to me that she could be in the main observatory, but I searched that too, as well as the solar tower and the Schmidt shed.

She was nowhere. By the time I had finished searching, it was sunset and there was no longer any use in my returning to my own instrument. I could only conclude that I had miscalculated the time lag between her exit and my pursuit, and that I would find her at home.

Yet, somehow I did not go home. All during my search of the grounds, another thought had been in my head: What if I was wrong? Suppose that there was no solar pulsation cycle? Suppose that my figures were meaningless? If this seems to you to be a strange thing for a man to be thinking, while searching for an inexplicably vanished wife, I can only say that the two subjects seemed to me to be somehow not unconnected.

And as it turned out, I was right. I have said that I have a sense of fate.

In the end, I went back to the observatory, now dark and, I supposed, deserted. But there was a light glowing softly inside: the evenly lit surface of the transparency viewer. Bent over it, his features floating eerily in nothingness, was Mario di Ferruci.

I groped for the switch, found it, and the fluorescents flashed on overhead. Mario straightened, blinking.

"Mario, what are you doing here? I thought you had left before sundown."

"I meant to," di Ferruci said slowly. "But I couldn't stop thinking about your theory. It isn't every day that one hears the end of the world announced by a man of your eminence. I decided I just had to run my own check, or else go nuts wondering."

"Why couldn't you have waited for me?" I said. "We could have done the work together much quicker and more easily."

"That's true," he said slowly. "But, Dr. Andresson, I'm just a graduate student, and you're a famous man; young as you are. I'm a little afraid of being overwhelmed—of missing an error because you've checked it already, or failing to check some point at all—that kind of thing. After all, we're all going to die if you're right, and that's hardly a minor matter; so I thought I'd try paddling my own canoe. Maybe I'll find the world just as far up the creek as you do. But I had to try."

It took me a while to digest this, distracted as I already was. After a while I said, as calmly as I could: "And what have you found?"

"Dr. Andresson—*you're wrong.*"

For an instant I could not see. All the red raw exploding universe of unstable stars went wheeling through my old head like maddened atoms. But I am a scientist; I conquered it.

"Wherein am I wrong?"

di Ferruci took a deep breath. His face was white and set under the fluorescents. "Dr. Andresson, forgive me; this is a hard thing for me to say. But the error in your calcs is way the hell back in the beginning, in your thermodynamic assumptions. It lies in the step between the Chapman-Cowling expression, and your derivation for the coefficient of mutual diffusion. Your derivation is perfectly sound in classical thermodynamics, but that isn't what we have to deal with here; we're dealing instead with a completely ionized binary gas, where your quantity D 12 becomes nothing more than a first approximation."

"I never called it anything else."

"Maybe not," di Ferruci said doggedly. "But your math handles it as an absolute. By the time your expanded equation 58 is reached, you've lost a complete set of subscripts and your expressions for the electron of charge wind up all as odd powers! I'm not impugning your logic—it's fantastically brilliant—but in so far as it derives from the bracketed expression D 12 it doesn't represent a real situation."

He stared at me, half-defiantly, half in a kind of anxiety the source of which I could not fathom. It had been many years since I had been young; now I was gravid with death—his, mine, yours, Marguerita's, everyone's. I said only: "Let's check it again."

But we never had the chance; at that moment the door opened soundlessly, and Marguerita came back.

"Theodor, Mario!" she said breathlessly. "Are you trying to work yourselves to death? Let's all live to our appointed times, whenever they come! Theodor, I was so frightened when you didn't come home—why didn't you call——"

"I'm not sure anyone would have answered," I said grimly. "Or if someone had, I would have suspected her of being an impostor—or a teleport."

She turned her strange look upon me. "I—don't understand you."

"I hope you don't, Marguerita. We'll take that matter up in private. Right now we're making a check. Dr. di Ferruci was about to knock the solar pulsation theory to flinders when you entered."

"Doc!" di Ferruci protested. "That wasn't the point at all. I just wanted to find——"

"*Don't call me 'Doc'!*"

"Very well," di Ferruci said. His face became whiter still. "But I insist on finishing my sentence. I'm not out to kick apart your theory; I think it's a brilliant theory and that it may still very well be right. There are holes in your math, that's all. They're big holes and they need filling; maybe, between us, we could fill them. But if you don't care enough to want to do the job, why should I?"

"Why, indeed?"

He stared at me with fury for a moment. Then he put his hand distractedly to his forehead, stood up slowly, and began to pace. "Look, Doc—Dr. Andresson. Believe me, I'm not hostile to the idea. It scares me, but that's only because I'm human. There's still a good chance that it's basically sound. If we could go to work on it now, really intensively, we might be able to have it in shape for the triple-A-S meeting in Chicago two months from now. It'd set every physicist, every astronomer, every scientist of any stripe by the ears!"

And there was the clue for which, all unconsciously, I had been waiting. "Indeed it would," I said. "And for four months, old Dr. Andresson and young Dr. Ferruci would be famous—as perhaps no scientists had ever been famous before. Old Dr. Andresson has had his measure of fame and has lost his faith in it—but for young Dr. Ferruci, even four months would be a deep draught. For that he is willing to impugn his senior's work, to force endless conferences, to call everything into question—all to get his own name added to the credits on the final paper."

"Theodor," Marguerita said. "Theodor, this isn't like you. If——"

"And there is even a touch of humour in this little playlet," I said. "The old man would have credited young Dr. Ferruci in the final paper in any case. The whole manœuvre was for nothing."

"There was no manœuvre," di Ferruci ground out, his fists clenched. His nervous movements of his hand across his forehead had turned his blue-black hair into a mare's nest. "I'm not an idiot. I know that if you're right, the whole world will be in ashes before the year is out—including any research papers which might carry my name, and any human eyes which might see them.

"What I want to do is to pin down this concept to the point where it's unassailable. The world will demand nothing less of it

70

than that. *Then* it can be presented to the AAAS—and the world will have four months during which the best scientific brains on Earth can look for an out, a way to save at least a part of the race, even if only two people. What's fame to me, or anyone else, if this theory is right? Gas, just gas. But if we can make the world believe it, utterly and completely, then the world will find a loophole. Nothing less than the combined brains of the whole of science could do the job—and we won't get those brains to work unless we convince them!"

"Nonsense," I said calmly. "There is no 'out', as you put it. But I'll agree that I looked deeper into you than I needed for a motive. Do you think that I have overlooked all these odd coincidences? Here is my wife, and here are you, both at improbable hours, neither of you expecting me; here is young Dr. di Ferruci interrupted at his task of stealing something more than just my work; here is Marguerita Andresson, emerged from wherever she has been hiding all evening, unable to believe that Earth's last picture is all but painted, but ready to help a young man with blue-black hair to steal the pretty notion and capitalize on it."

There was a faint sound from Marguerita. I did not look at her.

After a long while, di Ferruci said: "You are a great astronomer, Dr. Andresson. I owe you twenty years of inspiration from a distance, and five years of the finest training a master ever gave a tyro.

"You are also foul-minded, cruel-tongued, and very much mistaken. I resign from this University as of now; my obligation to you is wiped out by what you saw fit to say of me." He searched for his jacket, failed to find it, and gave up at once in trembling fury. "Good-bye, Mrs. Andresson, with my deepest sympathy. And Doc, good-bye—and God have mercy on you."

"Wait," I said. I moved then, after what seemed a century of standing frozen. The young man stopped, his hand half-way to the doorknob, and his back to me. Watching him, I found my way to a chart-viewer, and picked up the six-inch pair of dividers he had been using to check my charts.

"Well?" he said.

"It's not so easy as that, Mario. You don't walk out of a house with the stolen goods under your arm when the owner is present.

A strong man armed keepeth his house. You may not leave; you may not take my hard-won theory to another university; you may not leave Hamelin with pipes in your hand. You may not carry both my heart and my brains out of this observatory as easily as you would carry a sack of potatoes. In short—*you may not leave!*"

I threw the points of the dividers high and launched myself soul and body at that hunched, broad back. Marguerita's sudden scream rang deafeningly as a siren in the observatory dome.

The rest you know.

I have been honest with you. Tell me: where have you hidden her now?

2

I, Andrew, a servant of the Sun, who also am your brother, he who was called and was sanctified, say unto you, blessed be he that readeth, and keepeth the word; for behold, the time is at hand; be thou content.

2. For behold, it was given to me, in the City of Angels, upon a high hill, to look upon His face; whereupon I fell down and wept;

3. And He said, I am the Be-All and End-All; I am the Being and the Becoming; except that they be pure, none shall look upon Me else they die, for the time is at hand. And when He had spoken thus, I was sore afraid.

4. And He said, Rise up, and go forth unto the peoples, and say thou, Unless thou repent, I will come to thee quickly, and shine My countenance upon thee. I shall loosen the seals, and sound the trumpets, and open the vials, and the deaths which shall come upon thee will be numbered as seven times seven.

5. The sun shall become black as sackcloth of hair, and the moon become as blood; and the stars of heaven shall fall on to the earth, and the heaven depart as a scroll when it is rolled together, and every mountain and island be moved out of their places. And all men shall hide themselves, and say to the mountains and rocks, Fall on us, and hide us from the face of Him that sitteth on the throne.

6. There will be hail and fire mingled with blood, and these cast

upon the earth; a great mountain burning with fire shall be cast into the sea; and there will fall a great star from heaven, burning as it were a lamp, upon the fountains of waters; and the third part of the Sun shall be smitten, and the third part of the moon; and there shall arise a smoke out of the pit, so that the air and the day be darkened.

7. And if there be any who worship not Me, and who heed not, I say unto you all, woe, woe, for ye shall all die; ye shall feast without sacraments, ye shall batten upon each other; ye shall be clouds without water, driven by dry winds; ye shall be dry sterile trees, twice dead, and withered; wandering stars, to whom is given the dark of the emptiness of eternity; verily, I say unto you,

8. Ye shall be tormented with fire and brimstone, the third part of trees shall be burnt up, and all green grass be burnt up, and the third part of creatures which were in the sea, and had life, shall die; and the waters shall become blood, and many men die of the waters, because they be bitter; and the smoke of your torment shall ascend up for ever and ever, and thou shalt have no rest, neither day nor night; for the hour of judgment is come.

9. And saying thus, He that spake to me departed, and His dread spirit, and I went down among the people, and spoke, and bade men beware; and none heeded,

10. Neither those who worshipped the stars, and consulted, one among the others; nor those who worshipped man and his image; nor those who made prayers to the invisible spirits of the air; nor those who worshipped any other thing; and the spirit of Him who had spoken was heavy upon me, so that I went unto my chambers and lay me down in a swound.

11. And the angel of the Sun spoke to me as I lay, and spake with a voice like trombones, and said, Behold, all men are evil, but thou shalt redeem them, albeit thou remain a pure child of the Sun, and thou alone. Thou shalt have power; a two-edged sword shall go out of thy mouth, and thou shalt hold seven times seven stars in thy palm, and be puissant; this I shall give thee as thine own, if only thou remainest, and thou alone. And I said: Lord, I am Thine; do with me as Thou wilt.

12. And I went forth again, and spoke, and the nations of men

73

hearkened, and the kings of the world bent the knee, and the princes of the world brought tribute, seven times seven; and those who worshipped the stars, and the spirits of the air, and all other things, bowed down before Him; and it was well with them.

13. Now at this time there appeared a great wonder in heaven: a star clothed in a glory of hair, like a woman; and the people gathered and murmured of wonder, saying, Beware, for there is a god in the sky, clothed in hair like a woman, and with streaming of robes and bright garments; and behold, it draws near in the night, and fears not the Sun; the hem of this robe gathers about us.

14. And there arose a woman of the world, and came forward, preaching the gospel of the wild star, saying: Our god the Sun is a false god; his mate is this great star; they will devour us. There is no god but man.

15. And this woman, which was called Margo, summoned the people and made laughter with them, and derision, and scorned the Sun, and gave herself to the priests of the voices in the air, and to those who worshipped numbers, and to the kings and princes of the world; and there was whirling of tambourines in the high towers of the Sun.

16. And the angel of the Sun spoke to me with the sound of trombones, saying, Go with thy power which has been given to thee, and crush this woman, else thou shalt be given to the wild star, and to the flames of the wild star's hair, and with thee the world; I command thee, slay this woman, for thou hast been given the power, nor shall it be given thee again; I have spoken.

17. And I went, and the woman called Margo spoke unto me, saying: Thou art fair, and hath power. Give me of thy power, and I will give you of mine. Neither the wild star nor the Sun shall have such power as we have.

18. And I looked upon her, and she was fair, beyond all the daughters of the earth; and when she spoke, her voice was as the sounding of bells; and there was a spirit in her greater than the souls of men; and a star, clothed in a glory of hair, with streaming of robes and bright garments; and I kissed the hem of her robe.

19. And the voice of the angel of the Sun was heard like a sounding of trombones, saying, Thou hast yielded thy power to an

harlot, and given the earth to the fire; thy power is riven from thee, and all shall die;

20. So be it.

3

My name is George Anders. I have no hope that anyone will read this record, which will probably be destroyed with me—I have no safer place to put it than on my person—but I write it anyhow, if only to show that man was a talkative animal to his last gasp. If the day of glory which has been foretold comes about, there may will be a new and better world which will cherish what I put down here—but I am desperately afraid that the terrible here-and-now is the day the voices promised, and that there will be nothing else for ever and ever.

This is not to say that the voices lied. But since that first night when they spoke to me, I have come to know that they speak for forces of tremendous power, forces to which human life is as nothing. A day of glory we have already had, truly—but such a day as no man could long for.

It was on the morning of 18th March 1956 that that day dawned, with a sun so huge as to dominate the entire eastern sky—a flaring monster which made the memory of our accustomed sun seem like a match-flame. All the previous night had been as hot as high summer, although not four days before we had a blizzard. Now, with the rising of this colossal globe, we learned the real meaning of heat.

A day of glory, of glory incredible—and deadly. The heat grew and grew. By a little after noon the temperature in the shade was more than 150°, and in the open—it is impossible to describe what an inferno it was under the direct rays of that sun. A bucket of water thrown into the street from a window boiled in mid-air before it could strike the pavement.

In some parts of the city, where there were wooden buildings and asphalt or tarred-black streets, everything was burning. In the country, the radio said, it was worse; forests were ablaze, grasslands, wheatfields, everything. Curiously, it was this that saved many of us, for before the afternoon could reach its full fury the sky was grey with smoke, cutting off at least a little of the rays of that solar horror. Flakes of ash fell everywhere.

Millions died that day. Only a few in refrigerated rooms—meat-coolers, cold-storage warehouses, the blast-tunnels of frozen-food firms, underground fur-storage vaults—survived, where the refrigeration apparatus itself survived. By a little after midnight, the outside temperature had dropped to only slightly above 100°, and the trembling and half-mad wraiths who still lived emerged to look silently at the ruined world.

I was one of these; I had planned that I would be. Months before, I had known that this day of doom was to come upon us, for the voices had said so. I can still remember—for as long as I live I will remember, whether it be a day or forty years—the onset of that strange feeling, that withdrawal from the world around me, as if everything familiar had suddenly become as unreal as a stage-setting. What had seemed commonplace became strange, sinister: what was that man doing with the bottles which contained the white fluid? Why was the uniform he wore also white? Why not blood in the bottles? And the man with the huge assemblage of paper; why was he watching it so intently as he sat in the subway? Did he expect it to make some sudden move if he looked away? Were the black marks with which the paper was covered the footprints of some minuscule horde?

And as the world underwent its slow transformation, the voices came. I cannot write here what they said, because paper would not bear such words. But the meaning was clear. The destruction of the world was at hand. And beyond it—

Beyond it, the day of glory. A turn towards something new, something before which all men's previous knowledge of grandeur would pale; a new Apocalypse and Resurrection? So it seemed, then. But the voices spoke in symbol and parable, and perhaps the rising of the hellish sun was the only "day of glory" we would ever see.

And so I hid in my shelter, and survived that first day. When I first emerged into the boiling, choking midnight smoke I could see no one else, but after a while something white came out of the darkness towards me. It was a young girl, in what I took to be a nightgown—the lightest garment, at any event, which she could have worn in this intolerable heat.

"What will happen to us?" she said, as soon as she saw me. "What will happen to us? Will it be the same tomorrow?"

"I don't know," I said. "What's your name?"

"Margaret." She coughed. "This must be the end of the world. If the sun is like this tomorrow——"

"It *is* the end of the world," I said. "But maybe it's the beginning of another. You and I will live to see it."

"How do you know?"

"By your name. The voices call you the mother of the new gods. Have you heard the voices?"

She moved away from me a little bit. There was a sudden, furious gust of wind, and a long line of sparks flew through the lurid sky overhead. "The voices?" she said.

"Yes. The voices of the powers which have done all this. They have promised to save us, you and I. Together we can recreate——"

Suddenly, she was running. She vanished almost instantly into darkness and the smoke. I ran after her, calling, but it was hopeless; besides, my throat was already raw, and in the heat and the aftermath of the day I had no strength. I went back to my crypt. Tomorrow would tell the tale.

Sleep was impossible. I waited for dawn, and watched for it through my periscope, from the buried vault of the bank where, a day before, I had been a kind of teller. This had been no ordinary bank, and I had never taken or issued any money; but otherwise the terms are just. Perhaps you have already guessed, for no ordinary vault is equipped with periscopes to watch the surrounding countryside. This was Fort Knox, a bed of gold to be seeded with promise of the Age of Gold under this golden fire.

And, at last, the sun came up. It was immense. But I waited a while, and watched the image of it which was cast from the periscope eyepiece on to the opposite wall of the vault. It was not as big as it had been yesterday. And where yesterday the direct rays from the periscope had instantly charred a thousand-dollar bill, today they made only a slowly growing brown spot which never found its kindling-point.

The lesson was plain. Today most of what remained of mankind would be slain. But there would be survivors.

Then I slept.

I awoke towards the end of the day and set about the quest which I knew I must make. I took nothing with me but water, which I knew I could not expect to find. Then I left the vault for ever.

The world which greeted me as I came to the surface was a world transformed: blasted. Nearly everything had been levelled, and the rest lay in jumbled, smoking ruins. The sky was completely black. Near the Western horizon, the swollen sun sank, still monstrous, but now no hotter than the normal sun at the height of a tropic day. The great explosion, whatever it had been, was nearly over.

And now I had to find Margaret, and fulfil the millennium which the voices had promised. The tree of man had been blasted, but still it bore one flower. It was my great destiny to bring that flower to fruit.

Thus I bring this record to a close. I leave it here in the vault; then I shall go forth into the desert of the world. If any find it, remember: I am your father and the father of your race. If not, you will all be smoke.

Now I go. My knife is in my hand.

4

My name is Andy Virchow, but probably you know me better as Admiral Universe. Nowhere in the pages of galactic history has there ever been a greater champion of justice. Who do you know that doesn't know Universe, ruler of the spaceways, hero of science, bringer of law and order in the age of the conquest of space? Not a planetary soul, that's who.

Of course not everybody knows that Andy Virchow is Admiral Universe. Sometimes I have to go in disguise and fool criminals. Then I am Andy Virchow, and they think I am only 8 years old, until I have them where I want them and I whip out my Cosmic Smoke Gun and reveal my indentitification.

TESTAMENT OF ANDROS

Sometimes I don't say who I am but just clean the crooks up and ride off in my rocket, the *Margy II*. Then afterwards the people I have saved say, "He didn't even stay to be thanked. I wonder who he was?" and somebody else says, "There's only one man on the frontiers of space like him. That's Admiral Universe."

My rocket is called the *Margy II* partly because my secret interstellar base is on Mars and the Mars people we call Martians call themselves Margies and I like to think of myself as a Margy *too*, because the people of Earth don't understand me and I do good for them because I am champion of justice, not because I like them. Then they're sorry, but it's too late. Me and the Margies understand each other. They ask me for advice before they do anything important, and I tell them what to do. Earth people are always trying to tell other people what to do; the Margies aren't like that, they ask what to do instead of always giving orders.

Also Admiral Universe calls his rocket *Margy II*, because my patron saint is St. Margaret who gets me out of trouble if I do anything wrong. Admiral Universe never does anything wrong because St. Margaret is on his side all the time. St. Margaret is the patron saint of clocks and is called the Mother of Galaxies, because she was a mother—not like my mother, who is always shouting and sending me to bed too early—and mothers have milk and *galaxy* is Greek for milk. If you didn't know I was Admiral Universe you'd ask how I know what's Greek for anything, but Admiral Universe is a great scientist and knows everything. Besides, my father was a teacher of Greek before he died and he was Admiral Universe's first teacher.

In all the other worlds in the universe everything is pretty perfect except for a few crooks that have to be shot. It's not like Earth at all. The planets are different from each other, but they are all happy and have lots of science and the people are kind and never raise their hands to each other or send each other to bed without their supper.

Sometimes there are terrible accidents in the spacelanes and Admiral Universe arrives on the scene in the knick of time and saves everybody, and all the men shake his hand and all the girls kiss him and say mushy things to him, but he refuses their thanks in a polite way and disappears into the trackless wastes of outer space because he carries a medal of St. Margaret's in his pocket over his heart. She is his only girl, but she can't ever be anybody's girl because she is a saint, and this is Admiral Universe's great tragedy which he never tells anybody because it's his private business that he has to suffer all by himself, and besides if anybody else knew it they would think he was mushy too and wouldn't be so afraid of him, like crooks I mean.

Admiral Universe is always being called from all over outer space to help people and sometimes he can't be one place because he has to be in some other place. Then he has to set his jaw and do the best he can and be tough about the people he can't help because he is helping somebody else. First he asks St. Margaret what he should do and she tells him. Then he goes and does it, and he is very sorry for the people who get left out, but he knows that he did what was right.

This is why I wasn't there when the sun blew up, because I was helping people somewhere else at the time. I didn't even know it was the sun, because I was so far away that it was just another star, and I didn't see it blow up, because stars blow up all the time and if you're Admiral Universe you get used to it and hardly notice. Margaret might have told me, but she's a saint, and doesn't care.

If I'd of been there I would have helped. I would have saved my friends, and all the great scientists, and the girls who might be somebody's mothers some day, and everybody that was anybody except Dr. Ferguson, I would have left him behind to show him how wrong he was about me.

But I wasn't there at the time, and besides Admiral Universe never did like the Earth much. Nobody will really miss it.

5

My name is T. V. Andros. My father was an Athenian immigrant and a drunkard. After he came here he worked in the mines, but not very often because he was mostly soused.

Sometimes he beat my mother. She had TB but she took good care of us until I was 8; early that year, my father got killed in a brawl in a bar, and the doctor—his name I forget—sent her back to the little town in Pennsylvania where she was born. She died that March.

After that I worked in the mines. The law says a kid can't work in the mines but in company towns the law don't mean much. I got the cough too but the other miners took care of me and I grew up tough and could handle myself all right. When I was 14, I killed a man with a pick-handle, one blow. I don't remember what we was fighting about.

Mostly I kept out of fights, though. I had a crazy idea I wanted to educate myself and I read a lot—all kinds of things. For a while I read those magazines that tell about going to other planets and stuff like that. I didn't learn anything, except that to learn good you need a teacher, and the last one of those had been run out by the company cops. They said he was a Red.

It was tough in the mines. It's dark down there and hot, and you can't breathe sometimes for the dust. And you can't never wash the dirt off, it gets right down into your skin and makes you feel black even at noon on Sundays when you've scrubbed till your skin's raw.

I had a 16-year-old girl but I was too dirty for her. I tried to go to the priest about it but he wasn't looking for nothing but sin, and kept asking me had I done anything wrong with the girl. When I said I hadn't he wasn't interested no more. I hadn't, either, but he made me so mad he made me wish I had. After that I sort of drifted away from going to church because I couldn't stand his face. Maybe that was bad but it had its good side, too, I missed it and I took to cracking the Bible now and then. I never got much of the Bible when I was going to church.

After a while I took to drinking something now and then. It wasn't right for a kid but I wasn't a kid no more, I was eighteen and besides in the company towns there ain't nothing else to do. It helped some but not enough. All the guys in the bar ever talk about are wages and women. You got to drink yourself blind and stupid to keep from hearing them, otherwise you go nuts. After a while I was blind and stupid a lot of the time and didn't no longer know what I did or didn't.

TESTAMENT OF ANDROS

Once when I was drunk I mauled a girl younger than I was; I don't know why I did it. She was just the age I had been when my mother left me to go home and die. Then it was all up with me at the mines. I didn't mean her any harm but the judge gave me the works. Two years.

I got clean for once in my life while I was in the jug and I did some more reading but it just mixed me up more. Two years is a long time. When I got out I felt funny in my head. I couldn't stop thinking about the girl who thought I was too dirty for her. I was at the age when I needed girls.

But I wasn't going to mess with girls my age who could see the prison whiteness on the outside and all that ground-in coal dust underneath it. I couldn't forget Maggy, the girl that got me into the jam. That had been a hot night in summer, with a moon as big as the sun, as red as blood. I hadn't meant her any harm. She reminded me of myself when my mother had gone away.

I found another Maggy and when the cops caught me they worked me over. I can't hear in one ear now and my nose is skewed funny on my face. I had it coming because I hurt the girl. When they let me out again I got a job as a super, but there was another girl in the apartment above, and I went to fix a pipe there while her mother was away. It was a hot day with a big sun and no air moving, just like the day my mother left. I didn't really know nothing had happened until I saw that one of my hands was dark red. Then I tried to get her to talk to me but she wouldn't move. After a while I felt some woman's hands beating at my neck. She said, "Stop, you!"

This time they took me to a hospital and a Dr. Ferdinand talked to me. Write it all down, he said. It may help you. So I wrote it all down, like you see it here. Then they put me in a cell and said I would have to stay for a while. I don't talk to them much any more.

It is a real hot day. Outside the cell the sun is bigger. I don't breathe good any more but there's something wrong with the air. I pulled my mattress to pieces but I didn't find nothing. Maybe something is going to happen. Something is going to happen.

6

My name is Man. I will write my story if you wish.
I was . . .
Here the ashes blow away. The voices die.

Writers of fantasies are often suspected of transcribing material directly out of bad dreams. As a matter of fact this almost never happens, but sometimes a story will turn so sharply away from the way the writer thought it was going to go as to make it seem almost as independent as a dream. That happened in Part Three of this story: I had planned to confront my hero with something as unearthly as I could possibly manage, but I did not know what it would be until it began to appear on the page. Ordinarily I detest the products of automatic writing, but whatever my unconscious was up to here—and it has been the subject of reams of analysis by my friends—I think I still approve of it; the story frames and controls it, though perhaps just barely.

Common Time

"... the days went slowly round and round, endless and uneventful as cycles in space. Time, and time-pieces! How many centuries did my hammock tell, as pendulum-like it swung to the ship's dull roll, and ticked the hours and ages."

HERMAN MELVILLE in *Mardi*

I

Don't move.

It was the first thought that came into Garrard's mind when he awoke, and perhaps it saved his life. He lay where he was, strapped against the padding, listening to the round hum of the engines. That in itself was wrong; he should be unable to hear the overdrive at all.

He thought to himself: *Has it begun already?*

Otherwise everything seemed normal. The DFC-3 had crossed over into interstellar velocity, and he was still alive, and the ship was still functioning. The ship should at this moment be travelling at 22·4 times the speed of light—a neat 4,157,000 miles per second.

Somehow Garrard did not doubt that it was. On both previous tries, the ships had whiffed away towards Alpha Centauri at the proper moment when the overdrive should have cut in; and the split second of residual image after they had vanished, subjected to spectroscopy, showed a Doppler shift which tallied with the acceleration predicted for that moment by Haertel.

The trouble was not that Brown and Cellini hadn't gotten away in good order. It was simply that neither of them had ever been heard from again.

Very slowly, he opened his eyes. His eyelids felt terrifically heavy. As far as he could judge from the pressure of the couch against his skin, the gravity was normal; nevertheless, moving his eyelids seemed almost an impossible job.

After long concentration, he got them fully open. The instrument chassis was directly before him, extended over his diaphragm on its elbow joint. Still without moving anything but his eyes—and those only with the utmost patience—he checked each of the meters. Velocity: 22·4 c. Operating temperature: normal. Ship temperature: 37° C. Air pressure: 778 mm. Fuel: No. 1 tank full, No. 2 tank full, No. 3 tank full, No. 4 tank nine-tenths full. Gravity: 1 g. Calendar: stopped.

He looked at it closely, though his eyes seemed to focus very slowly, too. It was, of course, something more than a calendar—it was an all-purpose clock, designed to show him the passage of seconds, as well as of the ten months his trip was supposed to take to the double star. But there was no doubt about it: the second hand was motionless.

That was the second abnormality. Garrard felt an impulse to get up and see if he could start the clock again. Perhaps the trouble had been temporary and safely in the past. Immediately there sounded in his head the injunction he had drilled into himself for a full month before the trip had begun—

Don't move!

Don't move until you know the situation as far as it can be known without moving. Whatever it was that had snatched Brown and Cellini irretrievably beyond human ken was potent, and totally beyond anticipation. They had both been excellent men, intelligent, resourceful, trained to the point of diminishing returns and not a micron beyond that point—the best men in the Project. Preparations for every knowable kind of trouble had been built into their ships, as they had been built into the DFC-3. Therefore, if there was something wrong nevertheless, it would be something that might strike from some commonplace quarter—and strike only once.

He listened to the humming. It was even and placid, and not very loud, but it disturbed him deeply. The overdrive was supposed to be inaudible, and the tapes from the first unmanned test vehicles had recorded no such hum. The noise did not appear to interfere with the overdrive's operation, or to indicate any failure in it. It was just an irrelevancy for which he could find no reason.

But the reason existed. Garrard did not intend to do so much as draw another breath until he found out what it was.

Incredibly, he realized for the first time that he had not in fact drawn one single breath since he had first come to. Though he felt not the slightest discomfort, the discovery called up so overwhelming a flash of panic that he very nearly sat bolt upright on the couch. Luckily—or so it seemed, after the panic had begun to ebb—the curious lethargy which had affected his eyelids appeared to involve his whole body, for the impulse was gone before he could summon the energy to answer it. And the panic, poignant though it had been for an instant, turned out to be wholly intellectual. In a moment, he was observing that his failure to breathe in no way discommoded him as far as he could tell—it was just there, waiting to be explained. . . .

Or to kill him. But it hadn't, yet.

Engines humming; eyelids heavy; breathing absent; calendar stopped. The four facts added up to nothing. The temptation to move something—even if it were only a big toe—was strong, but Garrard fought it back. He had been awake only a'short while—half an hour at most—and already had noticed four abnormalities. There were bound to be more, anomalies more subtle than these four, but available to close examination before he had to move. Nor was there anything in particular that he had to do, aside from caring for his own wants; the Project, on the chance that Brown's and Cellini's failure to return had resulted from some tampering with the overdrive, had made everything in the DFC-3 subject only to the computer. In a very real sense, Garrard was just along for the ride. Only when the overdrive was off could he adjust——

Pock.

It was a soft, low-pitched noise, rather like a cork coming out of a wine-bottle. It seemed to have come just from the right of the control chassis. He halted a sudden jerk of his head on the cushions towards it with a flat fiat of will. Slowly, he moved his eyes in that direction.

He could see nothing that might have caused the sound. The ship's temperature dial showed no change, which ruled out a heat noise from differential contraction or expansion—the only possible explanation he could bring to mind.

He closed his eyes—a process which turned out to be just as difficult as opening them had been—and tried to visualize what the calendar had looked like when he had first come out of anaesthesia. After he got a clear and—he was almost sure—accurate picture, Garrard opened his eyes again.

The sound had been the calendar, advancing one second. It was now motionless again, apparently stopped.

He did not know how long it took the second hand to make that jump, normally; the question had never come up. Certainly the jump, when it came at the end of each second, had been too fast for the eye to follow.

Belatedly, he realized what all this cogitation was costing him in terms of essential information. The calendar had moved. Above all and before anything else, he *must* know exactly how long it took it to move again. . . .

He began to count, allowing an arbitrary five seconds lost. *One-and-a-six, one-and-a-seven, one-and-an-eight*——

Garrard had gotten only that far when he found himself plunged into hell.

First, and utterly without reason, a sickening fear flooded swiftly through his veins, becoming more and more intense. His bowels began to knot, with infinite slowness. His whole body became a field of small, slow pulses—not so much shaking him as putting his limbs into contrary joggling motions, and making his skin ripple

gently under his clothing. Against the hum another sound became
audible, a nearly subsonic thunder which seemed to be inside his
head. Still the fear mounted, and with it came the pain, and the
tenesmus—a boardlike stiffening of his muscles, particularly across
his abdomen and his shoulders, but affecting his forearms almost as
grievously. He felt himself beginning, very gradually, to double at
the middle, a motion about which he could do precisely nothing—a
terrifying kind of dynamic paralysis. . . .

It lasted for hours. At the height of it, Garrard's mind, even his
very personality, was washed out utterly; he was only a vessel of
horror. When some few trickles of reason began to return over that
burning desert of reasonless emotion, he found that he was sitting
up on the cushions, and that with one arm he had thrust the control
chassis back on its elbow so that it no longer jutted over his body.
His clothing was wet with perspiration, which stubbornly refused
to evaporate or to cool him. And his lungs ached a little, although
he could still detect no breathing.

What under God had happened? Was it this that had killed
Brown and Cellini? For it would kill Garrard, too—of that he was
sure, if it happened often. It would kill him even if it happened
only twice more, if the next two such things followed the first one
closely. At the very best it would make a slobbering idiot of him;
and though the computer might bring Garrard and the ship back
to Earth, it would not be able to tell the Project about this tornado
of senseless fear.

The calendar said that the eternity in hell had taken three seconds. As he looked at it in academic indignation, it said *pock* and
condescended to make the total seizure four seconds long. With
grim determination, Garrard began to count again.

He took care to establish the counting as an absolutely even,
automatic process which would not stop at the back of his mind no
matter what other problem he tackled along with it, or what emotional typhoons should interrupt him. Really compulsive counting
cannot be stopped by anything—not the transports of love nor the
agonies of empires. Garrard knew the dangers in deliberately setting
up such a mechanism in his mind, but he also knew how desperately

he needed to time that clock tick. He was beginning to understand what had happened to him—but he needed exact measurement before he could put that understanding to use.

Of course there had been plenty of speculation on the possible effect of the overdrive on the subjective time of the pilot, but none of it had come to much. At any speed below the velocity of light, subjective and objective time were exactly the same as far as the pilot was concerned. For an observer on Earth, time aboard the ship would appear to be vastly slowed at near-light speeds; but for the pilot himself there would be no apparent change.

Since flight beyond the speed of light was impossible—although for slightly differing reasons—by both the current theories of relativity, neither theory had offered any clue as to what would happen on board a translight ship. They would not allow that any such ship could even exist. The Haertel transformation, on which, in effect, the DFC-3 flew, was non-relativistic: it showed that the apparent elapsed time of a translight journey should be identical in ship-time, and in the time of observers at both ends of the trip.

But since ship and pilot were part of the same system, both covered by the same expression in Haertel's equation, it had never occurred to anyone that the pilot and the ship might keep different times. The notion was ridiculous.

One-and-a-sevenhundredone, one-and-a-sevenhundredtwo, one-and-a-sevenhundredthree, one-and-a-sevenhundredfour . . .

The ship was keeping ship-time, which was identical with observer-time. It would arrive at the Alpha Centauri system in ten months. But the pilot was keeping Garrard-time, and it was beginning to look as though he wasn't going to arrive at all.

It was impossible, but there it was. Something—almost certainly an unsuspected physiological side effect of the overdrive field on human metabolism, an effect which naturally could not have been detected in the preliminary, robot-piloted tests of the overdrive—had speeded up Garrard's subjective apprehension of time, and had done a thorough job of it.

The second hand began a slow, preliminary quivering as the calendar's innards began to apply power to it. *Seventy-hundred-forty-one, seventy-hundred-forty-two, seventy-hundred-forty-three . . .*

At the count of 7,058 the second hand began the jump to the next graduation. It took it several minutes to get across the tiny distance, and several more to come completely to rest. Later still, the sound came to him:

Pock.

In a fever of thought, but without any real physical agitation, his mind began to manipulate the figures. Since it took him longer to count an individual number as the number became larger, the interval between the two calendar ticks probably was closer to 7,200 seconds than to 7,058. Figuring backwards brought him quickly to the equivalence he wanted:

One second in ship-time was two hours in Garrard-time.

Had he really been counting for what was, for him, two whole hours? There seemed to be no doubt about it. It looked like a long trip ahead.

Just how long it was going to be struck him with stunning force. Time had been slowed for him by a factor of 7,200. He would get to Alpha Centauri in just 72,000 months.

Which was—

Six thousand years!

2

Garrard sat motionless for a long time after that, the Nessus-shirt of warm sweat swathing him persistently, refusing even to cool. There was, after all, no hurry.

Six thousand years. There would be food and water and air for all that time, or for sixty or six hundred thousand years; the ship would synthesize his needs, as a matter of course, for as long as the fuel lasted, and the fuel bred itself. Even if Garrard ate a meal every three seconds of objective, or ship, time (which, he realized suddenly, he wouldn't be able to do, for it took the ship several seconds of objective time to prepare and serve up a meal once it was ordered; he'd be lucky if he ate once a day, Garrard-time), there would be no reason to fear any shortage of supplies. That had been one of the earliest of the possibilities for disaster that the Project engineers had ruled out in the design of the DFC-3.

But nobody had thought to provide a mechanism which would indefinitely refurbish Garrard. After six thousand years, there would be nothing left of him but a faint film of dust on the DFC-3's dully gleaming horizontal surfaces. His corpse might outlast him a while, since the ship itself was sterile—but eventually he would be consumed by the bacteria which he carried in his own digestive tract. He needed those bacteria to synthesize part of his B-vitamin needs while he lived, but they would consume him without compunction once he had ceased to be as complicated and delicately balanced a thing as a pilot—or as any other kind of life.

Garrard was, in short, to die before the DFC-3 had gotten fairly away from Sol; and when, after 12,000 apparent years, the DFC-3 returned to Earth, not even his mummy would be still aboard.

The chill that went through him at that seemed almost unrelated to the way he thought he felt about the discovery; it lasted an enormously long time, and in so far as he could characterize it at all, it seemed to be a chill of urgency and excitement—not at all the kind of chill he should be feeling at a virtual death sentence. Luckily it was not as intolerably violent as the last such emotional convulsion; and when it was over, two clock ticks later, it left behind a residuum of doubt.

Suppose that this effect of time-stretching was only mental? The rest of his bodily processes might still be keeping ship-time; Garrard had no immediate reason to believe otherwise. If so, he would be able to move about only on ship-time, too; it would take many apparent months to complete the simplest task.

But he would live, if that were the case. His mind would arrive at Alpha Centauri six thousand years older, and perhaps madder, than his body, but he would live.

If, on the other hand, his bodily movements were going to be as fast as his mental processes, he would have to be enormously careful. He would have to move slowly and exert as little force as possible. The normal human hand movement, in such a task as lifting a pencil, took the pencil from a state of rest to another state of rest by imparting to it an acceleration of about two feet per second per second—and, of course, decelerated it by the same amount. If Garrard were to attempt to impart to a two-pound weight, which was keeping ship-time, an acceleration of 14,440 ft./sec.^{2} in his time, he'd have to exert a force of 900 pounds on it.

The point was not that it couldn't be done—but that it would take as much effort as pushing a stalled jeep. He'd never be able to lift that pencil with his forearm muscles alone; he'd have to put his back into the task.

And the human body wasn't engineered to maintain stresses of that magnitude indefinitely. Not even the most powerful professional weight-lifter is forced to show his prowess throughout every minute of every day.

Pock.

That was the calendar again; another second had gone by. Or another two hours. It had certainly seemed longer than a second, but less than two hours, too. Evidently subjective time was an intensively recomplicated measure. Even in this world of micro-time—in which Garrard's mind, at least, seemed to be operating—he could make the lapses between calendar ticks seem a little shorter by becoming actively interested in some problem or other. That would help, during the waking hours, but it would help only if the rest of his body were *not* keeping the same time as his mind. If it were not, then he would lead an incredibly active, but perhaps not intolerable, mental life during the many centuries of his awake-time, and would be mercifully asleep for nearly as long.

Both problems—that of how much force he could exert with his body, and how long he could hope to be asleep in his mind—emerged simultaneously into the forefront of his consciousness while he still sat inertly on the hammock, their terms still much muddled together. After the single tick of the calendar, the ship—or the part of it that Garrard could see from here—settled back into complete rigidity. The sound of the engines, too, did not seem to vary in frequency or amplitude, at least as far as his ears could tell. He was still not breathing. Nothing moved, nothing changed.

It was the fact that he could still detect no motion of his diaphragm or his rib cage that decided him at last. His body had to be keeping ship-time, otherwise he would have blacked out from oxygen starvation long before now. That assumption explained, too, those two incredibly prolonged, seemingly sourceless saturnalias of emotion through which he had suffered: they had been nothing more or less than the response of his endocrine glands to the purely intellectual reactions he had experienced earlier. He had discovered that he was not breathing, had felt a flash of panic and had tried to sit up. Long after his mind had forgotten those two impulses, they had inched their way from his brain down his nerves to the glands and muscles involved, and actual, *physical* panic had supervened. When that was over, he actually *was* sitting up, though the flood of adrenalin had prevented his noticing the motion as he had made it. The later chill—less violent, and apparently associated with the discovery that he might die long before the trip was completed—actually had been his body's response to a much earlier mental command—the abstract fever of interest he had felt while computing the time differential had been responsible for it.

Obviously, he was going to have to be very careful with apparently cold and intellectual impulses of any kind—or he would pay for them later with a prolonged and agonizing glandular reaction. Nevertheless, the discovery gave him considerable satisfaction, and Garrard allowed it free play; it certainly could not hurt him to feel pleased for a few hours, and the glandular pleasure might even prove helpful if it caught him at a moment of mental depression. Six thousand years, after all, provided a considerable number of opportunities for feeling down in the mouth; so it would be best to encourage all pleasure moments, and let the after-reaction last as long as it might. It would be the instants of panic, of fear, of gloom, which he would have to regulate sternly the moment they came into his mind; it would be those which would otherwise plunge him into four, five, six, perhaps even ten, Garrard-hours of emotional inferno.

Pock.

There now, that was very good: there had been two Garrard-hours which he had passed with virtually no difficulty of any kind, and without being especially conscious of their passage. If he could really settle down and become used to this kind of scheduling, the trip might not be as bad as he had at first feared. Sleep would take immense bites out of it; and during the waking periods he could put in one hell of a lot of creative thinking. During a single day of ship time, Garrard could get in more thinking than any philosopher of Earth could have managed during an entire lifetime. Garrard could, if he disciplined himself sufficiently, devote his mind for a century to running down the consequences of a single thought, down to the last detail, and still have millennia left to go on to the next thought. What panoplies of pure reason could he not have assembled by the time 6,000 years had gone by? With sufficient concentration, he might come up with the solution to the Problem of Evil between breakfast and dinner of a single ship's day, and in a ship's month might put his finger on the First Cause!

Pock.

Not that Garrard was sanguine enough to expect that he would remain logical or even sane throughout the trip. The vista was still grim, in much of its detail. But the opportunities, too, were there. He felt a momentary regret that it hadn't been Haertel, rather than himself, who had been given such an opportunity—

Pock.

—for the old man could certainly have made better use of it than Garrard could. The situation demanded someone trained in the highest rigours of mathematics to be put to the best conceivable use. Still and all Garrard began to feel—

Pock.

—that he would give a good account of himself, and it tickled him to realize that (as long as he held on to his essential sanity) he would return—

Pock.

—to Earth after ten Earth months with knowledge centuries advanced beyond anything—

Pock.

—that Haertel knew, or that anyone could know—

Pock.

—who had to work within a normal lifetime. *Pck.* The whole prospect tickled him. *Pck.* Even the clock tick seemed more cheerful. *Pck.* He felt fairly safe now *Pck* in disregarding his drilled-in command *Pck* against moving *Pck*, since in any *Pck* event he *Pck* had already *Pck* moved *Pck* without *Pck* being *Pck* harmed *Pck* Pck Pck Pck Pck *pckpckpckpckpckpckpck.* . . .

He yawned, stretched, and got up. It wouldn't do to be too pleased, after all. There were certainly many problems that still needed coping with, such as how to keep the impulse towards getting a ship-time task performed going, while his higher centres were following the ramifications of some purely philosophical point. And besides . . .

And besides, he had just moved.

More than that; he had just performed a complicated manœuvre with his body *in normal time*!

Before Garrard looked at the calendar itself, the message it had been ticking away at him had penetrated. While he had been enjoying the protracted, glandular backwash of his earlier feeling of satisfaction, he had failed to notice, at least consciously, that the calendar was accelerating.

Good-bye, vast ethical systems which would dwarf the Greeks. Good-bye, calculi aeons advanced beyond the spinor calculus of Dirac. Good-bye, cosmologies by Garrard which would allot the Almighty a job as third-assistant-waterboy in an *n*-dimensional backfield.

Good-bye, also, to a project he had once tried to undertake in college—to describe and count the positions of love, of which, according to under-the-counter myth, there were supposed to be at least forty-eight. Garrard had never been able to carry his tally beyond twenty, and he had just lost what was probably his last opportunity to try again.

The micro-time in which he had been living had worn off, only a few objective minutes after the ship had gone into overdrive and he had come out of the anaesthetic. The long intellectual agony, with its glandular counterpoint, had come to nothing. Garrard was now keeping ship-time.

Garrard sat back down on the hammock, uncertain whether to be bitter or relieved. Neither emotion satisfied him in the end; he simply felt unsatisfied. Micro-time had been bad enough while it lasted; but now it was gone, and everything seemed normal. How could so transient a thing have killed Brown and Cellini? They were stable men, more stable, by his own private estimation, than Garrard himself. Yet he had come through it. Was there more to it than this?

And if there was—what, conceivably, could it be?

There was no answer. At his elbow, on the control chassis which he had thrust aside during that first moment of infinitely protracted panic, the calendar continued to tick. The engine noise was gone. His breath came and went in natural rhythm. He felt light and strong. The ship was quiet, calm, unchanging.

The calendar ticked, faster and faster. It reached and passed the first hour, ship-time, of flight in overdrive.

Pock.

Garrard looked up in surprise. The familiar noise, this time, had been the hour-hand jumping one unit. The minute-hand was already sweeping past the past half-hour. The second-hand was whirling like a propeller—and while he watched it, it speeded up to complete invisibility—

Pock.

Another hour. The half-hour already passed. *Pock.* Another hour. *Pock.* Another. *Pock. Pock. Pock, Pock, Pock, Pock, pck-pck-pck-pck-pckpckpckpck.* . . .

The hands of the calendar swirled towards invisibility as time ran away with Garrard. Yet the ship did not change. It stayed there, rigid, inviolate, invulnerable. When the date tumblers reached a speed at which Garrard could no longer read them, he discovered that once more he could not move—and that, although his whole body seemed to be aflutter like that of a humming-bird, nothing coherent was coming to him through his senses. The room was dimming, becoming redder; or no, it was . . .

But he never saw the end of the process, never was allowed to look from the pinnacle of macro-time towards which the Haertel overdrive was taking him.

Pseudo-death took him first.

COMMON TIME

3

That Garrard did not die completely, and within a comparatively short time after the DFC-3 had gone into overdrive, was due to the purest of accidents; but Garrard did not know that. In fact, he knew nothing at all for an indefinite period, sitting rigid and staring, his metabolism slowed down to next to nothing, his mind almost utterly inactive. From time to time, a single wave of low-level metabolic activity passed through him—what an electrician might have termed a "maintenance turnover"—in response to the urgings of some occult survival urge; but these were of so basic a nature as to reach his consciousness not at all. This was the pseudo-death.

When the observer actually arrived, however, Garrard woke. He could make very little sense out of what he saw or felt even now; but one fact was clear: the overdrive was off—and with it the crazy alterations in time rates—and there was strong light coming through one of the ports. The first leg of the trip was over. It had been these two changes in his environment which had restored him to life.

The thing (or things) which had restored him to consciousness, however, was—it was what? It made no sense. It was a construction, a rather fragile one, which completely surrounded his hammock. No, it wasn't a construction, but evidently something alive—a living being, organized horizontally, that had arranged itself in a circle about him. No, it was a number of beings. Or a combination of all of these things.

How it had gotten into the ship was a mystery, but there it was. Or there they were.

"How do you hear?" the creature said abruptly. Its voice, or their voices, came at equal volume from every point in the circle, but not from any particular point in it. Garrard could think of no reason why that should be unusual.

"I—" he said. "Or we—we hear with our ears. Here."

His answer, with its unintentionally long chain of open vowel sounds, rang ridiculously. He wondered why he was speaking such an odd language.

97

"We-they wooed to pitch you-yours thisways," the creature said. With a thump, a book from the DFC-3's ample library fell to the deck beside the hammock. "We wooed there and there and there for a many. You are the being-Garrard. We-they are the clinesterton beademung, with all of love."

"With all of love," Garrard echoed. The beademung's use of the language they both were speaking was odd; but again Garrard could find no logical reason why the beademung's usage should be considered wrong.

"Are—are you-they from Alpha Centauri?" he said hesitantly.

"Yes, we hear the twin radioceles, that show there beyond the gift-orifices. We-they pitched that the being-Garrard heard with most adoration these twins and had mind to them, soft and loud alike. How do you hear?"

This time the being-Garrard understood the question. "I hear Earth," he said. "But that is very soft, and does not show."

"Yes," said the beademung. "It is a harmony, not a first, as ours. The All-Devouring listens to lovers there, not on the radioceles. Let me-mine pitch you-yours so to have mind of the rodalent beademung and other brothers and lovers, along the channel which is fragrant to the being-Garrard."

Garrard found that he understood the speech without difficulty. The thought occurred to him that to understand a language on its own terms—without having to put it back into English in one's own mind—is an ability that is won only with difficulty and long practice. Yet, instantly his mind said, "But it *is* English," which of course it was. The offer the clinesterton beademung had just made was enormously hearted, and he in turn was much minded and of love, to his own delighting as well as to the beademungen; that almost went without saying.

There were many matings of ships after that, and the being-Garrard pitched the harmonies of the beademungen, leaving his ship with the many gift-orifices in harmonic for the All-Devouring to love, while the beademungen made show of they-theirs.

He tried, also, to tell how he was out of love with the overdrive, which wooed only spaces and times, and made featurelings. The

rodalent beademung wooed the overdrive, but it did not pitch
he-them.

Then the being-Garrard knew that all the time was devoured,
and he must hear Earth again.

"I pitch you-them to fullest love," he told the beademungen. "I
shall adore the radioceles of Alpha and Proxima Centauri, 'on
Earth as it is in Heaven'. Now the overdrive my-other must woo
and win me, and make me adore a featureling much like silence."

"But you will be pitched again," the clinesterton beademung
said. "After you have adored Earth. You are much loved by Time,
the All-Devouring. We-they shall wait for this othering."

Privately Garrard did not faith as much, but he said, "Yes, we-
they will make a new wooing of the beademungen at some other
radiant. With all of love."

On this the beademungen made and pitched adorations, and in
the midst the overdrive cut in. The ship with the many gift-orifices
and the being-Garrard him-other saw the twin radioceles sundered
away.

Then, once more, came the pseudo-death.

4

When the small candle lit in the endless cavern of Garrard's
pseudo-dead mind, the DFC-3 was well inside the orbit of Uranus.
Since the sun was still very small and distant, it made no spectacular
display through the nearby port, and nothing called him from the
post-death sleep for nearly two days.

The computers waited patiently for him. They were no longer
immune to his control; he could now tool the ship back to Earth
himself if he so desired. But the computers were also designed to
take into account the fact that he might be truly dead by the time
the DFC-3 got back. After giving him a solid week, during which
time he did nothing but sleep, they took over again. Radio signals
began to go out, tuned to a special channel.

An hour later, a very weak signal came back. It was only a
directional signal, and it made no sound inside the DFC-3—but it
was sufficient to put the big ship in motion again.

COMMON TIME

It was that which woke Garrard. His conscious mind was still glazed over with the icy spume of the pseudo-death; and as far as he could see the interior of the cabin had not changed one whit, except for the book on the deck—

The book. The clinesterton beademung had dropped it there. But what under God was a clinesterton beademung? And what was he, Garrard, crying about? It didn't make sense. He remembered dimly some kind of experience out there by the Centauri twins—

—the twin radioceles—

There was another one of those words. It seemed to have Greek roots, but he knew no Greek—and besides, why would Centaurians speak Greek?

He leaned forward and actuated the switch which would roll the shutter off the front port, actually a telescope with a translucent viewing screen. It showed a few stars, and a faint nimbus off on one edge which might be the Sun. At about one o'clock on the screen was a planet about the size of a pea which had tiny projections, like teacup handles, on each side. The DFC-3 hadn't passed Saturn on its way out; at that time it had been on the other side of the Sun from the route the starship had had to follow. But the planet was certainly difficult to mistake.

Garrard was on his way home—and he was still alive and sane. Or was he still sane? These fantasies about Centaurians—which still seemed to have such a profound emotional effect upon him— did not argue very well for the stability of his mind.

But they were fading rapidly. When he discovered, clutching at the handiest fragments of the "memories", that the plural of *beademung* was *beademungen*, he stopped taking the problem seriously. Obviously a race of Centaurians who spoke Greek wouldn't also be forming weak German plurals. The whole business had obviously been thrown up by his unconscious.

But what *had* he found by the Centaurus stars?

There was no answer to that question but that incomprehensible garble about love, the All-Devouring, and beademungen. Possibly, he had never seen the Centaurus stars at all, but had been lying here, cold as a mackerel, for the entire twenty months.

Or had it been 12,000 years? After the tricks the overdrive had played with time, there was no way to tell what the objective date actually was. Frantically Garrard put the telescope into action. Where was the Earth? After 12,000 years—

The Earth was there. Which, he realized swiftly, proved nothing. The Earth had lasted for many millions of years; 12,000 years was nothing to a planet. The Moon was there, too; both were plainly visible, on the far side of the Sun—but not too far to pick them out clearly, with the telescope at highest power. Garrard could even see a clear sun-highlight on the Atlantic Ocean, not far east of Greenland; evidently the computers were bringing the DFC-3 in on the Earth from about 23° north of the plane of the ecliptic.

The Moon, too, had not changed. He could even see on its face the huge splash of white, mimicking the sun-highlight on Earth's ocean, which was the magnesium hydroxide landing beacon, which had been dusted over the Mare Vaporum in the earliest days of space flight, with a dark spot on its southern edge which could only be the crater Monilius.

But that again proved nothing. The Moon never changed. A film of dust laid down by modern man on its face would last for millennia —what, after all, existed on the Moon to blow it away? The Mare Vaporum beacon covered more than 4,000 square miles; age would not dim it, nor could man himself undo it—either accidentally, or on purpose—in anything under a century. When you dust an area that large on a world without atmosphere, it stays dusted.

He checked the stars against his charts. They hadn't moved; why should they have, in only 12,000 years? The pointer stars in the Dipper still pointed to Polaris. Draco, like a fantastic bit of tape, wound between the two Bears, and Cepheus and Cassiopeia, as it always had done. These constellations told him only that it was spring in the northern hemisphere of Earth.

But spring of what year?

Then, suddenly, it occurred to Garrard that he had a method of finding the answer. The Moon causes tides in the Earth, and action and reaction are always equal and opposite. The Moon cannot move things on Earth without itself being affected—and that effect shows up in the moon's angular momentum. The Moon's distance from the Earth increases steadily by 0·6 inches every year. At the end of 12,000 years, it should be 600 feet farther away from the Earth.

Was it possible to measure? Garrard doubted it, but he got out his ephemeris and his dividers anyhow, and took pictures. While he worked, the Earth grew nearer. By the time he had finished his first calculation—which was indecisive, because it allowed a margin for error greater than the distances he was trying to check—Earth and Moon were close enough in the telescope to permit much more accurate measurements.

Which were, he realized wryly, quite unnecessary. The computer had brought the DFC-3 back, not to an observed sun or planet, but simply to a calculated point. That Earth and Moon would not be near that point when the DFC-3 returned was not an assumption that the computer could make. That the Earth was visible from here was already good and sufficient proof that no more time had elapsed than had been calculated for from the beginning.

This was hardly new to Garrard; it had simply been retired to the back of his mind. Actually he had been doing all this figuring for one reason, and one reason only: because deep in his brain, set to work by himself, there was a mechanism that demanded counting. Long ago, while he was still trying to time the ship's calendar, he had initiated compulsive counting—and it appeared that he had been counting ever since. That had been one of the known dangers of deliberately starting such a mental mechanism; and now it was bearing fruit in these perfectly useless astronomical exercises.

The insight was healing. He finished the figures roughly, and that unheard moron deep inside his brain stopped counting at last. It had been pawing its abacus for twenty months now, and Garrard imagined that it was as glad to be retired as he was to feel it go.

His radio squawked, and said anxiously, "DFC-3, DFC-3. Garrard, do you hear me? Are you still alive? Everybody's going wild down here. Garrard, if you hear me, call us!"

It was Haertel's voice. Garrard closed the dividers so convulsively that one of the points nipped into the heel of his hand. "Haertel, I'm here. DFC-3 to the Project. This is Garrard." And then, without knowing quite why, he added: "With all of love."

Haertel, after all the hoopla was over, was more than interested in the time effects. "It certainly enlarges the manifold in which I was working," he said. "But I think we can account for it in the transformation. Perhaps even factor it out, which would eliminate it as far as the pilot is concerned. We'll see, anyhow."

Garrard swirled his highball reflectively. In Haertel's cramped old office, in the Project's administration shack, he felt both strange and as old, as compressed, constricted. He said, "I don't think I'd do that, Adolph. I think it saved my life."

"How?"

"I told you that I seemed to die after a while. Since I got home, I've been reading; and I've discovered that the psychologists take far less stock in the individuality of the human psyche than you and I do. You and I are physical scientists, so we think about the world as being all outside our skins—something which is to be observed, but which doesn't alter the essential *I*. But evidently, that old solipsistic position isn't quite true. Our very personalities, really, depend in large part upon *all* the things in our environment, large and small, that exist outside our skins. If by some means you could cut a human being off from every sense impression that comes to him from outside, he would cease to exist as a personality within two or three minutes. Probably he would die."

"Unquote: Harry Stack Sullivan," Haertel said, dryly. "So?"

"So," Garrard said, "think of what a monotonous environment the inside of a spaceship is. It's perfectly rigid, still, unchanging, lifeless. In ordinary interplanetary flight, in such an environment, even the most hardened spaceman may go off his rocker now and then. You know the typical spaceman's psychosis as well as I do, I suppose. The man's personality goes rigid, just like his surroundings. Usually he recovers as soon as he makes port, and makes contact with a more-or-less normal world again.

"But in the DFC-3, I was cut off from the world around me much more severely. I couldn't look outside the ports—I was in overdrive, and there was nothing to see. I couldn't communicate with home, because I was going faster than light. And then I found I couldn't move either, for an enormous long while; and that even the instruments that are in constant change for the usual spaceman wouldn't be in motion for me. Even those were fixed.

"After the time rate began to pick up, I found myself in an even more impossible box. The instruments moved, all right, but then they moved too *fast* for me to read them. The whole situation was now utterly rigid—and, in effect, I died. I froze as solid as the ship around me, and stayed that way as long as the overdrive was on."

"By that showing," Haertel said dryly, "the time effects were hardly your friends."

"But they were, Adolph. Look. Your engines act on subjective time; they keep it varying along continuous curves—from far-too-slow to far-too-fast—and, I suppose, back down again. Now, this is a *situation of continuous change*. It wasn't marked enough, in the long run, to keep me out of pseudo-death; but it was sufficient to protect me from being obliterated altogether, which I think is what happened to Brown and Cellini. Those men knew that they could shut down the overdrive if they could just get to it, and they killed themselves trying. But I knew that I just had to sit and take it—and, by my great good luck, your sine-curve time variation made it possible for me to survive."

"Ah, ah," Haertel said. "A point worth considering—though I doubt that it will make interstellar travel very popular!"

He dropped back into silence, his thin mouth pursed. Garrard took a grateful pull at his drink.

At last Haertel said: "Why are you in trouble over these Centaurians? It seems to me that you have done a good job. It was nothing that you were a hero—any fool can be brave—but I see also that you *thought*, where Brown and Cellini evidently only reacted. Is there some secret about what you found when you reached those two stars?"

Garrard said, "Yes, there is. But I've already told you what it is. When I came out of the pseudo-death, I was just a sort of plastic palimpsest upon which anybody could have made a mark. My own environment, my ordinary Earth environment, was a hell of a long way off. My present surroundings were nearly as rigid as they had ever been. When I met the Centaurians—if I did, and I'm not at all sure of that—*they* became the most important thing in my world, and my personality changed to accommodate and understand them. That was a change about which I couldn't do a thing.

"Possibly I did understand them. But the man who understood them wasn't the same man you're talking to now, Adolph. Now that I'm back on Earth, I don't understand that man. He even spoke English in a way that's gibberish to me. If I can't understand myself during that period—and I can't; I don't even believe that that man was the Garrard I know—what hope have I of telling you or the Project about the Centaurians? They found me in a controlled environment, and they altered me by entering it. Now that they're gone, nothing comes through; I don't even understand why I think they spoke English!"

"Did they have a name for themselves?"

"Sure," Garrard said. "They were the beademungen."

"What did they look like?"

"I never saw them."

Haertel leaned forward. "Then . . ."

"I heard them. I think." Garrard shrugged, and tasted his Scotch again. He was home, and on the whole he was pleased.

But in his malleable mind he heard someone say, *On Earth, as it is in Heaven*; and then, in another voice, which might also have been his own (why had he thought "him-other"?), *It is later than you think*.

"Adolph," he said, "is this all there is to it? Or are we going to go on with it from here? How long will it take to make a better starship, a DFC-4?"

"Many years," Haertel said, smiling kindly. "Don't be anxious, Garrard. You've come back, which is more than the others managed to do, and nobody will ask you to go out again. I really think that it's hardly likely that we'll get another ship built during your lifetime; and even if we do, we'll be slow to launch it. We really have very little information about what kind of playground you found out there."

"I'll go," Garrard said. "I'm not afraid to go back—I'd like to go. Now that I know how the DFC-3 behaves, I could take it out again, bring you back proper maps, tapes, photos."

"Do you really think", Haertel said, his face suddenly serious, "that we could let the DFC-3 go out again? Garrard, we're going to take that ship apart practically molecule by molecule; that's preliminary to the building of any DFC-4. And no more can we let you go. I don't mean to be cruel, but has it occurred to you that this desire to go back may be the result of some kind of post-hypnotic suggestion? If so, the more badly you want to go back, the more dangerous to us all you may be. We are going to have to examine you just as thoroughly as we do the ship. If these beade-mungen wanted you to come back, they must have had a reason—and we have to know that reason."

Garrard nodded, but he knew that Haertel could see the slight movement of his eyebrows and the wrinkles forming in his forehead, the contractions of the small muscles which stop the flow of tears only to make grief patent on the rest of the face.

"In short," he said, "*don't move.*"

Haertel looked politely puzzled. Garrard, however, could say nothing more. He had returned to humanity's common time, and would never leave it again.

Not even, for all his dimly remembered promise, with all there was left in him of love.

Ostensibly this is a story about the future of serious music (by which adjective I mean to exclude dance music both good—Ellington and the Strausses—and bad—Beatles and other coleoptera); but actually it proposes no novelties in that field. Its real subject is the creative process itself. I chose a composer for my hero because I dislike stories about writers, but I might have used any art in which I felt at home. The story adopts a radical scientific assumption in order to make a philosophical and emotional point that could have been made in no other way—which is the highest form of science fiction, and the most difficult to bring off. This sample so satisfies me that I regard it as a testament; and, also, as

A Work of Art

Instantly, he remembered dying. He remembered it, however, as if at two removes—as though he were remembering a memory, rather than an actual event; as though he himself had not really been there when he died.

Yet the memory was all from his own point of view, not that of some detached and disembodied observer which might have been his soul. He had been most conscious of the rasping, unevenly drawn movements of the air in his chest. Blurring rapidly, the doctor's face had bent over him, loomed, come closer, and then had vanished as the doctor's head passed below his cone of vision, turned sideways to listen to his lungs.

It had become rapidly darker, and then, only then, had he realized that these were to be his last minutes. He had tried dutifully to say Pauline's name, but his memory contained no record of the sound—only of the rattling breath, and of the film of sootiness thickening in the air, blotting out everything for an instant.

Only an instant, and then the memory was over. The room was bright again, and the ceiling, he noticed with wonder, had turned a soft green. The doctor's head lifted again and looked down at him.

A WORK OF ART

It was a different doctor. This one was a far younger man, with an ascetic face and gleaming, almost fey eyes. There was no doubt about it. One of the last conscious thoughts he had had was that of gratitude that the attending physician, there at the end, had not been the one who secretly hated him for his one-time associations with the Nazi hierarchy. The attending doctor, instead, had worn an expression amusingly proper for that of a Swiss expert called to the deathbed of an eminent man: a mixture of worry at the prospect of losing so eminent a patient, and complacency at the thought that, at the old man's age, nobody could blame this doctor if he died. At 85, pneumonia is a serious matter, with or without penicillin.

"You're all right now," the new doctor said, freeing his patient's head of a whole series of little silver rods which had been clinging to it by a sort of network cap. "Rest a minute and try to be calm. Do you know your name?"

He drew a cautious breath. There seemed to be nothing at all the matter with his lungs now; indeed, he felt positively healthy. "Certainly," he said, a little nettled. "Do you know yours?"

The doctor smiled crookedly. "You're in character, it appears," he said. "My name is Barkun Kris; I am a mind sculptor. Yours?"

"Richard Strauss."

"Very good," Dr. Kris said, and turned away. Strauss, however, had already been diverted by a new singularity. *Strauss* is a word as well as a name in German; it has many meanings—an ostrich, a bouquet; von Wolzogen had had a high old time working all the possible puns into the libretto of *Feuersnot*. And it happened to be the first German word to be spoken either by himself or by Dr. Kris since that twice-removed moment of death. The language was not French or Italian, either. It was most like English, but not the English Strauss knew; nevertheless, he was having no trouble speaking it and even thinking in it.

Well, he thought, *I'll be able to conduct* The Loves of Danae *after all. It isn't every composer who can première his own opera posthumously.* Still, there was something queer about all this—the queerest part of all being that conviction, which would not go away, that he had actually been dead for just a short time. Of course medicine was making great strides, but . . .

"Explain all this," he said, lifting himself to one elbow. The bed was different, too, and not nearly as comfortable as the one in which he had died. As for the room, it looked more like a dynamo shed than a sickroom. Had modern medicine taken to reviving its corpses on the floor of the Siemanns-Schuckert plant?

"In a moment," Dr. Kris said. He finished rolling some machine back into what Strauss impatiently supposed to be its place, and crossed to the pallet. "Now. There are many things you'll have to take for granted without attempting to understand them, Dr. Strauss. Not everything in the world today is explicable in terms of your assumptions. Please bear that in mind."

"Very well. Proceed."

"The date", Dr. Kris said, "is 2161 by your calendar—or, in other words, it is now two hundred and twelve years after your death. Naturally, you'll realize that by this time nothing remains of your body but the bones. The body you have now was volunteered for your use. Before you look into a mirror to see what it's like, remember that its physical difference from the one you were used to is all in your favour. It's in perfect health, not unpleasant for other people to look at, and its physiological age is about fifty."

A miracle? No, not in this new age, surely. It was simply a work of science. But what a science! This was Nietzsche's eternal recurrence and the immortality of the superman combined into one.

"And where is this?" the composer said.

"In Port York, part of the State of Manhattan, in the United States. You will find the country less changed in some respects than I imagine you anticipate. Other changes, of course, will seem radical to you; but it's hard for me to predict which ones will strike you that way. A certain resilience on your part will bear cultivating."

"I understand," Strauss said, sitting up. "One question, please; is it still possible for a composer to make a living in this century?"

"Indeed it is," Dr. Kris said, smiling. "As we expect you to do. It is one of the purposes for which we've—brought you back."

"I gather, then," Strauss said somewhat dryly, "that there is still a demand for my music. The critics in the old days——"

"That's not quite how it is," Dr. Kris said. "I understand some of your work is still played, but frankly I know very little about your current status. My interest is rather——"

A door opened somewhere, and another man came in. He was older and more ponderous than Kris and had a certain air of academicism; but he too was wearing the oddly tailored surgeon's gown, and looked upon Kris's patient with the glowing eyes of an artist.

"A success, Kris?" he said. "Congratulations."

"They're not in order yet," Dr. Kris said. "The final proof is what counts. Dr. Strauss, if you feel strong enough, Dr. Seirds and I would like to ask you some questions. We'd like to make sure your memory is clear."

"Certainly. Go ahead."

"According to our records," Kris said, "you once knew a man whose initials were RKL; this was while you were conducting at the Vienna *Staatsoper*." He made the double "a" at least twice too long, as though German were a dead language he was striving to pronounce in some "classical" accent. "What was his name, and who was he?"

"That would be Kurt List—his first name was Richard, but he didn't use it. He was assistant stage manager."

The two doctors looked at each other. "Why did you offer to write a new overture to *The Woman Without Shadows*, and give the manuscript to the City of Vienna?"

"So I wouldn't have to pay the garbage removal tax on the Maria Theresa villa they had given me."

"In the back yard of your house at Garmisch-Partenkirchen there was a tombstone. What was written on it?"

Strauss frowned. That was a question he would be happy to be unable to answer. If one is to play childish jokes upon oneself, it's best not to carve them in stone, and put the carving where you can't help seeing it every time you go out to tinker with the Mercedes. "It says," he replied wearily, "*Sacred to the memory of Guntram, Minnesinger, slain in a horrible way by his father's own symphony orchestra*."

"When was *Guntram* premièred?"

"In—let me see—1894, I believe."

"Where?"

"In Weimar."

"Who was the leading lady?"

"Pauline de Ahna."

"What happened to her afterwards?"

"I married her. Is she . . ." Strauss began anxiously.

"No," Dr. Kris said. "I'm sorry, but we lack the data to reconstruct more or less ordinary people."

The composer sighed. He did not know whether to be worried or not. He had loved Pauline, to be sure; on the other hand, it would be pleasant to be able to live the new life without being forced to take off one's shoes every time one entered the house, so as not to scratch the polished hardwood floors. And also pleasant, perhaps, to have two o'clock in the afternoon come by without hearing Pauline's everlasting, *"Richard—jetzt komponiert!"*

"Next question," he said.

For reasons which Strauss did not understand, but was content to take for granted, he was separated from Drs. Kris and Seirds as soon as both were satisfied that the composer's memory was reliable and his health stable. His estate, he was given to understand, had long since been broken up—a sorry end for what had been one of the principal fortunes of Europe—but he was given sufficient money to set up lodgings and resume an active life. He was provided, too, with introductions which proved valuable.

It took longer than he had expected to adjust to the changes that had taken place in music alone. Music was, he quickly began to suspect, a dying art, which would soon have a status not much above that held by flower arranging back in what he thought of as his own century. Certainly it couldn't be denied that the trend towards fragmentation, already visible back in his own time, had proceeded almost to completion in 2161.

He paid no more attention to American popular tunes than he had bothered to pay in his previous life. Yet it was evident that their assembly-line production methods—all the ballad composers openly used a slide-rule-like device called a Hit Machine—

now had their counterparts almost throughout serious music.

The conservatives these days, for instance, were the twelve-tone composers—always, in Strauss's opinions, a dryly mechanical lot but never more so than now. Their gods—Berg, Schoenberg, Webern—were looked upon by the concert-going public as great masters, on the abstruse side perhaps, but as worthy of reverence as any of the Three B's.

There was one wing of the conservatives, however, which had gone the twelve-tone procedure one better. These men composed what was called "stochastic music", put together by choosing each individual note by consultation with tables of random numbers. Their bible, their basic text, was a volume called *Operational Aesthetics*, which in turn derived from a discipline called information theory; and not one word of it seemed to touch upon any of the techniques and customs of composition which Strauss knew. The ideal of this group was to produce music which would be "universal"—that is, wholly devoid of any trace of the composer's individuality, wholly a musical expression of the universal Laws of Chance. The Laws of Chance seemed to have a style of their own, all right; but to Strauss it seemed the style of an idiot child being taught to hammer a flat piano, to keep him from getting into trouble.

By far the largest body of work being produced, however, fell into a category misleadingly called "science-music". The term reflected nothing but the titles of the works, which dealt with space flight, time travel, and other subjects of a romantic or an unlikely nature. There was nothing in the least scientific about the music, which consisted of a *mélange* of clichés and imitations of natural sounds, in which Strauss was horrified to see his own time-distorted and diluted image.

The most popular form of science-music was a nine-minute composition called a concerto, though it bore no resemblance at all to the classical concerto form; it was instead a sort of free rhapsody after Rachmaninoff—long after. A typical one—"Song of Deep Space" it was called, by somebody named H. Valerion Krafft—began with a loud assault on the tam-tam, after which all the strings rushed up the scale in unison, followed at a respectful distance by the harp and one clarinet in parallel 6/4's. At the top of the scale cymbals were bashed together, *forte possibile*, and the whole orchestra launched itself into a major-minor, wailing sort of melody; the whole orchestra, that is, except for the French horns, which were plodding back down the scale again in what was evidently supposed to be a countermelody. The second phrase of the theme was picked up by a solo trumpet with a suggestion of tremolo; the orchestra died back to its roots to await the next cloudburst, and at this point—as any 4-year-old could have predicted—the piano entered with the second theme.

Behind the orchestra stood a group of thirty women, ready to come in with a wordless chorus intended to suggest the eeriness of Deep Space—but at this point, too, Strauss had already learned to get up and leave. After a few such experiences he could also count upon meeting in the lobby Sindi Noniss, the agent to whom Dr. Kris had introduced him, and who was handling the reborn composer's output—what there was of it thus far. Sindi had come to expect these walkouts on the part of his client, and patiently awaited them, standing beneath a bust of Gian Carlo Menotti; but he liked them less and less, and lately had been greeting them by turning alternately red and white like a toti-potent barber pole.

"You shouldn't have done it," he burst out after the Krafft incident. "You can't just walk out on a new Krafft composition. The man's the president of the Interplanetary Society for Contemporary Music. How am I ever going to persuade them that you're a contemporary if you keep snubbing them?"

"What does it matter?" Strauss said. "They don't know me by sight."

"You're wrong; they know you very well, and they're watching every move you make. You're the first major composer the mind sculptors ever tackled, and the ISCM would be glad to turn you back with a rejection slip."

"Why?"

"Oh," said Sindi, "there are lots of reasons. The sculptors are snobs; so are the ISCM boys. Each of them wants to prove to the other that their own art is the king of them all. And then there's the competition; it would be easier to flunk you than to let you into the market. I really think you'd better go back in. I could make up some excuse——"

"No," Strauss said shortly. "I have work to do."

"But that's just the point, Richard. How are we going to get an opera produced without the ISCM? It isn't as though you wrote theremin solos, or something that didn't cost so——"

"I have work to do," he said, and left.

And he did: work which absorbed him as had no other project during the last thirty years of his former life. He had scarcely touched pen to music paper—both had been astonishingly hard to find—when he realized that nothing in his long career had provided him with touchstones by which to judge what music he should write *now*.

The old tricks came swarming back by the thousands, to be sure: the sudden, unexpected key changes at the crest of a melody; the interval stretching; the piling of divided strings, playing in the high harmonics, upon the already tottering top of a climax; the scurry and bustle as phrases were passed like lightning from one choir of the orchestra to another; the flashing runs in the brass, the chuckling in the clarinets, the snarling mixtures of colours to emphasize dramatic tension—all of them.

But none of them satisfied him now. He had been content with them for most of a lifetime, and had made them do an astonishing amount of work. But now it was time to strike out afresh. Some of the tricks, indeed, actively repelled him: where had he gotten the notion, clung to for decades, that violins screaming out in unison somewhere in the stratosphere was a sound interesting enough to be worth repeating inside a single composition, let alone in all of them?

And nobody, he reflected contentedly, ever approached such a new beginning better equipped. In addition to the past lying available in his memory, he had always had a technical armamentarium second to none; even the hostile critics had granted him that. Now that he was, in a sense, composing his first opera—his first after fifteen of them!—he had every opportunity to make it a masterpiece.

And every such intention.

A WORK OF ART

There were, of course, many minor distractions. One of them was that search for old-fashioned score paper, and a pen and ink with which to write on it. Very few of the modern composers, it developed, wrote their music at all. A large bloc of them used tape, patching together snippets of tone and sound snipped from other tapes, superimposing one tape on another, and varying the results by twirling an elaborate array of knobs this way or that. Almost all the composers of 3-V scores, on the other hand, wrote on the sound track itself, rapidly scribbling jagged wiggly lines which, when passed through a photocell-audio circuit, produced a noise reasonably like an orchestra playing music, overtones and all.

The last-ditch conservatives who still wrote notes on paper, did so with the aid of a musical typewriter. The device, Strauss had to admit, seemed perfected at last; it had manuals and stops like an organ, but it was not much more than twice as large as a standard letter-writing typewriter, and produced a neat page. But he was satisfied with his own spidery, highly legible manuscript and refused to abandon it, badly though the one pen nib he had been able to buy coarsened it. It helped to tie him to his past.

Joining the ISCM had also caused him some bad moments, even after Sindi had worked him around the political road blocks. The Society man who examined his qualifications as a member had run through the questions with no more interest than might have been shown by a veterinarian examining his four thousandth sick calf.

"Had anything published?"

"Yes, nine tone poems, about three hundred songs, an——"

"Not when you were alive," the examiner said, somewhat disquietingly. "I mean since the sculptors turned you out again."

"Since the sculptors—ah, I understand. Yes, a string quartet, two song cycles, a——"

"Good. Alfie, write down 'songs'. Play an instrument?"

"Piano."

"Hm." The examiner studied his finger-nails. "Oh, well. Do you read music? Or do you use a Scriber, or tape clips? Or a Machine?"

"I read."

"Here." The examiner sat Strauss down in front of a viewing lectern, over the lit surface of which an endless belt of translucent paper was travelling. On the paper was an immensely magnified sound track. "Whistle me the tune of that, and name the instruments it sounds like."

"I don't read that *Musiksticheln*," Strauss said frostily, "or write it, either. I use standard notation, on music paper."

"Alfie, write down 'Reads notes only'." He laid a sheet of greyly printed music on the lectern above the ground glass. "Whistle me that."

"That" proved to be a popular tune called "Vangs, Snifters and Store-Credit Snooky" which had been written on a Hit Machine in 2159 by a guitar-faking politician who sang it at campaign rallies. (In some respects, Strauss reflected, the United States had indeed not changed very much.) It had become so popular that anybody could have whistled it from the title alone, whether he could read the music or not. Strauss whistled it, and to prove his bona fides added. "It's in the key of B flat."

The examiner went over to the green-painted upright piano and hit one greasy black key. The instrument was horribly out of tune—the note was much nearer to the standard 440/cps A than it was to B flat—but the examiner said, "So it is. Alfie, write down, 'Also read flats'. All right, son, you're a member. Nice to have you with us; not many people can read that old-style notation any more. A lot of them think they're too good for it."

"Thank you," Strauss said.

"My feeling is, if it was good enough for the old masters, it's good enough for us. We don't have people like them with us these days, it seems to me. Except for Dr. Krafft, of course. They were *great* back in the old days—men like Shilkrit, Steiner, Tiomkin, and Pearl . . . and Wilder and Jannsen. Real goffin."

"*Doch gewiss*," Strauss said politely.

But the work went forward. He was making a little income now, from small works. People seemed to feel a special interest in a composer who had come out of the mind sculptors' laboratories; and in addition the material itself, Strauss was quite certain, had merits of its own to help sell it.

It was the opera which counted, however. That grew and grew

under his pen, as fresh and new as his new life, as founded in knowledge and ripeness as his long full memory. Finding a libretto had been troublesome at first. While it was possible that something existed that might have served among the current scripts for 3-V—though he doubted it—he found himself unable to tell the good from the bad through the fog cast over both by incomprehensibly technical production directions. Eventually, and for only the third time in his whole career, he had fallen back upon a play written in a language other than his own, and—for the first time—decided to set it in that language.

The play was Christopher Fry's *Venus Observed*, in all ways a perfect Strauss opera libretto, as he came gradually to realize. Though nominally a comedy, with a complex farcical plot, it was a verse play with considerable depth to it, and a number of characters who cried out to be brought by music into three dimensions, plus a strong undercurrent of autumnal tragedy, of leaf-fall and apple-fall—precisely the kind of contradictory dramatic mixture which von Hofmannsthal had supplied him with in *The Knight of the Rose*, in *Ariadne at Naxos*, and in *Arabella*.

Alas for von Hofmannsthal, but here was another long-dead playwright who seemed nearly as gifted; and the musical opportunities were immense. There was, for instance, the fire which ended act two; what a gift for a composer to whom orchestration and counterpoint were as important as air and water! Or take the moment where Perpetua shoots the apple from the Duke's hand; in that one moment a single passing reference could add Rossini's marmoreal *William Tell* to the musical texture as nothing but an ironic footnote! And the Duke's great curtain speech, beginning:

> *Shall I be sorry for myself? In Mortality's name*
> *I'll be sorry for myself. Branches and boughs,*
> *Brown hills, the valleys faint with brume,*
> *A burnish on the lake . . .*

There was a speech for a great tragic comedian, in the spirit of Falstaff; the final union of laughter and tears, punctuated by the sleepy comments of Reedbeck, to whose sonorous snore (trombones,

no less than five of them, *con sordini*?) the opera would gently
end. . . .

What could be better? And yet he had come upon the play only
by the unlikeliest series of accidents. At first he had planned to do
a straight knockabout farce, in the idiom of *The Silent Woman*, just
to warm himself up. Remembering that Zweig had adapted that
libretto for him, in the old days, from a play by Ben Jonson, Strauss
had begun to search out English plays of the period just after
Jonson's, and had promptly run aground on an awful specimen in
heroic couplets called *Venice Preserv'd*, by one Thomas Otway. The
Fry play had directly followed the Otway in the card catalogue, and
he had looked at it out of curiosity; why should a Twentieth Century playwright be punning on a title from the Eighteenth?

After two pages of the Fry play, the minor puzzle of the pun
disappeared entirely from his concern. His luck was running again;
he had an opera.

Sindi worked miracles in arranging for the performance. The
date of the première was set even before the score was finished,
reminding Strauss pleasantly of those heady days when Fuerstner
had been snatching the conclusion of *Elektra* off his work table a
page at a time, before the ink was even dry, to rush it to the
engraver before publication deadline. The situation now, however,
was even more complicated, for some of the score had to be scribed,
some of it taped, some of it engraved in the old way, to meet the
new techniques of performance; there were moments when Sindi
seemed to be turning quite grey.

But *Venus Observed* was, as usual, forthcoming complete from
Strauss's pen in plenty of time. Writing the music in first draft had
been hellishly hard work, much more like being reborn than had
been that confused awakening in Barkun Kris's laboratory, with
its overtones of being dead instead; but Strauss found that he still
retained all of his old ability to score from the draft almost effort-
lessly, as undisturbed by Sindi's half-audible worrying in the room
with him as he was by the terrifying supersonic bangs of the rockets
that bulleted invisibly over the city.

When he was finished, he had two days still to spare before the

beginning of rehearsals. With those, furthermore, he would have
nothing to do. The techniques of performance in this age were so
completely bound up with the electronic arts as to reduce his own
experience—he, the master *Kapellmeister* of them all—to the hopelessly primitive.

He did not mind. The music, as written, would speak for itself.
In the meantime he found it grateful to forget the months'-long
preoccupation with the stage for a while. He went back to the
library and browsed lazily through old poems, vaguely seeking
texts for a song or two. He knew better than to bother with recent
poets; they could not speak to him, and he knew it. The Americans
of his own age, he thought, might give him a clue to understanding
this America of 2161; and if some such poem gave birth to a song,
so much the better.

The search was relaxing and he gave himself up to enjoying it.
Finally he struck a tape that he liked: a tape read in a cracked old
voice that twanged of Idaho as that voice had twanged in 1910, in
Strauss's own ancient youth. The poet's name was Pound; he said,
on the tape:

> . . . *the souls of all men great*
> *At times pass through us,*
> *And we are melted into them, and are not*
> *Save reflexions of their souls.*
> *Thus I am Dante for a space and am*
> *One François Villon, ballad-lord and thief*
> *Or am such holy ones I may not write,*
> *Lest Blasphemy be writ against my name;*
> *This for an instant and the flame is gone.*
> *'Tis as in midmost us there glows a sphere*
> *Translucent, molten gold, that is the "I"*
> *And into this some form projects itself:*
> *Christus, or John, or eke the Florentine;*
> *And as the clear space is not if a form's*
> *Imposed thereon,*
> *So cease we from all being for the time,*
> *And these, the Masters of the Soul, live on.*

He smiled. That lesson had been written again and again, from Plato onwards. Yet the poem was a history of his own case, a sort of theory for the metempsychosis he had undergone, and in its formal way it was moving. It would be fitting to make a little hymn of it, in honour of his own rebirth, and of the poet's insight.

A series of solemn, breathless chords framed themselves in his inner ear, against which the words might be intoned in a high, gently bending hush at the beginning . . . and then a dramatic passage in which the great names of Dante and Villon would enter ringing like challenges to Time. . . . He wrote for a while in his notebook before he returned the spool to its shelf.

These, he thought, are good auspices.

And so the night of the première arrived, the audience pouring into the hall, the 3-V cameras riding on no visible supports through the air, and Sindi calculating his share of his client's earnings by a complicated game he played on his fingers, the basic law of which seemed to be that one plus one equals ten. The hall filled to the roof with people from every class, as though what was to come would be a circus rather than an opera.

There were, surprisingly, nearly fifty of the aloof and aristocratic mind sculptors, clad in formal clothes which were exaggerated black versions of their surgeon's gowns. They had bought a block of seats near the front of the auditorium, where the gigantic 3-V figures which would shortly fill the "stage" before them (the real singers would perform on a small stage in the basement) could not but seem monstrously out of proportion; but Strauss supposed that they had taken this into account and dismissed it.

There was a tide of whispering in the audience as the sculptors began to trickle in, and with it an undercurrent of excitement the meaning of which was unknown to Strauss. He did not attempt to fathom it, however; he was coping with his own mounting tide of opening-night tension, which, despite all the years, he had never quite been able to shake.

The sourceless, gentle light in the auditorium dimmed, and Strauss mounted the podium. There was a score before him, but he doubted that he would need it. Directly before him, poking up from among the musicians, were the inevitable 3-V snouts, waiting to carry his image to the singers in the basement.

The audience was quiet now. This was the moment. His baton swept up and then decisively down, and the prelude came surging up out of the pit.

For a little while he was deeply immersed in the always tricky business of keeping the enormous orchestra together and sensitive to the flexing of the musical web beneath his hand. As his control firmed and became secure, however, the task became slightly less demanding, and he was able to pay more attention to what the whole sounded like.

There was something decidedly wrong with it. Of course there were the occasional surprises as some bit of orchestral colour emerged with a different *Klang* than he had expected; that happened to every composer, even after a lifetime of experience. And there were moments when the singers, entering upon a phrase more difficult to handle than he had calculated, sounded like someone about to fall off a tightrope (although none of them actually fluffed once; they were as fine a troupe of voices as he had ever had to work with).

But these were details. It was the overall impression that was wrong. He was losing not only the excitement of the première— after all, that couldn't last at the same pitch all evening—but also his very interest in what was coming from the stage and the pit. He was gradually tiring; his baton arm becoming heavier; as the second act mounted to what should have been an impassioned outpouring of shining tone, he was so bored as to wish he could go back to his desk to work on that song.

Then the act was over; only one more to go. He scarcely heard the applause. The twenty minutes' rest in his dressing-room was just barely enough to give him the necessary strength.

And suddenly, in the middle of the last act, he understood.

There was nothing new about the music. It was the old Strauss all over again—but weaker, more dilute than ever. Compared with the output of composers like Krafft, it doubtless sounded like a masterpiece to this audience. But he knew.

The resolutions, the determination to abandon the old clichés and mannerisms, the decision to say something new—they had all come to nothing against the force of habit. Being brought to life again meant bringing to life as well all those deeply graven reflexes of his style. He had only to pick up his pen and they overpowered him with easy automatism, no more under his control than the jerk of a finger away from a flame.

His eyes filled; his body was young, but he was an old man, an old man. Another thirty-five years of this? Never. He had said all this before, centuries before. Nearly a half-century condemned to saying it all over again, in a weaker and still weaker voice, aware that even this debased century would come to recognize in him only the burnt husk of greatness?—no; never, never.

He was aware, dully, that the opera was over. The audience was screaming its joy. He knew the sound. They had screamed that way when *Day of Peace* had been premièred, but they had been cheering the man he had been, not the man that *Day of Peace* showed with cruel clarity he had become. Here the sound was even more meaningless: cheers of ignorance, and that was all.

He turned slowly. With surprise, and with a surprising sense of relief, he saw that the cheers were not, after all, for him.

They were for Dr. Barkun Kris.

Kris was standing in the middle of the bloc of mind sculptors, bowing to the audience. The sculptors nearest him were shaking his hand one after the other. More grasped at it as he made his way to the aisle, and walked forward to the podium. When he mounted the rostrum and took the composer's limp hand, the cheering became delirious.

Kris lifted his arm. The cheering died instantly to an intent hush.

"Thank you," he said clearly. "Ladies and gentlemen, before we take leave of Dr. Strauss, let us again tell him what a privilege it has been for us to hear this fresh example of his mastery. I am sure no farewell could be more fitting."

A WORK OF ART

The ovation lasted five minutes, and would have gone another five if Kris had not cut it off.

"Dr. Strauss," he said, "in a moment, when I speak a certain formulation to you, you will realize that your name is Jerom Busch, born in our century and with a life in it all your own. The super-imposed memories which have made you assume the mask, the *persona*, of a great composer will be gone. I tell you this so that you may understand why these people here share your applause with me."

A wave of assenting sound.

"The art of mind sculpture—the creation of artificial personalities for aesthetic enjoyment—may never reach such a pinnacle again. For you should understand that as Jerom Busch you had no talent for music at all; indeed, we searched a long time to find a man who was utterly unable to carry even the simplest tune. Yet we were able to impose upon such unpromising material not only the personality, but the genius, of a great composer. That genius belongs entirely to you—to the *persona* that thinks of itself as Richard Strauss. None of the credit goes to the man who volunteered for the sculpture. That is your triumph, and we salute you for it."

Now the ovation could no longer be contained. Strauss, with a crooked smile, watched Dr. Kris bow. This mind sculpturing was a suitably sophisticated kind of cruelty for this age; but the impulse, of course, had always existed. It was the same impulse that had made Rembrandt and Leonardo turn cadavers into art works.

It deserved a suitably sophisticated payment under the *lex talionis*: an eye for an eye, a tooth for a tooth—and a failure for a failure.

No, he need not tell Dr. Kris that the "Strauss" he had created was as empty of genius as a hollow gourd. The joke would always be on the sculptor, who was incapable of hearing the hollowness of the music now preserved on the 3-V tapes.

But for an instant a surge of revolt poured through his blood-stream. *I am I*, he thought. *I am Richard Strauss until I die, and will never be Jerom Busch, who was utterly unable to carry even the simplest tune.* His hand, still holding the baton, came sharply up, though whether to deliver or to ward off a blow he could not tell.

He let it fall again, and instead, at last, bowed—not to the audience, but to Dr. Kris. He was sorry for nothing, as Kris turned to him to say the word that would plunge him back into oblivion, except that he would now have no chance to set that poem to music.

Rockets, nuclear weapons and space travel have so invaded the news-
papers that they have left the science-fiction writer gasping for subjects
—and much of the popular fiction the public at large devours today,
from On the Beach *to* Seven Days in May, *is science fiction which has*
escaped the onus—still anachronistically with us—of the sf label. If the
science-fiction writer still has any toe-hold on such subjects as the post-
Armageddon world, it probably lies in the opportunity to use his
familiarity with the subject and the territory to question our emblems
of conduct, without distracting the reader with spurious problems of
technical feasibility. (For example: the authors of Fail-Safe *spoiled*
their central question by making its circumstances impossible; whereas
the competent science-fiction writer begins by putting the circumstances
where they belong: beyond doubt, and hence on the periphery of the
story proper.) The questions I set out to raise in the next two stories
were not, Can such things be?, *but,* If they can, how then shall we
live with ourselves?

Tomb Tapper

The distant glare of the atomic explosion had already faded from
the sky as McDonough's car whirred away from the blacked-out
town of Port Jervis and turned north. He was making fifty m.p.h.
on U.S. Route 209 using no lights but his parkers, and if a deer
should bolt across the road ahead of him he would never see it
until the impact. It was hard enough to see the road.

But he was thinking, not for the first time, of the old joke about
the men who tapped train wheels.

He had been doing it, so the story ran, for thirty years. On every
working day he would go up and down both sides of every loco-
motive that pulled into the yards and hit the wheels with a hammer:
first the drivers, then the trucks. Each time, he would cock his
head, as though listening for something in the sound. On the day
of his retirement, he was given a magnificent dinner, as befitted a

man with long seniority in the Brotherhood of Railway Trainmen—and somebody stopped to ask him what he had been tapping for all those years.

He had cocked his head as though listening for something, but evidently nothing came. "I don't know," he said.

That's me, McDonough thought. I tap tombs, not trains. But what am I listening for?

The speedometer said he was close to the turnoff for the airport, and he pulled the dimmers on. There it was. There was at first nothing to be seen, as the headlights swept along the dirt road, but a wall of darkness deep as all night, faintly edged at the east by the low domed hills of the Neversink Valley. Then another pair of lights snapped on behind him, on the main highway, and came jolting after McDonough's car, clear and sharp in the dust clouds he had raised.

He swung the car to a stop beside the airport fence and killed the lights; the other car followed. In the renewed blackness the faint traces of dawn on the hills were wiped out, as though the whole universe had been set back an hour. Then the yellow eye of a flashlight opened in the window of the other car and stared into his face.

He opened the door. "Martinson?" he said tentatively.

"Right here," the adjutant's voice said. The flashlight's oval spoor swung to the ground. "Anybody else with you?"

"No. You?"

"No. Go ahead and get your equipment out. I'll open up the shack."

The oval spot of light bobbed across the parking area and came to uneasy rest on the combination padlock which held the door of the operations shack secure. McDonough flipped the dome light of his car on long enough to locate the canvas sling which held the components of his electroencephalograph, and eased the sling out on to the sand.

He had just slammed the car door and taken up the burden when little chinks of light sprang into being in the blind windows of the shack. At the same time, cars came droning out on to the field from the opposite side, four of them, each with its wide-spaced unblinking slits of paired parking lights, and ranked themselves on either side of the landing strip. It would be dawn before long, but if the planes were ready to go before dawn, the cars could light the strip with their brights.

We're fast, McDonough thought, with brief pride. Even the Air Force thinks the Civil Air Patrol is just a bunch of amateurs, but we can put a mission in the air ahead of any other C.A.P. squadron in this county. We can scramble.

He was getting his night vision back now, and a quick glance showed him that the windsock was flowing straight out above the black, silent hangar against the pearly false dawn. Aloft, the stars were paling without any cloud-dimming, or even much twinkling. The wind was steady north up the valley; ideal flying weather.

Small lumpy figures were running across the field from the parked cars towards the shack. The squadron was scrambling.

"Mac!" Martinson shouted from inside the shack. "Where are you? Get your junk in here and get started!"

McDonough slipped inside the door, and swung his EEG components on to the chart table. Light was pouring into the briefing room from the tiny office, dazzling after the long darkness. In the briefing room the radio blinked a tiny red eye, but the squadron's communications officer hadn't yet arrived to answer it. In the office, Martinson's voice rumbled softly, urgently, and the phone gave him back thin unintelligible noises, like an unteachable parakeet.

Then, suddenly, the adjutant appeared at the office door and peered at McDonough. "What are you waiting for?" he said. "Get that mind reader of yours into the Cub on the double."

"What's wrong with the Aeronica? It's faster."

"Water in the gas; she ices up. We'll have to drain the tank. This is a hell of a time to argue." Martinson jerked open the squealing door which opened into the hangar, his hand groping for the light switch. McDonough followed him, supporting his sling with both hands, his elbows together. Nothing is quite so concentratedly heavy as an electronics chassis with a transformer mounted on it, and four of them make a back-wrenching load.

The adjutant was already hauling the servicing platform across the concrete floor to the cowling of the Piper Cub. "Get your stuff set," he said. "I'll fuel her up and check the oil."

"All right. Doesn't look like she needs much gas."

"Don't you ever stop talkin'? Let's move!"

McDonough lowered his load to the cold floor beside the plane's cabin, feeling a brief flash of resentment. In daily life Martinson was a job printer who couldn't, and didn't, give orders to anybody, not even his wife. Well, those were usually the boys who let rank go to their heads, even in a volunteer outfit. He got to work.

Voices sounded from the shack, and then Andy Persons, the commanding officer, came bounding over the sill, followed by two sleepy-eyed cadets. "What's up?" he shouted. "That you, Martinson?"

"It's me. One of you cadets, pass me up that can. Andy, get the doors open, hey? There's a Russki bomber down north of us, somewhere near Howells. Part of a flight that was making a run on Schenectady."

"Did they get it?"

"No, they overshot, *way* over—took out Kingston instead. Stewart Field hit them just as they turned to regroup, and knocked this baby down on the first pass. We're supposed to——"

The rest of the adjutant's reply was lost in a growing, echoing roar, as though they were all standing underneath a vast trestle over which all the railroad trains in the world were crossing at once. The 64-foot organ-reeds of jets were being blown in the night zenith above the field—another hunting pack, come from Stewart Field to avenge the hydrogen agony that had been Kingston.

His head still inside the plane's greenhouse, McDonough listened transfixed. Like most C.A.P. officers, he was too old to be a jet pilot, his reflexes too slow, his eyesight too far over the line, his belly muscles too soft to take the five-gravity turns; but now and then he thought about what it might be like to ride one of those flying blowtorches, cruising at six hundred miles an hour before a thin black wake of kerosene fumes, or being followed along the ground at top speed by the double wave-front of the "supersonic bang". It was a noble notion, almost as fine as that of piloting the one-man Niagara of power that was a rocket fighter.

The noise grew until it seemed certain that the invisible jets were going to bullet directly through the hangar, and then dimmed gradually.

"The usual orders?" Persons shouted up from under the declining roar. "Find the plane, pump the live survivors, pick the corpses' brains? Who else is up?"

"Nobody," Martinson said, coming down from the ladder and hauling it clear of the plane. "Middletown squadron's de-activated; Montgomery hasn't got a plane; Newburgh hasn't got a field."

"Warwick has Group's L-16——"

"They snapped the undercarriage off it last week," Martinson said with gloomy satisfaction. "It's our baby, as usual. Mac, you got your ghoul-tools all set in there?"

"In a minute," McDonough said. He was already wearing the Walter goggles, pushed back up on his helmet, and the detector, amplifier and power pack of the EEG were secure in their frames on the platform behind the Cub's rear seat. The "hair net"—the flexible network of electrodes which he would jam on the head of any dead man whose head had survived the bomber crash—was connected to them and hung in its clips under the seat, the leads strung to avoid fouling the plane's exposed control cables. Nothing remained to do now but to secure the frequency analyser, which was the heaviest of the units and had to be bolted down just forward of the rear joystick so that its weight would not shift in flight. If the apparatus didn't have to be collimated after every flight, it could be left in the plane—but it did, and that was that.

"O.K.," he said, pulling his head out of the greenhouse. He was trembling slightly. These tomb-tapping expeditions were hard on the nerves. No matter how much training in the art of reading a dead mind you may have had, the actual experience is different, and cannot be duplicated from the long-stored corpses of the laboratory. The newly dead brain is an inferno, almost by definition.

"Good," Persons said. "Martinson, you'll pilot. Mac, keep on the air; we're going to refuel the Airoknocker and get it up by ten o'clock if we can. In any case we'll feed you any spottings we get from the Air Force as fast as they come in. Martinson, refuel at Montgomery if you have to; don't waste time coming back here. Got it?"

"Roger," Martinson said, scrambling into the front seat and buckling his safety belt. McDonough put his foot hastily into the stirrup and swung into the back seat.

"Cadets!" Persons said. "Pull chocks! Roll 'er!"

Characteristically, Persons himself did the heavy work of lifting and swinging the tail. The Cub bumped off the apron and out on the grass into the brightening morning.

"Switch off!" the cadet at the nose called. "Gas! Brakes!"

"Switch off, brakes," Martinson called back. "Mac, where to? Got any ideas?"

While McDonough thought about it, the cadet pulled the prop backwards through four turns. "Brakes! Contact!"

"Let's try up around the Otisville tunnel. If they were knocked down over Howells, they stood a good chance to wind up on the side of that mountain."

Martinson nodded and reached a gloved hand over his head. "Contact!" he shouted, and turned the switch. The cadet swung the prop, and the engine barked and roared; at McDonough's left, the duplicate throttle slid forward slightly as the pilot "caught" the engine. McDonough buttoned up the cabin, and then the plane began to roll towards the far, dim edge of the grassy field.

The sky got brighter. They were off again, to tap on another man's tomb, and ask of the dim voice inside it what memories it had left unspoken when it had died.

The Civil Air Patrol is, and has been since 1941, an auxiliary of the United States Air Force, active in coastal patrol and in air-sea rescue work. By 1954—when its ranks totalled more than eighty thousand men and women, about fifteen thousand of them licensed pilots—the Air Force had nerved itself up to designating C.A.P. as its Air Intelligence arm, with the job of locating downed enemy planes and radioing back information of military importance.

Aerial search is primarily the task of planes which can fly low and slow. Air Intelligence requires speed, since the kind of tactical information an enemy wreck may offer can grow cold within a few hours. The C.A.P.'s planes, most of them single-engine, private-flying models, had already been proven ideal aerial search instruments; the C.A.P.'s radio net, with its more than seventy-five hundred fixed, mobile and airborne stations, was more than fast enough to get information to wherever it was needed while it was still hot.

But the expected enemy, after all, was Russia; and how many civilians, even those who know how to fly, navigate or operate a radio transmitter, could ask anyone an intelligent question in Russian, let alone understand the answer?

It was the astonishingly rapid development of electrical methods for probing the brain which provided the answer—in particular the development, in the late fifties, of flicker-stimulus aimed at the visual memory. Abruptly, EEG technicians no longer needed to use language at all to probe the brain for visual images, and read them; they did not even need to know how their apparatus worked, let alone the brain. A few moments of flicker into the subject's eyes, on a frequency chosen from a table, and the images would come swarming into the operator's toposcope goggles—the frequency chosen without the slightest basic knowledge of electrophysiology, as a woman choosing an ingredient from a cookbook is ignorant of—and indifferent to—the chemistry involved in the choice.

It was that engineering discovery which put tomb-tappers into the back seats of the C.A.P.'s putt-putts when the war finally began —for the images in the toposcope goggles did not stop when the brain died.

The world at dawn, as McDonough saw it from 3,000 feet, was a world of long sculptured shadows, almost as motionless and three-dimensional as a lunar landscape near the daylight terminator. The air was very quiet, and the Cub droned as gently through the blue haze as any bee, gaining altitude above the field in a series of wide climbing turns. At the last turn the plane wheeled south over a farm owned by someone Martinson knew, a man already turning his acres from the seat of his tractor, and Martinson waggled the plane's wings at him and got back a wave like the quivering of an insect's antenna. It was all deceptively normal.

Then the horizon dipped below the Cub's nose again and Martinson was climbing out of the valley. A lake passed below them, spotted with islands, and with the brown barracks of Camp Cejwin, once a children's summer camp but now full of sleeping soldiers. Martinson continued south, skirting Port Jervis, until McDonough was able to pick up the main line of the Erie Railroad, going northeast towards Otisville and Howells. The mountain through which the Otisville tunnel ran was already visible as a smoky hulk to the far left of the dawn.

McDonough turned on the radio, which responded with a rhythmical sputtering; the Cub's engine was not adequately shielded. In the background, the C.O.'s voice was calling them: "Huguenot to L-4. Huguenot to L-4."

"L-4 here. We read you, Andy. We're heading towards Otisville. Smooth as glass up here. Nothing to report yet."

"We read you weak but clear. We're dumping the gas in the Airoknocker *crackle* ground. We'll follow as fast as possible. No new A.F. spottings yet. If *crackle*, call us right away. Over."

"L-4 to Huguenot. Lost the last sentence, Andy. Cylinder static. Lost the last sentence. Please read it back."

"All right, Mac. If you see the bomber, *crackle* right away. Got it? If you see *crackle*, call us right away. Got it? Over."

"Got it, Andy. L-4 to Huguenot, over and out."

"Over and out."

The railroad embankment below them went around a wide arc and separated deceptively into two. One of the lines had been pulled up years back, but the marks of the long-ago stacked and burned ties still striped the gravel bed, and it would have been impossible for a stranger to tell from the air whether or not there were any rails running over those marks; terrain from the air can be deceptive unless you know what it is supposed to look like, rather than what it does look like. Martinson, however, knew as well as McDonough which of the two rail spurs was the discontinued one, and banked the Cub in a gentle climbing turn towards the mountain.

The rectangular acres wheeled slowly and solemnly below them, brindled with tiny cows as motionless as toys. After a while the deceptive spur-line turned sharply east into a woolly green woods and never came out again. The mountain got larger, the morning ground haze rising up its nearer side, as though the whole forest were smouldering sullenly there.

Martinson turned his head and leaned it back to look out of the corner of one eye at the back seat, but McDonough shook his head. There was no chance at all that the crashed bomber could be on this side of that heavy-shouldered mass of rock.

Martinson shrugged and eased the stick back. The plane bored up into the sky, past 4,000 feet, past 4,500. Lake Hawthorne passed under the Cub's fat little tyres, an irregular sapphire set in the pommel of the mountain. The altimeter crept slowly past 5,000 feet; Martinson was taking no chances on being caught in the downdraught on the other side of the hill. At 6,000, he edged the throttle back and levelled out, peering back through the plexiglass.

But there was no sign of any wreck on that side of the mountain, either.

Puzzled, McDonough forced up the top cabin flap on the right side, buttoned it into place against the buffeting slipstream, and thrust his head out into the tearing gale. There was nothing to see on the ground. Straight down, the knife-edge brow of the cliff from which the railroad tracks emerged again drifted slowly away from the Cub's tail; just an inch farther on was the matchbox which was the Otisville siding shack. A sort of shaking of pepper around the matchbox meant people, a small crowd of them—though there was no train due until the Erie's No. 6, which didn't stop at Otisville anyhow.

He thumped Martinson on the shoulder. The adjutant tilted his head back and shouted, "What?"

"Bank right. Something going on around the Otisville station. Go down a bit."

The adjutant jerked out the carburettor-heat toggle and pulled back the throttle. The plane, idling, went into a long, whistling glide along the railroad right of way.

"Can't go too low here," he said. "If we get caught in the downdraught, we'll get slammed right into the mountain."

"I know that. Go on about four miles and make an airline approach back. Then you can climb into the draught. I want to see what's going on down there."

Martinson shrugged and opened the throttle again. The Cub clawed for altitude, then made a half-turn over Howells for the bogus landing run.

The plane went into normal glide and McDonough craned his neck. In a few moments he was able to see what had happened down below. The mountain from this side was steep and sharp; a wounded bomber couldn't possibly have hoped to clear it. At night, on the other hand, the mouth of the railroad tunnel was marked on all three sides, by the lights of the station on the left, the neon sign of the tavern which stood on the brow of the cliff in Otisville ("Pop. 3,000—High and Healthy"), and on the right by the Erie's own signal standard. Radar would have shown the rest: the long regular path of the embankment leading directly into that cul-de-sac of lights, the beetling mass of contours which was the mountain. All these signs would mean "tunnel" in any language.

And the bomber pilot had taken the longest of all possible chances: to come down gliding along the right of way, in the hope of shooting his fuselage cleanly into that tunnel, leaving behind his wings with their dangerous engines and fuel tanks. It was absolutely insane, but that was what he had done.

And, miracle of miracles, he had made it. McDonough could see the wings now, buttered into two-dimensional profiles over the two pilasters of the tunnel. They had hit with such force that the fuel in them must have been vaporized instantly; at least, there was no sign of a fire. And no sign of a fuselage, either.

The bomber's body was inside the mountain, probably half-way or more down the tunnel's one-mile length. It was inconceivable that there could be anything intelligible left of it; but where one miracle has happened, two are possible.

No wonder the little Otisville station was peppered over with the specks of wondering people.

"L-4 to Huguenot. L-4 to Huguenot. Andy, are you there?"

"We read you, Mac. Go ahead."

"We've found your bomber. It's in the Otisville tunnel. Over."

"*Crackle* to L-4. You've lost your mind."

"That's where it is, all the same. We're going to try to make a landing. Send us a team as soon as you can. Out."

"Huguenot to L-4. Don't be a *crackle* idiot, Mac, you can't land there."

"Out," McDonough said. He pounded Martinson's shoulder and gestured urgently downwards.

"You want to land?" Martinson said. "Why didn't you say so? We'll never get down on a shallow glide like this." He cleared the engine with a brief burp on the throttle, pulled the Cub up into a sharp stall, and slid off on one wing. The whole world began to spin giddily.

Martinson was losing altitude. McDonough closed his eyes and hung on to his back teeth.

Martinson's drastic piloting got them down to a rough landing, on the wheels, on the road leading to the Otisville station, slightly under a mile away from the mountain. They taxied the rest of the way. The crowd left the mouth of the tunnel to cluster around the airplane the moment it had come to a stop, but a few moments' questioning convinced McDonough that the Otisvilleans knew very little. Some of them had heard "a turrible noise" in the early morning, and with the first light had discovered the bright metal coating the sides of the tunnel. No, there hadn't been any smoke. No, nobody heard any sounds in the tunnel. You couldn't see the other end of it, though. Something was blocking it.

"The signal's red on this side," McDonough said thoughtfully while he helped the adjutant tie the plane down. "You used to run the PBX board for the Erie in Port, didn't you, Marty? If you were to phone the station master there, maybe we could get him to throw a block on the other end of the tunnel."

"If there's wreckage in there, the block will be on automatically."

"Sure. But we've got to go in there. I don't want the Number Six piling in after us."

Martinson nodded, and went inside the railroad station. McDonough looked around. There was, as usual, a motorized hand-truck parked off the tracks on the other side of the embankment. Many willing hands helped him set it on the right of way, and several huskies got the one-lung engine started for him. Getting his own apparatus out of the plane and on to the truck, however, was a job for which he refused all aid. The stuff was just too delicate, for all its weight, to be allowed in the hands of laymen—and never mind that McDonough himself was almost as much of a layman in neurophysiology as they were; he at least knew the collimating tables and the cookbook.

"O.K.," Martinson said, rejoining them. "Tunnel's blocked at both ends. I talked to Ralph at the dispatcher's; he was steaming—says he's lost four trains already, and another due in from Buffalo in forty-four minutes. We cried a little about it. Do we go now?"

"Right now."

Martinson drew his automatic and squatted down on the front of the truck. The little car growled and crawled towards the tunnel. The spectators murmured and shook their heads knowingly.

Inside the tunnel it was as dark as always, and cold, with a damp chill which struck through McDonough's flight jacket and dungarees. The air was still, and in addition to its musty smell it had a peculiar metallic stench. Thus far, however, there was none of the smell of fuel or of combustion products which McDonough had expected. He found suddenly that he was trembling again, although he did not really believe that the EEG would be needed.

"Did you notice those wings?" Martinson said suddenly, just loud enough to be heard above the popping of the motor. The echoes distorted his voice almost beyond recognition.

"Notice them? What about them?"

"Too short to be bomber wings. Also, no engines."

McDonough swore silently. To have failed to notice a detail as gross as that was a sure sign that he was even more frightened than he had thought. "Anything else?"

"Well, I don't think they were aluminium; too tough. Titanium, maybe, or stainless steel. What have we got in here, anyhow? You *know* the Russkies couldn't get a fighter this far."

There was no arguing that. There was no answering the question, either—not yet.

McDonough unhooked the torch from his belt. Behind them, the white aperture of the tunnel's mouth looked no bigger than a nickel, and the twin bright lines of the rails looked forty miles long. Ahead, the flashlight revealed nothing but the slimy walls of the tunnel, coated with soot.

And then there was a fugitive bluish gleam. McDonough set the motor back down as far as it would go. The truck crawled painfully through the stifling blackness. The thudding of the engine was painful, as though his own heart were trying to move the heavy platform.

The gleam came closer. Nothing moved around it. It was metal, reflecting the light from his torch. Martinson lit his own and brought it into play.

The truck stopped, and there was absolute silence except for the ticking of water on the floor of the tunnel.

"It's a rocket," Martinson whispered. His torch roved over the ridiculously inadequate tail empennage facing them. It was badly crumpled. "In fair shape, considering. At the clip he was going, he must have slammed back and forth like an alarm clapper."

Cautiously they got off the truck and prowled around the gleaming, badly dented spindle. There were clean shears where the wings had been, but the stubs still remained, as though the metal itself had given to the impact before the joints could. That meant welded construction throughout, McDonough remembered vaguely. The vessel rested now roughly in the centre of the tunnel, and the railroad tracks had spraddled under its weight. The fuselage bore no identifying marks, except for a red star at the nose; or rather, a red asterisk.

Martinson's torch lingered over the star for a moment, but the adjutant offered no comment. He went around the nose, McDonough trailing.

On the other side of the ship was the death wound: a small, ragged tear in the metal, not far forward of the tail. Some of the raw curls of metal were partially melted. Martinson touched one.

"Flak," he muttered. "Cut his fuel lines. Lucky he didn't blow up."

"How do we get in?" McDonough said nervously. "The cabin didn't even crack. And we can't crawl through that hole."

Martinson thought about it. Then he bent to the lesion in the ship's skin, took a deep breath, and bellowed at the top of his voice:

"*Hey* in there! Open up!"

It took a long time for the echoes to die away. McDonough was paralysed with pure fright. Any one of those distorted, ominous rebounding voices could have been an answer. Finally, however, the silence came back.

"So he's dead," Martinson said practically. "I'll bet even his foot-bones are broken, every one of 'em. Mac, stick your hairnet in there and see if you can pick up anything."

"N-not a chance. I can't get anything unless the electrodes are actually t-touching the skull."

"Try it anyhow, and then we can get out of here and let the experts take over. I've about made up my mind it's a missile, anyhow. With this little damage, it could still go off."

McDonough had been repressing that notion since his first sight of the spindle. The attempt to save the fuselage intact, the piloting skill involved, and the obvious cabin windshield all argued against it; but even the bare possibility was somehow twice as terrifying, here under a mountain, as it would have been in the open. With so enormous a mass of rock pressing down on him, and the ravening energies of a sun perhaps waiting to break loose by his side—

No, no; it was a fighter, and the pilot might somehow still be alive. He almost ran to get the electrode net off the truck. He dangled it on its cable inside the flak tear, pulled the goggles over his eyes, and flicked the switch with his thumb.

The Walter goggles made the world inside the tunnel no darker than it actually was, but knowing that he would now be unable to see any gleam of light in the tunnel, should one appear from some-where—say, in the ultimate glare of hydrogen fusion—increased the pressure of blackness on his brain. Back on the truck the fre-quency-analyser began its regular, meaningless peeping, scanning the possible cortical output bands in order of likelihood: First the 0·5 to 3·5 cycles/second band, the delta wave, the last activity of the brain detectable before death; then the four to seven c.p.s. theta channel, the pleasure-scanning waves which went on even during sleep; the alpha rhythm, the visual scanner at eight to thirteen c.p.s.; the beta rhythms at fourteen to thirty c.p.s. which mirror the tensions of conscious computation, not far below the level of real thought; the gamma band, where—

The goggles lit.

... And still the dazzling sky-blue sheep are grazing in the red field under the rainbow-billed and pea-green birds ...

McDonough snatched the goggles up with a gasp, and stared frantically into the blackness, now swimming with residual images in contrasting colours, melting gradually as the rods and cones in his retina gave up the energy they had absorbed from the scene in the goggles. Curiously, he knew at once where the voice had come from; it had been his mother's, reading to him, on Christmas Eve, a story called "A Child's Christmas in Wales". He had not thought of it in well over two decades, but the scene in the toposcope goggles had called it forth irresistibly.

"What's the matter?" Martinson's voice said. "Get anything? Are you sick?"

"No," McDonough muttered. "Nothing."

"Then let's beat it. Do you make a noise like that over nothing every day? My Uncle Crosby did, but then, *he* had asthma."

Tentatively, McDonough lowered the goggles again. The scene came back, still in the same impossible colours, and almost completely without motion. Now that he was able to look at it again, however, he saw that the blue animals were not sheep; they were too large, and they had faces rather like those of kittens. Nor were the enormously slow-moving birds actually birds at all, except that they did seem to be flying—in unlikely straight lines, with slow, mathematically even flappings of unwinglike wings; there was something vegetable about them. The red field was only a dazzling blur, hazing the feet of the blue animals with the huge, innocent kitten's faces. As for the sky, it hardly seemed to be there at all; it was as white as paper.

"Come on," Martinson muttered, his voice edged with irritation. "What's the sense of staying in this hole any more? You bucking for pneumonia?"

"There's ... something alive in there."

"Not a chance," Martinson said. His voice was noticeably more ragged. "You're dreaming. You said yourself you couldn't pick up——"

"I know what I'm doing," McDonough insisted, watching the scene in the goggles. "There's a live brain in there. Something nobody's ever hit before. It's powerful—no mind in the books ever put out a broadcast like this. It isn't human."

"All the more reason to call in the A.F. and quit. We can't get in there anyhow. What do you mean, it isn't human? It's a Red, that's all."

"No it isn't," McDonough said evenly. Now that he thought he knew what they had found, he had stopped trembling. He was still terrified, but it was a different kind of terror: the fright of a man who has at last gotten a clear idea of what it is he is up against. "Human beings just don't broadcast like this. Especially not when they're near dying. And they don't remember huge blue sheep with cat's heads on them, or red grass, or a white sky. Not even if they come from the U.S.S.R. Whoever it is in there comes from some place else."

"You read too much. What about the star on the nose?"

McDonough drew a deep breath. "What about it?" he said steadily. "It isn't the insignia of the Red Air Force. I saw that it stopped you, too. No air force I ever heard of flies a red asterisk. It isn't a cocarde at all. It's just what it is."

"An asterisk?" Martinson said angrily.

"No, Marty, I think it's a star. A symbol for a *real* star. The A.F.'s gone and knocked us down a spaceship." He pushed the goggles up and carefully withdrew the electrode net from the hole in the battered fuselage.

"And", he said carefully, "the pilot, whatever he is, is still alive—and thinking about home, wherever *that* is."

In the ensuing silence, McDonough realized belatedly that Martinson was as frightened as he was.

Though the Air Force had been duly notified by the radio net of McDonough's preposterous discovery, it took its own time about getting a technical crew over to Otisville. It had to, regardless of how much stock it took in the theory. The nearest source of advanced Air Force EEG equipment was just outside Newburgh, at Stewart Field, and it would have to be driven to Otisville by truck; no A.F. plane slow enough to duplicate Martinson's landing on the road could have handled the necessary payload.

For several hours, therefore, McDonough could do pretty much as he liked with his prize. After only a little urging, Martinson got the Erie dispatcher to send an oxy-acetylene torch to the Port Jervis side of the tunnel, on board a Diesel camelback. Persons, who had subsequently arrived in the Aeronica, was all for trying it immediately in the tunnel, but McDonough was restrained by some dim memory of high-school experiments with magnesium, a metal which looked very much like this. He persuaded the C.O. to try the torch on the smeared wings first.

The wings didn't burn. They carried the torch into the tunnel, and Persons got to work with it, enlarging the flak hole.

"Is that what-is-it still alive?" Persons asked, cutting steadily.

"I think so," McDonough said, his eyes averted from the tiny sun of the torch. "I've been sticking the electrodes in there about once every five minutes. I get essentially the same picture. But it's getting steadily weaker."

"D'you think we'll reach it before it dies?"

"I don't know. I'm not even sure I want to."

Persons thought that over, lifting the torch from the metal. Then he said, "You've got something there. Maybe I better try that gadget and see what I think."

"No," McDonough said. "It isn't tuned to you."

"Orders, Mac. Let me give it a try. Hand it over."

"It isn't that, Andy. I wouldn't buck you, you know that; you made this squadron. But it's dangerous. Do you want to have an epileptic fit? The chances are nine to five that you would."

"Oh," Persons said. "All right. It's your show." He resumed cutting.

After a while McDonough said, in a remote, emotionless voice: "That's enough. I think I can get through there now, as soon as it cools."

"Suppose there's no passage between the tail and the nose?"

Martinson said. "More likely there's a firewall, and we'd never be able to cut through that."

"Probably," McDonough agreed. "We couldn't run the torch near the fuel tanks, anyhow, that's for sure."

"Then what good——"

"If these people think anything like we do, there's bound to be some kind of escape mechanism—something that blows the pilot's capsule free of the ship. I ought to be able to reach it."

"And fire it in *here*?" Persons said. "You'll smash the cabin against the tunnel roof. That'll kill the pilot for sure."

"Not if I disarm it. If I can get the charge out of it, all firing it will do is open the locking devices; then we can take the windshield off and get in. I'll pass the charge out back to you; handle it gently. Let me have your flashlight, Marty, mine's almost dead."

Silently, Martinson handed him the light. He hesitated a moment, listening to the water dripping in the background. Then, with a deep breath, he said, "Well. Here goes nothin'."

He clambered into the narrow opening.

The jungle of pipes, wires and pumps before him was utterly unfamiliar in detail, but familiar in principle. Human beings, given the job of setting up a rocket motor, set it up in this general way. McDonough probed with the light beam, looking for a passage large enough for him to wiggle through.

There didn't seem to be any such passage, but he squirmed his way forward regardless, forcing himself into any opening that presented itself, no matter how small and contorted it seemed. The feeling of entrapment was terrible. If he were to wind up in a cul-de-sac, he would never be able to worm himself backwards out of this jungle of piping—

He hit his head a sharp crack on a metal roof, and the metal resounded hollowly. A tank of some kind, empty, or nearly empty. Oxygen? No, unless the stuff had evaporated long ago; the skin of the tank was no colder than any of the other surfaces he had encountered. Propellant, perhaps, or compressed nitrogen—something like that.

Between the tank and what he took to be the inside of the hull, there was a low freeway, just high enough for him to squeeze through if he turned his head sideways. There were occasional supports and ganglions of wiring to be writhed around, but the going was a little better than it had been, back in the engine compartment. Then his head lifted into a slightly larger space, made of walls that curved gently against each other: the front of the tank, he guessed, opposed to the floor of the pilot's capsule and the belly of the hull. Between the capsule and the hull, up rather high, was the outside curve of a tube, large in diameter but very short; it was encrusted with motors, small pumps, and wiring.

An air lock? It certainly looked like one. If so, the trick with the escape mechanism might not have to be worked at all—if indeed the escape device existed.

Finding that he could raise his shoulders enough to rest on his elbows, he studied the wiring. The thickest of the cables emerged from the pilot's capsule; that should be the power line, ready to activate the whole business when the pilot hit the switch. If so, it could be shorted out—provided that there was still any juice in the batteries.

He managed to get the big nippers free of his belt, and dragged forward into a position where he could use them, with considerable straining. He closed their needlelike teeth around the cable and squeezed with all his might. The jaws closed slowly, and the cusps bit in.

There was a deep, surging hum, and all the pumps and motors began to whirr and throb. From back the way he had come, he heard a very muffled distant shout of astonishment.

He hooked the nippers back into his belt and inched forward, raising his back until he was almost curled into a ball. By careful, small movements, as though he were being born, he managed to somersault painfully in the cramped, curved space, and get his head and shoulders back under the tank again, face up this time. He had to trail the flashlight, so that his progress backwards through the utter darkness was as blind as a mole's; but he made it, at long last.

The tunnel, once he had tumbled out into it again, seemed miraculously spacious—almost like flying.

"The damn door opened right up, all by itself," Martinson was chattering. "Scared me green. What'd you do—say 'Open sesame' or something?"

"Yeah," McDonough said. He rescued his electrode net from the handtruck and went forward to the gaping air lock. The door had blocked most of the rest of the tunnel, but it was open wide enough.

It wasn't much of an air lock. As he had seen from inside, it was too short to hold a man; probably it had only been intended to moderate the pressure-drop between inside and outside, not prevent such a drop absolutely. Only the outer door had the proper bank-vault heaviness of a true air lock. The inner one, open, was now nothing but a narrow ring of serrated blades, machined to a Johannsen-block finish so fine that they were air-tight by virtue of molecular cohesion alone—a highly perfected iris diaphragm. McDonough wondered vaguely how the pinpoint hole in the centre of the diaphragm was plugged when the iris was fully closed, but his layman's knowledge of engineering failed him entirely there; he could come up with nothing better than a vision of the pilot plugging that hole with a wad of well-chewed bubblegum.

He sniffed the damp, cold, still air. Nothing. If the pilot had breathed anything alien to Earth-normal air, it had already dissipated without trace in the organ pipe of the tunnel. He flashed his light inside the cabin.

The instruments were smashed beyond hope, except for a few at the sides of the capsule. The pilot had smashed them—or rather, his environment had.

Before him in the light of the torch was a heavy, transparent tank of iridescent greenish brown fluid, with a small figure floating inside it. It had been the tank, which had broken free of its moorings, which had smashed up the rest of the compartment. The pilot was completely enclosed in what looked like an ordinary G-suit, inside the oil; flexible hoses connected to bottles on the ceiling fed him his atmosphere, whatever it was. The hoses hadn't broken, but something inside the G-suit had; a line of tiny bubbles was rising from somewhere near the pilot's neck.

He pressed the EEG electrode net against the tank and looked into the Walter goggles. The sheep with the kitten's faces were still there, somewhat changed in position; but almost all of the colour had washed out of the scene. McDonough grunted involuntarily. There was now an atmosphere about the picture which hit him like a blow, a feeling of intense oppression, of intense distress—

"Marty," he said hoarsely. "Let's see if we can't cut into that tank from the bottom somehow." He backed down into the tunnel.

"Why? If he's got internal injuries——"

"The suit's been breached. It's filling with that oil from the bottom. If we don't drain the tank, he'll drown first."

"All right. Still think he's a man-from-Mars, Mac?"

"I don't know. It's too small to be a man, you can see that. And the memories aren't like human memories. That's all I know. Can we drill the tank some place?"

"Don't need to," Persons's echo-distorted voice said from inside the air lock. The reflections of his flashlight shifted in the opening like ghosts. "I just found a drain pet cock. Roll up your trouser cuffs, gents."

But the oil didn't drain out of the ship. Evidently it went into storage somewhere inside the hull, to be pumped back into the pilot's cocoon when it was needed again.

It took a long time. The silence came flooding back into the tunnel.

"That oil-suspension trick is neat," Martinson whispered edgily. "Cushions him like a fish. He's got inertia still, but no mass—like a man in free fall."

McDonough fidgeted, but said nothing. He was trying to imagine what the multi-coloured vision of the pilot could mean. Something about it was nagging at him. It was wrong. Why would a still-conscious and gravely injured pilot be solely preoccupied with remembering the fields of home? Why wasn't he trying to save himself instead—as ingeniously as he had tried to save the ship? He still had electrical power, and in that litter of smashed apparatus which he alone could recognize, there must surely be expedients which still awaited his trial. But he had already given up, though he knew he was dying.

Or did he? The emotional aura suggested a knowledge of things desperately wrong, yet there was no real desperation, no frenzy, hardly any fear—almost as though the pilot did not know what death was, or, knowing it, was confident that it could not happen to him. The immensely powerful, dying mind inside the G-suit seemed curiously uncaring and passive, as though it awaited rescue with supreme confidence—so supreme that it could afford to drift, in an oil-suspended floating-dream of home, nostalgic and unhappy, but not really afraid.

And yet it was dying!

"Almost empty," Andy Persons's quiet, garbled voice said into the tunnel.

Clenching his teeth, McDonough hitched himself into the air lock again and tried to tap the fading thoughts on a higher frequency. But there was simply nothing to hear or see, though with a brain so strong, there should have been, at as short a range as this. And it was peculiar, too, that the visual dream never changed. The flow of thoughts in a powerful human mind is bewilderingly rapid; it takes weeks of analysis by specialists before its essential pattern emerges. This mind, on the other hand, had been holding tenaciously to this one thought—complicated though it was—for a minimum of two hours. A truly sub-idiot performance—being broadcast with all the drive of a super genius.

Nothing in the cookbook provided McDonough with any precedent for it.

The suited figure was now slumped against the side of the empty tank, and the shapes inside the toposcope goggles suddenly began to be distorted with regular, wrenching blurs: pain waves. A test at the level of the theta waves confirmed it; the unknown brain was responding to the pain with terrible knots of rage, real blasts of it, so strong and uncontrolled that McDonough could not endure them for more than a second. His hand was shaking so hard that he could hardly tune back to the gamma level again.

"We should have left the oil there," he whispered. "We've moved him too much. The internal injuries are going to kill him in a few minutes."

"We couldn't let him drown, you said so yourself," Persons said practically. "Look, there's a seam on this tank that looks like a torsion seal. If we break it, it ought to open up like a tired clam. Then we can get him out of here."

As he spoke, the empty tank parted into two shell-like halves. The pilot lay slumped and twisted at the bottom, like a doll, his suit glistening in the light of the C.O.'s torch.

"Help me. By the shoulders, real easy. That's it; lift. Easy, now."

Numbly, McDonough helped. It was true that the oil would have drowned the fragile, pitiful figure, but this was no help, either. The thing came up out of the cabin like a marionette with all its strings cut. Martinson cut the last of them: the flexible tubes which kept it connected to the ship. The three of them put it down, sprawling bonelessly.

. . . AND STILL THE DAZZLING SKY-BLUE SHEEP ARE GRAZING IN THE RED FIELD . . .

Just like that, McDonough saw it.

A colouring book!

That was what the scene was. That was why the colours were wrong, and the size referents. Of course the sheeplike animals did not look much like sheep, which the pilot could never have seen except in pictures. Of course the sheep's heads looked like the heads of kittens; everyone has seen kittens. Of course the brain was powerful out of all proportion to its survival drive and its knowledge of death; it was the brain of a genius, but a genius without experience. And of course, *this* way, the U.S.S.R. could get a rocket fighter to the United States on a one-way trip.

The helmet fell off the body, and rolled off into the gutter which carried away the water condensing on the wall of the tunnel. Martinson gasped, and then began to swear in a low, grinding monotone. Andy Persons said nothing, but his light, as he played it on the pilot's head, shook with fury.

McDonough, his fantasy of spaceships exploded, went back to the handtruck and kicked his tomb-tapping apparatus into small shards and bent pieces. His whole heart was a fuming cauldron of pity and grief. He would never knock upon another tomb again.

The blonde head on the floor of the tunnel, dreaming its waning dream of a coloured paper field, was that of a little girl, barely 8 years old.

The Oath

Remembering conscientiously to use the handbrake as well as the foot, Dr. Frank Tucci began to slow down towards the middle of the bridge, examining the toll-booths ahead with a cold eye. He despised everything about scouting by motor-scooter—though he agreed, when forced to it, that a man on a scooter made the smallest possible target consistent with getting anywhere—but most of all he despised crossing bridges. It made him feel even more exposed than usual, and toll-booths made natural ambushes.

These, however, were as deserted as they looked. The glass had been broken and the tills rifled. Without question the man who took the money—had there been any left there after the Day—had not lived long enough afterwards to discover that it was worthless. The looting of money was unusual, for there had been little time for it. Most people had died during the first two days; the forty-eight-hour dose in the open had averaged 9,100 röntgens.

Naturally the small town ahead would be thoroughly looted of food and other valuables, but that was different. There was a doctor in the area—that was the man Tucci had come all this uncomfortable and dangerous way to see—and as usual, people would have drifted in to settle around him. People meant looting, necessarily. For one thing, they were accustomed to getting 70 per cent of their calcium from milk, and the only milk that was drinkable out here was canned stuff from before the Day. There might still be a cow or two alive outside the Vaults, but that meant nothing, since her milk would be lethal.

There would be no more dairy products of any kind for the lifetime of anyone now living, once the lootables were gone. There was too much strontium-90 in the soil. The Nutrition Board had worked out some way around the calcium supply problem, Tucci had heard, but he knew nothing about it; that wasn't his province.

His province was in the valley ahead, in the large reddish frame-house where, all the reports assured him, he would find a doctor—or somebody who was passing for one. The house, he noted professionally, was fairly well situated. There was a broad creek running rapidly over a stone bed not far away, and the land was arable and in cultivation: truck crops for the most part, a good acre of them, enough to supply a small family by today's starvation standards. The family was there, that was evident: two children in the 4-to-7 age bracket—hence, survivors, both of them—were playing a stalking game in the rows of corn to which the other acre was planted.

The position was not optimum for defence; though the centrally located house did offer clear shots all around, anyone could have put it into siege almost indefinitely from the high ground which surrounded it. But presumably a doctor did not need to conduct a lonely defence against the rare roving mob, since his neighbours would help him. A "neighbour" in that sense would include anyone within a hundred miles who could pick up a weapon and get to the scene fast enough.

Even a mob might pause before it could come to that. The first sight of the house it could have would be from here, looking down into the valley; and on the roof of the house, over green paint much streaked by repeated anti-fallout hosings, was painted a large red cross.

That would hardly have protected the owner during the first six months after the Day, but that had been more than a year ago. Things had settled somewhat since then. Initially a good deal of venom had expressed itself against doctors, when the dying had discovered that they could not be saved; that was why, now, rumours of the existence of a doctor could bring Tucci sixty bumpy miles on a rusty Lambretta whose side panels had fallen off, sweating inside a bullet-proof suit in whose efficacy he thoroughly disbelieved.

He gunned the motor three times in neutral before putting the scooter back in gear and starting it slowly down the hill. The last thing he wanted to do was to seem to be sneaking up on anybody. Sure enough, as he clambered down from his perch on to the road in front of the house and lurched the scooter up on to its kickstand, he saw someone watching him from a ground-floor window.

He knew that he was an odd sight. Short dumpy men look particularly short and dumpy on a motor-scooter, and he doubted that his white crash helmet and dark goggles made him look any less bizarre. But those, at least, he could take off; there was nothing he could do, right now, about the putatively bullet-proof coverall.

He was met at the door by a woman. She was a tall, muscular blonde, wearing shorts and a halter, and a cloth tying up her hair in the back. He approved of her on sight. She was rather pretty in her own heroic fashion, but more than that, she was obviously strong and active. That was what counted these days, though animal cunning was also very helpful.

"Good morning," he said. He produced from his pocket the ritual gift of canned beans without which it was almost impossible to open negotiations with a stranger. "My name is Frank Tucci, from up north. I'm looking for someone named Gottlieb, Nathan Gottlieb, I think."

"Thank you, this is where he lives," the woman said, with unusual graciousness. Obviously, she was not afraid. "I'm Sigrid

Gottlieb. You'll have to wait a while, I'm afraid; he's seeing another patient now, and there are several others waiting."

"Patient?" Tucci said, without attempting to look surprised. He knew that he would overdo it; just speaking slowly should be sufficient for an unwarned audience. "But it's—of course everything's different now, but the Gottlieb I'm looking for is a poet. 'Er, was a poet."

"Is a poet," Sigrid said. "Well, please come in. He'll be astonished. At least, *I'm* astonished—hardly anybody knew his name, even Back Then."

Score one—thanks to the Appalachian Vaults' monstrous library. Out of a personal crotchet, Tucci checked with the library each name that rumour brought him, and this time it had paid off. It never had before.

From here on out, it ought to be easy.

Nathan Gottlieb listened with such intensity that he reduced every other listener in Tucci's memory to little better than a catatonic. His regard made Tucci acutely aware of the several small lies upon which his story rested, and of the fact that Gottlieb was turning over and over in his hands the ritual can of beans Tucci had given his wife. In a while, perhaps, Gottlieb would see that it had been made *after* the Day, and draw the appropriate conclusions. There would be no harm in that after he had been hooked, but it would be awkward if he actually *saw* that can too early. Well, there was no help for it; onward and upward.

Physically, Gottlieb was small and gaunt, nearly a foot shorter than his wife. He looked as though, nude, you might be able to count all his bones. His somatotype suggested that he had not looked much plumper Back Then. But the body hardly mattered; what overwhelmed Tucci was the total, balanced alertness which informed its every muscle.

". . . Then when the word was brought in that there was not only a settlement here, but that a man named Nathan Gottlieb was some sort of key figure in it, it rang a bell. Sheer accident, since really I've never been much of a reader; but right away a line came to me and I couldn't get rid of it."

"A line?"

"Yes. It goes: 'And the duned gold clean drifted over the forelock of time.' It had haunted me for years, and when I saw your name, it came back, full force."

"As a last line, it's a smasher," Gottlieb said thoughtfully. "Too bad the rest of the poem wasn't up to it. The trouble was, the minute I thought of it, I knew it was a last line, and I waited around for two years for a poem to come along to go with it. None ever did, so finally I constructed one synthetically, with the predictable bad results."

"Nobody would ever know if you didn't tell them," Tucci said with genuine warmth. He had, as a matter of fact, particularly admired that poem for the whole two days since he first had read it. "In any event, I was sufficiently curious to don my parachute-silk underwear and come jolting down here to see if you were the same man as the one who wrote *The Coming-Forth*. I'm delighted to find that you are, but I'm overwhelmed to find you practising medicine as well! We're terribly short of physicians, and that happens to be my particular department. So all in all it's an enormous coincidence."

"That's for true," Gottlieb said, turning the can around in his hands. "And there's still a part of it that I don't understand. Who is this 'we' you mention?"

"Well. We just call it the Corporation now, since it's the last there is. Originally it was the Bryan Moving and Warehouse Corporation. If you lived in this area Back Then, you may remember our radio commercials on WASF-FM, for our Appalachian Mountain Vaults. Business men, what would happen to your records if some (unnamed) disaster struck? Put them in our mountain vaults, and die happy. That was the general pitch."

"I remember. I didn't think you meant it."

"We did. Oddly enough, a good many corporation executives took us at face value, too. When the Day came, it was obvious that the papers were going to be no good to anybody; we threw them out and moved in ourselves, instead. We had thought that was the most likely outcome and had been planning on it."

Gottlieb nodded, and set the can on the floor between his feet, as though the question it had posed him was now answerèd. "A sane procedure, that's for sure. Go on."

"Well, since the Reds saturated Washington and the ten 'hard' missile sites out west, we appear to be the only such major survival project that came through. We've had better than a year to hear differently, and haven't heard a whisper. Now we're out and doing. We're trying to organize a—well, not a government exactly, since we don't want to make laws and don't want to give orders—but at least the service functions of government, to bring things into some kind of shape. Doing for people, in short, what they can't do for themselves, especially with things in their present shambles."

"I see. And how do you profit?"

"Profit? Hardly at all. We attract specialists, which we need. This indebts the community to us and helps us manage it better; it's a large community now, about as big as New York and Pennsylvania combined, though it's shaped rather more like Texas. Every specialist we recruit is, so to speak, an argument for reviving the institution of government." He paused, counted to ten, and added: "I hope you are persuaded. Now that I've found you out, I'd be most reluctant to let you go."

Gottlieb said, "I'm flattered, but I think you're wrong. I'm still only a poet, and as such, quite useless. I'm the world's worst medical man."

"Ah. Now that's something I've been burning to ask you. How *did* you get into this profession?"

"Deliberately. When Sigrid and I got alarmed by all those Berlin crises, and decided to start on a basement shelter, I had to start thinking of what I might be able to do if we did survive. There wasn't any way to make a living as a poet Back Then, either, but I'd always been able to turn a marginal dollar as a flack—you know, advertising, the trade papers, popular articles, all those dodges. But obviously there wasn't going to be anything going in those lines after the Day."

"So you chose medicine instead?" Tucci said. "But why? Surely you had *some* training in it?"

"Some," Gottlieb said. "I was a medical laboratory technician for four years in World War II—the Army's idea of what to do with a poet, I suppose. I did urinalyses, haemotology, blood chemistry, bacteriology, serology and so on; it involved some ward visiting too, so I got to see the patients, not just their body fluids. At first I did it all by the cookbook, but after a while I began to understand it, and by God I seemed to have a feeling for it. I think most literary people might, if they'd just have been able to get rid of their notion that the humanities were superior to the sciences—you know, the pride of the professor of medieval Latin, really a desperately complicated language, in the fact that he couldn't 'do' simple multiplication. Hell, *anybody* can do multiplication; my oldest daughter could 'do' algebra at the age of nine, and I think she's a little retarded. Anyhow, you're probably familiar with the kind of inverse snobbery I'm talking about. And that's why I chose medicine. Nowadays I understand why the medicos had the interne system Back Then, though. There's nothing that turns you into a doctor like actually working at it, accumulating patient-hours and diagnostic experience."

"A fair decision," Tucci said, "but rather abstract. What did you do for equipment, materia medica, and so on?"

"I don't have any equipment to speak of. I don't do even simple surgery; I have to be hyper-conservative out of sheer ignorance—lancing a boil and installing a tube drain is as far in that line as I dare to go. As for supplies, that was easy. I simply looted the local drugstore first crack out of the box, while everybody else who survived was busy lifting canned goods and clothing and hardware. I was lucky that the whole dodge hadn't occurred to the pharmacist himself before the Day came, but it didn't. And I figured that anything I missed in the line of consumer goods would come my way later, if the doctor business paid off. You'd be surprised how much of my medical knowledge comes from the package inserts the manufacturers used to include with the drugs."

"Hmm. How long will your supplies hold out?" Tucci said.

"Quite a while, I think. I'm being conservative there too. In infectious cases, for instance, if I have a choice between an antibiotic and a synthetic—such as a sulpha drug—I use the antibiotic, since it has an expiration date and the synthetic drug doesn't. In another year most of my antibiotics will be useless, but so will all the others in the world, so there's no use worrying about it—and I'll still have the synthetics."

Tucci thought about it, conscientiously; it was a strange case and he was not sure that he liked it. Most of the few "doctors" he tracked down in the field were simple quacks, practising folk medicine to fill a gap left by the unavailability of any other kind. Occasionally he hit a survivor who had been a real physician Back Then; those were great discoveries, and instantly recruited. Gottlieb was neither the one nor the other, obviously, for though he had no right to practise by the old, extinct standards, he seemed to be trying to do an honest job from a limited but real basis of knowledge.

"I think we can solve at least some of your problems," he said at last. "So far as shelf life of antibiotics is concerned, we keep them in cold storage and have enough to last a good fifty years. And we can give you the use of a great deal of equipment that's absolutely out of the question in your situation: for example, X-rays, fluoroscopes, electrocardiographs, EEGs. I think we need you, Mr. Gottlieb, and it's self-evident that you need us."

Gottlieb shook his head, slowly, but not at all hesitantly. "It doesn't attract me," he said.

"For heaven's sake, why not? I don't like to be importunate, but you ought at least to think of what the other advantages might be. You could give up farming; we have a large enough community so we can leave that to experienced farmers. We use specialists in their specialties. You and your family could live in the Vaults, and breathe filtered air—that alone should run your children's life expectancy up by a decade or more. And above all, you'd be able to practise medicine in a way that's quite impossible here, and help many more people than you're helping now."

Gottlieb stood up. "I could explain, easily enough," he said, "but it would be faster in the long run if you first took a look at the kind of medicine I'm actually practising now. After that, the explanations can be shorter, and probably more convincing. I've still got three patients out there; why don't you just sit quietly and watch? You may not want me so badly when we're through."

THE OATH

The first patient was a burly, bearded, twisted man with heavily calloused hands who might always have been a farmer; in any event, everybody was a farmer now. He stank mightily, and part of the stench seemed to Tucci to be alcohol. His troubles, which he explained surlily, were intimate.

"Before we go on, there's something we have to get clear, Mr. Herwood," Gottlieb told him, in what subsequently proved to be a set speech. "I'm not a doctor and I can't promise to help you. I know something about medicine and I'll do the best I can, as I see it. If it doesn't work, you don't pay me. O.K.?"

"I don't give a damn," the patient said. "You do what you can, that's O.K. with me."

"Good." Gottlieb took a smear and rang a little handbell on his desk. His 15-year-old daughter popped her head in through the swinging door that led to the kitchen, and Gottlieb handed her the slide. "Check this for gram-positive diplococci," he told her. She nodded and disappeared. Gottlieb filled in the time discussing payment with the patient; Herwood had, it turned out, a case of anchovy fillets which he had liberated in the first days, when people were grabbing up anything, and had subsequently discovered that nobody in his surviving family would eat them.

The girl pushed open the swinging door again. "Positive," she reported.

"Thanks, honey. Now, Mr. Herwood, who's your contact?"

"Don't follow you."

"Who'd you get this from?"

"I don't have to tell you that."

"Of course you don't," Gottlieb said. "I don't have to treat you, either."

Herwood shifted in his seat; he was obviously in considerable physical discomfort. "You got no right to blackjack me," he growled. "I thought you was here to help people, not t'make trouble."

"That's right. But I already told you, I'm not a doctor. I never took the Hippocratic Oath and I'm not *bound* to help anybody. I make up my own mind. In this case, I want to see that woman, and if I don't get to see her, I don't treat."

"Well. . . ." Herwood shifted again in the chair. "All right, damn you. You got me over a barrel and you know it. I'll tell her to come in."

"That's only a start," Gottlieb said patiently. "That leaves it up to her, which isn't good enough. I want to know her name, so if she doesn't show up here for treatment herself, I can do something about it."

The argument continued for several minutes more, but it was already clear to Tucci that Gottlieb had won it. He gave the man an injection with matter-of-fact skill.

"That should start clearing up the trouble, but don't jump to conclusions when you begin to feel better; it will only be temporary. These things are stubborn; I'll need to see you three more times, at least. So don't forget to tell your friend that I want to see her—and that I know who she is."

As Herwood left, muttering, Gottlieb turned to his observer. "I see a lot of that kind of thing, and I'm doing my best to stamp it out—which I might even be able to do in a population as small as this," he said. "I don't have any moral strictures on the subject, incidentally; illegitimacy is probably the only way we can re-populate before we're extinct. But the diseases involved cost us an enormous sum in man-hours; and some of them have long latent periods that store up hell for the next generations."

"True," Tucci said non-committally.

The next patient was also a man, shockingly plump, though as work-worn as his predecessor. His symptoms made up an odd constellation, obviously meaningless to the patient himself; and after a while Tucci began to suspect that they meant very little to Gottlieb, either.

"How did that toe clear up?" Gottlieb was saying.

"All right, fine, Nat. It's just that I keep getting these infections every time I hit a splinter, looks like. And lately I'm always thirsty, I can't seem to get enough water; and the more I drink the more it cuts into my sleep, so I'm tired all the time too. And the same with food. People these days don't like pigs, and it's showing on me, but I can't seem to help it."

"I see. Well, it's pretty indefinite now, Hal; I think we'll have to

wait and see what develops." Gottlieb stopped, and quite sur-
reptitiously drew a deep breath. "Try to cut down a little on the
intake, I'll give you some pills that will help that, and some sleeping-
tablets. Don't hit the sleepy-pills too hard, though."

Payment was arranged; it was only nominal this time.

"Are you aware", Tucci said when they were alone again, "that
you've just committed manslaughter—at the very least?"

"Perfectly so," Gottlieb said in a low voice. "I wondered if you'd
be aware of it too. The man's a new diabetic. There's nothing I can
do for him."

"Nothing? Surely that's not so. I'm aware that you can't store
insulin without any refrigeration, but surely there are some of the
oral hypoglycemic agents in your stock—tolbutamide, carbutamide,
chlorpropamide? If you don't recognize them by their old trade
names, I can help you. In the meantime, you could have put the
man on a rational diet."

"I threw them all out," Gottlieb said flatly. "I don't treat diabetics. You heard what I told Herwood: I never took the Hippocratic Oath and I don't subscribe to it. In the present instance,
we're having a hard enough time with the new anti-survival muta-
tions that have cropped up. I am not going to have any hand in
preserving any of the old ones. If I ever hit a hemophiliac, the first
thing I'll do is puncture him for a test—and forget to put a patch
over the hole."

"It isn't easy," Gottlieb added after a moment, almost to himself.
"Hal's a friend of mine. But as far as I'm concerned, his heredity
has just shot him dead."

Tucci subsided without further comment. He was beginning to
have some second thoughts, and even a few third ones.

The last patient was relatively commonplace: she had frequent,
incapacitating headaches—and had earned them, for she had five
children, two survivors and three new ones. While Gottlieb doled
out aspirin to her, for which he charged a price so stiff that Tucci
suspected it was intended to discourage a further visit, Tucci
studied her fascies and certain revealing tics, tremors and failures
of co-ordination which were more eloquent to him than anything
she had said.

"There, that does it for today," Gottlieb said. "And with no more telephones, I'm almost never called out at night. I'll clean up and then we can talk further; you'll eat with us, of course. I have a canned Polish ham I've been saving for our first guest after the Day, and you've earned the right to be that guest."

"I'd be honoured," Tucci said. "But first, one question: have you a diagnosis for the last patient?"

"Oh, migraine, I suppose, though that's as good as no diagnosis at all. Possibly menopausal—or maybe just copelessness. That's a disease I invented, but I see a lot of it. Why?"

"It's not copelessness. It's glioblastoma multiforme—a runaway malignant tumour of the brain. At the moment that's only a provisional opinion, but I think an X-ray would confirm it. Aspirin won't last her long, and in the end, neither will morphine."

"Well, I'm sorry; Annie's a warm and useful woman. But if you're right, that's that."

"No. We have a treatment. We give the patient a boric acid injection—boron won't cross the blood-brain barrier, but it will concentrate in the tumour. Then we irradiate her whole head with slow neutrons. The boron atoms split, emitting two quanta of gamma radiation per atom, and the tumour is destroyed; the fission fragments are non-toxic, and the neutrons don't harm the normal brain tissue. As for the secondary gammas, they can't get through more than a layer of tissue a single cell thick. It works very well—one of our inheritances from Back Then."

"What you mean me to understand", Gottlieb said slowly, "is that you also have an atomic pile. That's the only possible source of slow neutrons."

"Yes, we do. It generates our electricity."

"All right," Gottlieb said. "I'll go and change, and then we'll talk. But the purpose of my demonstration, Mr. Tucci, is what I mean *you* to understand; and I wish you'd think about it a while."

The dinner was enormously pleasant—remarkably good even by the standards of the Vaults, and almost a unique experience for the field. Sigrid Gottlieb proved to be a witty table companion as well as an imaginative cook; and the children—the one prospect of the meal to which Tucci had not been looking forward, for as a bachelor he was categorically frightened of children—were not even in evidence: they were fed in the kitchen by the eldest, the same girl who served as her father's laboratory technician.

There was no medical talk until dinner was over. Instead, Gottlieb talked of poetry, which kept his guest a little on guard; Tucci knew more than most Americans about the subject, but far less than he had pretended to know.

Afterwards, however, Gottlieb got directly to the point.

"Any conclusions?" he said.

"A few," Tucci said, refusing to be rushed. "I'm not terribly alarmed by your odd brand of medicine—and I don't know whether you were afraid I would be, or whether you meant me to be. In the Vaults, we sometimes have to short-circuit the Oath too, for roughly similar reasons. I'm still quite convinced that you'd be better off with us."

"Yes, I don't doubt that you do; the Oath was full of traps even Back Then," Gottlieb said. "But I hoped you'd see that there's more to my refusal to join you than that. To begin with, Mr. Tucci, *I don't like medicine*; so I don't care whether I could do it better in the Vaults, or not."

"Oh? Well, then, you're quite right, I have somehow missed the point."

"It's this. You say you are so well organized that you can use specialists as specialists, rather than requiring them to do their own subsistence farming, and so on. But: could you use me *as a poet*? No, of course not. I'd have to practise medicine in the Vaults. But I really hate medicine—no, I shouldn't say that, but I'm certainly no fonder of it than I am of farming. I picked it as a profession because I knew it would be in demand after the Day, that's all!

"In your Vaults I'd be an apprentice, to a trade I don't much like. After all, you're sure to have real M.D.s there. I'd lose status. And more than that, I'd lose control over policy, over the kind of medicine *I* think suitable for the world we live in now—which is the only aspect of my practice that does interest me. I don't want to save diabetics at your behest; I want to let them die, at mine.

Call it playing God if you like, but it makes sense to me. Do you follow me?"

"I'm afraid I do; but go on."

"There isn't much further to go. I'm satisfied where I am, that's the essence of it. My patients may not be as well served by me as they think they are, but all the same they swear by me and come back for more. And I'm the only one of my kind in these parts. I don't have to farm my place to the hilt because most of my fees are in kind—which is lucky, because I have a brown thumb; I don't have to fortify it because my patients wouldn't dare let anything happen to me; I don't need the facilities you're offering me because I wouldn't know how to use them. And I think I'll keep on this way."

"I'm sure", Tucci said slowly, "that you'd find plenty of time to practise poetry as well, and many people who value it. I doubt that you find either here."

"What of it? Poetry has been a private art for a century, anyhow," Gottlieb said bitterly. "Certainly it's no art for a captive audience, which wants to pat the poet on the head because it thinks he's valuable for something quite different, like writing advertising copy, or practising medicine. I'm not interested in being tolerated; I wrote that off the day after the Day, and I'm not going back to it. Listen to me, Mr. Tucci: If you are really running a sort of Institute for Advanced Study, and can promise me *all* my time to perfect myself as a poet, I'll go with you. Otherwise I'll stay here. If I *have* to practise medicine, I may as well do so under conditions that I myself have laid down."

"I can't make such a promise," Tucci said. "So we have no more to say to each other. I'm truly sorry that it worked out this way, but in a way I'm on your side. And besides, were you to come with us, you'd leave your own people without a doctor—and though many of them would doubtless follow you into our community, there must be almost as many who wouldn't be able to do so."

"That's true," Gottlieb said; but he said it with a sort of convulsive shrug, as of a man who would dismiss the question, but only with doubt. "Thank you anyhow for the offer; I must say that you've made me feel like a boy getting a diploma. And it's run so late that you will have to spend the night with us; I don't want the Vaults to lose you on my account. Come back again when you can, and we'll talk poetry."

"Thank you," Tucci said. And that was all. He was guided up to bed, in the wake of a hurricane-lamp.

Or was it all? In the insect-strident night, so full of reminders of how many birds had died after the Day, and how loaded with insensible latent death the black air that he breathed as he lay tense in the big cool bed, Tucci was visited by a whole procession of phantoms. Mostly, they were images of himself. Some of them were dismissable as nightmares, surfacing during brief shallow naps from which he was awakened by convulsive starts which made his whole body leap against the sheets, as though his muscles were crazily trying to relax in a single bound the moment sleep freed them from the tensions of his cortex. He was used to that; it had been going on for years, and he had come to take it as a sign that though he was not thoroughly asleep yet, he would be shortly. In the meantime, the nightmares were fantastic and entertaining, not at all like the smothering, dread-loaded replays of the Day which woke him groaning and drenched with sweat many mornings just after dawn.

But this time the starts did not presage deep sleep; instead, they left him wide awake, and considering images of himself more disquieting than any he could remember having seen in dreams. One of the shallow nightmares had been a fantasy of what might be going on in the Gottliebs' bedroom—evidently Sigrid had marked Tucci's celibate psyche more profoundly than he had realized—but from this he awoke suddenly to find himself staring at the invisible ceiling and straining to visualize, not the passages of love between the poet and his wife about which he had been dreaming, but what they might be saying about Dr. Frank Tucci and his errand.

That errand hadn't looked hard, to begin with. By all the rules of this kind of operation, Sigrid should now be bringing all possible feminine pressures to bear against Gottlieb's stand, and furthermore, she should be winning; after all, she would think first of her children, an argument of almost absolute potency compared with Gottlieb's abstract and selfish reasons for refusing to go to the Vaults. That was generally how it went.

But Gottlieb was not typical; he was, in fact, decidedly hard upon Tucci's image of himself. He was a quack, by his own admission, but he was not a charlatan—a distinction without a difference before the Day, but presently one of the highest importance, now that Tucci was forced to think about it. And in this cool darkness after the preliminary, complacent nightmares, Tucci was beginning to see himself with horror as a flipped coin. Not a quack, no . . . he was an authentic doctor with a pre-Day degree, nobody could take that away from him; but he *was* a charlatan, or at the very least a shill. When, after all, had Tucci last practised medicine? Not since the Day. Ever since, he had been scooting about the empty, menacingly quiet countryside on recruiting errands—practising trickery, not medicine.

Outside, a cloud rolled off the moon, and somewhere nearby a chorus of spring peepers began to sing: *Here we are, here we are, here we are.* . . . They had been tadpoles in the mud when the hot water had come down toward the rivers in the spring floods; they might be bearing heavy radiation loads, but that was not something they were equipped to think about; they were celebrating only the eternal *now* in which they had become inch-long frogs, each with a St. Andrew's cross upon its back. . . . *Here we are, we made it.* . . .

Here we are. We made it. Some are quacks, and nevertheless practise medicine as best they can. Some are flacks, for all their qualifications, and do nothing but shill . . . and burden the practitioners with hard decisions the Tuccis have become adroit at ducking. The Tuccis can always say that they were specialists before the Day—Tucci himself had been an electrophysiologist, and most of the machines that he needed to continue down that road were still unavailable in the Vaults—but every doctor *begins* as a general practitioner; was there any excuse, now, for shilling instead of practicing?

The phantoms marched whitely across the ceiling. Their answer was *No*, and again: *No*.

In this world, in fact, Gottlieb was a doctor—and Dr. Frank Tucci was not. That was the last nightmare of all.

He was ruminatively tying his gear on to the baggage rack of the scooter, very early the next morning, when he heard the screen door bang and looked up to see Gottlieb coming down the front walk towards him. There were, he saw for the first time, lilies of the valley in bloom all along the side of the house. It was hard to believe that the world had ended years ago, even here in Gottlieb's valley. He straightened painfully and lifted his bubble goggles.

"Nice of you," he said. "But you needn't have seen me off. Keeping doctor's hours, you need all the sleep you can get."

"Yes," Gottlieb said abstractedly, leaning on the gate. "I had trouble sleeping, anyhow; I was thinking. I woke up this morning on the floor—that hasn't happened to me since just before my final exams. Could we talk a minute?"

"Well, certainly. But I'd like to get on the road before too long, to skip some of the heat of the day. This helmet absolutely fries my brains when the sun is high."

"Sure. I only wanted to say, I've changed my mind."

"Well. *That* was worth waiting for." Tucci took the helmet off and dropped the goggles carefully into it. "I hope you won't mind if I'm in a hurry. We'll have trucks down here for you in about a week at the latest; it takes a while to get a convoy organized. We'll also send a bus, since I think you'll find that about half your patients will want to follow you, once you explain the proposition."

"That'll be fine," Gottlieb said. He seemed embarrassed and disturbed. Tucci waited a moment, and then said, very gently:

"If you don't mind, Mr. Gottlieb, would you tell me why you reversed yourself?"

"It's my own fault," Gottlieb broke out, in a transport of anger. "I've given that speech about the Hippocratic Oath two thousand times in the last year or so. I never took the Oath, that's a fact, and I don't believe in it. But. . . . You said I'd be able to treat more patients, and treat them better, if I went to work for you. That's been on my mind all night. And I can't get away from it. It began to look to me as though a man can't be half a doctor, whether he

164

likes it or not. And I did go into this doctor business by my own choice."

He scuffed at the foot of the gate with one broganned toe, as though he might kick it if no one were watching him.

"So there I am. I have to go with you—and never mind that I'm giving up everything I've won so far—and a lot more that I hoped for. I may stop hating you five or ten years from now. But I could have spared myself, if I hadn't been so superior about Hippocrates all this time, and just minded my own business."

"The oath that you don't take", Tucci agreed, resuming his goggles and helmet again, "is often more binding than the one you do."

He stamped on the kick starter. For a miracle, the battered old Lambretta spat and began to snarl on the first try. Gottlieb stepped back, with a gesture of farewell. At the last moment, however, something else seemed to occur to him.

"Mr. Tucci!" he shouted above the noise of the one-lung engine.

"Yes? Better make it loud, Mr. Gottlieb—I'm almost deaf on this thing."

"It's not 'the forelock of time', you know," Gottlieb said. He did not seem to be yelling, but Tucci could hear him quite plainly. "The word in the poem is 'forepaws'."

Tucci nodded gravely, and put the scooter in gear. As he tooled off up the hill, his methodical mind began to chew gently on the question of who had been manipulating whom.

He knew that it would be many years before he had an answer.

A good many years ago, Damon Knight discovered that—unbeknownst to me—two early stories of mine were heavily loaded with symbols; and that these symbols showed that the stories, despite quite different overt contents, were about the same basic theme. When Damon later asked me to write a story for the first issue of his book-magazine Orbit, *I thought it appropriate to give the piece such a symbol system consciously, and this is the result.*

How Beautiful with Banners

I

Feeling as naked as a peppermint soldier in her transparent film wrap, Dr. Ulla Hillström watched a flying cloak swirl away towards the black horizon with a certain consequent irony. Although nearly transparent itself in the distant dim arc-light flame that was Titan's sun, the fluttering creature looked warmer than what she was wearing, for all that reason said it was at the same minus 316° F. as the thin methane it flew in. Despite the virus space-bubble's warranted and eerie efficiency, she found its vigilance—itself probably as close to alive as the flying cloak was—rather difficult to believe in, let alone to trust.

The machine—as Ulla much preferred to think of it—was inarguably an improvement on the old-fashioned pressure suit. Fashioned (or more accurately, cultured) of a single colossal protein molecule, the vanishingly thin sheet of lifestuff processed gases, maintained pressure, monitored radiation through almost the whole of the electromagnetic spectrum, and above all did not get in the way. Also, it could not be cut, punctured, or indeed sustain any damage short of total destruction; macroscopically, it was a single, primary unit, with all the physical integrity of a crystal of salt or steel.

If it did not actually think, Ulla was grateful; often it almost seemed to, which was sufficient. Its primary drawback for her was that much of the time it did not really seem to be there.

Still, it seemed to be functioning; otherwise, Ulla would in fact have been as solid as a stick of candy, toppled forever across the confectionery whiteness that frosted the knife-edge stones of this cruel moon, layer upon layer. Outside—only a perilous few inches from the lightly clothed warmth of her skin—the brief gust the cloak had been soaring on died, leaving behind a silence so cataleptic that she could hear the snow creaking in a mockery of motion. Impossible though it is to comprehend, it was getting still colder out there; Titan was swinging out across Saturn's orbit towards eclipse, and the apparently fixed sun was secretly going down, its descent sensed by the snows no matter what her Earthly eyes, accustomed to the nervousness of living skies, tried to tell her. In another two Earth days it would be gone, for an eternal week.

At the thought, Ulla turned to look back the way she had come that morning. The virus bubble flowed smoothly with the motion, and the stars became brighter as it compensated for the fact that the sun was now at her back. She still could not see the base camp, of course. She had come too far for that, and in any event it was wholly underground except for a few wiry palps, hollowed out of the bitter rock by the blunt-nosed ardour of prolapse drills; the repeated nannosecond birth and death of primordial ylem the drills had induced while that cavern was being imploded had seemed to convulse the whole demon womb of this world, but in the present silence the very memory of the noise seemed false.

Now there was no sound but the creaking of the methane snow; and nothing to see but a blunt, faint spearhead of hazy light, deceptively like an Earthly aurora or the corona of the sun, pushing its way from below the edge of the cold into the indifferent company of the stars. Saturn's rings were rising, very slightly awaver in the dark-blue air, like the banners of a spectral army. The idiot face of the giant gas planet itself, faintly striped with meaningless storms as though trying to remember a childhood passion, would be glaring down at her before she could get home if she didn't get herself in motion soon. Obscurely disturbed, Dr. Hillström faced front and began to unlimber her sled.

The touch and clink of the instruments cheered her a little, even in this ultimate loneliness. She was efficient—many years, and a good many suppressed impulses had seen to that; it was too late for temblors, especially so far out from the sun that had warmed her Stockholm streets and her silly friendships. All those null-adventures were gone now like a sickness. The phantom embrace of the virus suit was perhaps less satisfying—only *perhaps*—but it was much more reliable. Much more reliable; she could depend on that.

Then, as she bent to thrust the spike of a thermocouple into the wedding-cake soil, the second flying cloak (or was it that same one?) hit her in the small of the back and tumbled her into nightmare.

2

With the sudden darkness there came a profound, ambiguous emotional blow—ambiguous, yet with something shockingly familiar about it. Instantly exhausted, she felt herself go flaccid and unstrung, and her mind, adrift in nowhere, blurred and spun downward too into the swamps of trance.

The long fall slowed just short of unconsciousness, lodged precariously upon a shelf of a dream, a mental buttress founded four years in the past—a long distance, when one recalls that in a four-dimensional plenum every second of time is one hundred eighty-six thousand miles of space — and eight hundred millions of miles away. The memory was curiously inconsequential to have arrested her, let alone supported her; not of her home, of her few triumphs, or even of her aborted marriage, but of a sordid little encounter with a reporter that she had talked herself into at the Madrid genetics conference, when she herself had already been an associate professor, a Swedish Government delegate, a twenty-five-year-old divorcee, and altogether a woman who should have known better.

But better than what? The life of science even in those days had been almost by definition the life of the eternal campus exile; there was so much to learn—or, at least to show competence in—that people who wanted to be involved in the ordinary, vivid concerns of human beings could not stay with it long, indeed often could not even be recruited; they turned aside from the prospect with a shudder, or even a snort of scorn. To prepare for the sciences had become a career in indefinitely protracted adolescence, from which one awakened fitfully to find one's self spending a one-night stand in the body of a stranger. It had given her no pride, no self-love, no defences of any sort; only a queer kind of virgin numbness, highly dependent upon familiar surroundings and valueless habits, and easily breached by any normally confident siege in print, in person, anywhere—and remaining just as numb as before when the seizure of fashion, politics, or romanticism had swept by and left her stranded, too easy a recruit to have been allowed into the centre of things or even considered for it.

Curious—most curious—that in her present remote terror she should find even a moment's rest upon so wobbling a pivot. The Madrid incident had not been important; she had been through with it almost at once. Of course, as she had often told herself, she had never been promiscuous, and had often described the affair, defiantly, as that one (or at worst, second) test of the joys of impulse which any woman is entitled to have in her history. Nor had it really been that joyous: She could not now recall the boy's face, and remembered how he had felt primarily because he had been in so casual and contemptuous a hurry.

But now that she came to dream of it, she saw with a bloodless, lightless eye that all her life, in this way and in that, she had been repeatedly seduced by the inconsequential. She had nothing else to remember even in this hour of her presumptive death. Acts have consequences, a thought told her, but not ours; we have done, but never felt. We are no more alone on Titan, you and I, than we have ever been. *Basta, per carita!*—so much for Ulla.

Awakening in this same darkness as before, Ulla felt the virus bubble snuggling closer to her blind skin, and recognized the shock that had regressed her: a shock of recognition, but recognition of something she had never felt herself. Alone in a Titanic snowfield, she had eavesdropped on an . . .

No. Not possible. Sniffling, and still blind, she pushed the cozy bubble away from her breasts and tried to stand up. Light flushed briefly around her, as though the bubble had cleared just above her forehead and then clouded agian. She was still alive, but everything else was utterly problematical. What had happened to her? She simply could not know.

Therefore, she thought, begin with ignorance. No one begins anywhere else . . . but I didn't know even that, once upon a time. Hence:

3

Though the virus bubble ordinarily regulated itself, there was a control box on her hip—actually an ultrashort-range microwave transmitter—by which it could be modulated, against more special environments than the bubble itself could cope with alone. She had never had to use it before, but she tried it now.

The fogged bubble cleared patchily, but it would not stay cleared. Crazy moires and herringbone patterns swept over it, changing direction repeatedly, and outside the snowy landscape kept changing colour like a delirium. She found, however, that by continuously working the frequency knob on her box—at random, for the responses seemed to bear no relation to the Braille calibrations on the dial—she could maintain outside vision of a sort in pulses of two or three seconds each.

This was enough to show her, finally, what had happened. There was a flying cloak around her. This in itself was unprecedented; the cloaks had never attacked a man before, or indeed paid any of them the least attention during their brief previous forays. On the other hand, this was the first time anyone had ventured more than five or ten minutes outdoors in a virus suit.

It occurred to her suddenly that in so far as anything was known about the nature of the cloaks, they were in some respects much like the bubbles. It was almost as though the one were a wild species of the other.

It was an alarming notion and possibly only a trope, containing as little truth as most poetry. Annoyingly, she found herself wondering if, once she got out of this mess, the men at the base camp would take to referring to it as "the cloak and suit business".

The snowfield began to turn brighter; Saturn was rising. For a moment the drifts were a pale straw colour, the normal hue of

170

Saturnlight through an atmosphere; then it turned a raving Kelly green. Muttering, Ulla twisted the potentiometer dial, and was rewarded with a brief flash of normal illumination which was promptly overridden by a torrent of crimson lake, as though she were seeing everything in terms of a series of lithographer's colour separations.

Since she could not help this, she clenched her teeth and ignored it. It was much more important to find out what the flying cloak had done to her bubble, if she were to have any hope of shucking the thing.

There was no clear separation between the bubble and the Titanian creature. They seemed to have blended into a mélange which was neither one nor the other, but a sort of coarse burlesque of both. Yet the total surface area of the integument about her did not seem to be any greater—only more ill-fitting, less responsive to her own needs. Not *much* less; after all, she was still alive, and any really gross insensitivity to the demands and cues of her body would have been instantly fatal; but there was no way to guess how long the bubble would stay even that obedient. At the moment the wild thing that had enslaved it was perhaps most like a bear sark, dangerous to the wearer only if she panicked, but the change might well be progressive, pointed ultimately towards some Saturnine equivalent of the shirt of Nessus.

And that might be happening very rapidly. She might not be allowed the time to think her way out of this fix by herself. Little though she wanted any help from the men at the base camp, and useless though she was sure they would prove, she'd damn well better ask for it now, just in case.

But the bubble was not allowing any radio transmission through its roiling unicell wall today. The earphone was dead; not even the hiss of the stars came through it—only an occasional pop of noise that was born of entropy loss in the circuits themselves.

She was cut off. *Nun denn, allein!*

With the thought, the bubble cloak shifted again around her. A sudden pressure at her lower abdomen made her stumble forward over the crisp snow, four or five steps. Then it was motionless once more, except within itself.

That it should be able to do this was not surprising, for the cloaks had to be able to flex voluntarily at least a little in order to catch the thermals they rode, and the bubble had to be able to vary its dimensions and surface tension over a wide range to withstand pressure changes, outside and in, and do it automatically. No, of course the combination would be able to move by itself; what was disquieting was that it should want to.

Another stir of movement in the middle distance caught her eye: a free cloak, seemingly riding an updraught over a fixed point. For a moment she wondered what on that ground could be warm enough to produce so localized a thermal. Then, abruptly, she realized that she was shaking with hatred, and fought furiously to drive the spasm down, her fingernails slicing into her naked palms.

A raster of jagged black lines, like a television interference pattern, broke across her view and brought her attention fully back to the minutely solipsistic confines of her dilemma. The wave of emotion, nevertheless, would not quite go away, and she had a vague but persistent impression that it was being imposed from outside, at least in part—a cold passion she was interpreting as fury because its real nature, whatever it was, had no necessary relevance to her own imprisoned soul. For all that it was her own life and no other that was in peril, she felt guilty, as though she was eavesdropping, and as angry with herself as with what she was overhearing; yet burning as helplessly as the forbidden lamp in the bedchamber of Psyche and Eros.

Another trope—but was it, after all, so far-fetched? She was a mortal present at the mating of inhuman essences; mountainously far from home; borne here like the invisible lovers upon the arms of the wind; empalaced by a whole virgin-white world, over which flew the banners of a high god and a father of gods; and, equally appropriately, Venus was very far away from whatever love was being celebrated here.

What ancient and coincidental nonsense! Next she would be thinking herself degraded at the foot of some cross.

Yet the impression, of an eerie tempest going on just slightly outside any possibility of understanding what it was, would not pass away. Still worse, it seemed to mean something, to be important, to mock her with subtle clues to matters of great moment, of which her own present trap was only the first and not necessarily the most significant.

And suppose that all these impressions were in fact not extraneous or irrelevant, but did have some import—not just as an abstract puzzle, but to that morsel of displaced life that was Ulla Hillström? She was certainly no Freudian—that farrago of poetry and tosh had been passé for so long that it was now hard to understand how anybody, let alone a whole era, had been bemused by it—but it was too late now to rule out the repulsive possibility. No matter how frozen her present world, she could not escape the fact that, from the moment the cloak had captured her, she had been equally ridden by a Sabbat of specifically erotic memories, images, notions, analogies, myths, symbols, and frank physical sensations, all the more obtrusive because they were both inappropriate and disconnected. It might well have to be faced that a season of love can fall due in the heaviest weather—and never mind the terrors that flow in with it, or what deep damnations. At the very least, it was possible that somewhere in all this was the clue that would help her to divorce herself at last even from this violent embrace.

But the concept was preposterous enough to defer consideration of it if there were any other avenues open, and at least one seemed to be: the source of the thermal. The virus bubble, like many of the Terrestrial micro-organisms to which it was analogous, could survive temperatures well above boiling, but it seemed reasonable to assume that the flying cloaks, evolved on a world where even words congealed, might be sensitive to a relatively slight amount of heat.

Now, could she move inside this shroud of her own volition? She tried a step. The sensation was tacky, as though she were ploughing in thin honey, but it did not impede her except for a slight imposed clumsiness which experience ought to obviate. She was able to mount the sled with no trouble.

The cogs bit into the snow with a dry, almost inaudible squeaking, and the sled inched forward. Ulla held it to as slow a crawl as possible, because of her interrupted vision.

The free cloak was still in sight, approximately where it had been before, in so far as she could judge against this featureless snow-scape—which was fortunate, since it might well be her only flag for the source of the thermal, whatever it was.

A peculiar fluttering in her surroundings—a whisper of sound, of motion, of flickering in the light—distracted her. It was as though her compound sheath were trembling slightly. The impression grew slowly more pronounced as the sled continued to lurch forward. As usual, there seemed to be nothing she could do about it except, possibly, to retreat; but she could not do that either, now; she was committed. Outside, she began to hear the soft soughing of a steady wind.

The cause of the thermal, when she finally reached it, was almost bathetic: a pool of liquid. Placid and deep blue, it lay inside a fissure in a low, heart-shaped hummock, rimmed with feathery snow. It looked like nothing more or less than a spring, though she did not for a moment suppose that the liquid could be water. She could not see the bottom of it; evidently, it was welling up from a fair depth. The spring analogy was probably completely false; the existence of anything in a liquid state on this world had to be thought of as a form of vulcanism. Certainly the column of heat rising from it was considerable; despite the thinness of the air, the wind here nearly howled. The free cloak floated up and down, about a hundred feet above her, like the last leaf of a long, cruel autumn. Nearer home, the bubble cloak shook with something comically like subdued fury.

Now, what to do? Should she push boldly into that cleft, hoping that the alien part of the bubble cloak would be unable to bear the heat? Close up, that course now seemed foolish, as long as she was ignorant of the real nature of the magma down there. And, besides, any effective immersion would probably have to surround at least half of the total surface area of the bubble, which wasn't practicable— the well wasn't big enough to accommodate it, even supposing that the compromised virus suit did not fight back, as in the pure state it had been obliged to do. On the whole, she was reluctantly glad that the experiment was impossible, for the mere notion of risking a new immolation in that problematical hole gave her the horrors.

Yet the time left for decision was obviously now very short, even supposing—as she had no right to do—that the environment-maintaining functions of the suit were still in perfect order. The quivering of the bubble was close to being explosive, and even were it to remain intact, it might shut her off from the outside world at any second.

The free cloak dipped lower, as if in curiosity. That only made the trembling worse. She wondered why.

Was it possible—was it possible that the thing embracing her companion was jealous?

4

There was no time left to examine the notion, no time even to sneer at it. Act—act! Forcing her way off the sled, she stumbled to the mound and looked frantically for some way of stopping it up. If she could shut off the thermal, bring the free cloak still closer—but how?

Throw rocks. But were there any? Yes, there were two, not very big, but at least she could move them. She bent stiffly and tumbled them into the crater.

The liquid froze around them with soundless speed. In seconds, the snow rimming the pool had drawn completely over it, like lips closing, leaving behind only a faint dimpled streak of shadow on a white ground.

The wind moaned and died, and the free cloak, its hems outspread to the uttermost, sank down as if to wrap her in still another deadly swath. Shadow spread around her; the falling cloak, its colour deepening, blotted Saturn from the sky, and then was sprawling over the beautiful banners of the rings—

The virus bubble convulsed and turned black, throwing her to the frozen ground beside the hummock like a bead doll. A blast of wind squalled over her.

Terrified, she tried to curl into a ball. The suit puffed up around her.

Then at last, with a searing, invisible wrench at its contained kernel of space-time, which burned out the control box instantly, the single creature that was the bubble cloak tore itself free of Ulla and rose to join its incomplete fellow.

In the single second before she froze forever into the livid back-drop of Titan, she failed even to find time to regret what she had never felt; for she had never known it, and only died as she had lived, an artifact of successful calculation. She never saw the cloaks go flapping away downwind—nor could it ever have occurred to her that she had brought heterosexuality to Titan, thus beginning that long evolution the end of which, sixty millions of years away, no human being would see.

No; her last thought was for the virus bubble, and it was only three words long:

You goddam philanderer—

Almost on the horizon, the two cloaks, the two Titanians, flailed and tore at each other, becoming smaller and smaller with distance. Bits and pieces of them flaked off and fell down the sky like ragged tears. Ungainly though the cloaks normally were, they courted even more clumsily.

Beside Ulla, the well was gone; it might never have existed. Over-head, the banners of the rings flew changelessly, as though they too had seen nothing—or perhaps, as though in the last six billion years they had seen everything, siftings upon siftings in oblivion, until nothing remained but the banners of their own mirrored beauty.

[*This story is dedicated to Philip K. Dick, who once suggested that something like it would be the logical successor to such novels as* The Space Merchants, Gladiator at Law *and* Preferred Risk—*to say nothing of* If This Goes On. *At the time, I thought he was kidding.*— *JB*]

We All Die Naked

The good is oft interred with their bones;
So let it be with Caesar.

When Alexei-Aub Kehoe Salvia Sun-Moon-Lake Stewart, San. D., went out for lunch, he found half a dozen men with jackhammers tearing up the street in front of the building, the chisel blades of their drills cutting the slowly bubbling asphalt into sagging rectangular chunks. The din was fearsome, and a sizable necklace of teenagers was dancing to it, protected from the traffic by the police barricades across both ends of the block. In their gas masks they reminded him, after a moment's assiduous mental groping, of some woodcut from the *Totentanz* of Hans Holbein the Younger.

Not that he was any beauty himself, even out of a gas mask, as he had long ago resigned himself. He was fairheaded, but no Viking— in fact, he was on the short side even by modern undernourished standards, and what was worse, chubby, which caused strangers to look at him with that mixture of jealousy and hatred the underfed reserve for people whom they suspect of stuffing themselves at the public trough. In Alex's case, as all his acquaintances knew, they were absolutely right: as the head of a union under stringent government control, he was even technically only one step removed from being a public employee, *and* he could not blame his chubbiness on a metabolic defect, either; the fact was that he felt about food the way Shakespeare had felt about words. Nor, at forty, was he about to undertake any vast program of dietary reform. As for his face, it had been broad to begin with, and the accumulation of a faint

177

double chin now made it look as though it had been sat upon by some creature with gentle instincts but heavy hindquarters. Oh well; since like everyone else he had been born into an atmosphere, and an ecology in general, which was a veritable sea of mutagens, he felt he had to think himself lucky that his nose wasn't on upside down, or equipped with an extra nostril.

As for the dancing teenagers, they also made passage along the sidewalk even more difficult than it usually was at this hour, but Alex didn't mind. He watched them fondly. They consumed, but did not produce. And it was a privilege to be allowed to walk at all. In downtown Manhattan, you either owned a canoe (if you were wealthy) or travelled by TA barge, and left your office by a second-story window.

Twenty years ago, he liked to remember, Morningside Heights had consisted mostly of some (by modern standards) rather mild slums, completely surrounding the great university which had been their landlord. Today, like all other high ground in the city, the Heights was a vast skyscraper complex in which worked only the most powerful of the Earth. Lesser breeds had to paddle for it in the scummy, brackish canals of Times Square, Wall Street, Rockefeller Center, and other unimportant places, fending off lumps of offal and each other as best they could, or jamming over the inter-building bridges, or trying to flag down an occasional blimp. Flatlands like Brooklyn—once all by itself one of the largest cities in the world—were of course completely flooded, which was probably just as well, for the earthquakes had been getting worse there lately.

The most powerful of the Earth. Alex liked the sound of the phrase. He was one of Them. As the General President of Local 802 of the International Brotherhood of Sanitation Engineers, he had in fact few peers, and not only in his own estimation. Doubtless such a figure as Everett Englebert Loosli Vladimir Bingovitch Felice de Tohil Vaca, by virtue of his higher lineage and his still higher post of U.S. Secretary of Health, Education, Welfare, and Resources (Disposal of), was the more honoured; but it was doubtful that with all his hereditary advantages he could be the more cultured . . . and the next few weeks, Alex thought, would show which of them was truly the more powerful.

Adjusting his mask—no matter how new a mask was, it seemed to let in more free radicals from the ambient air every day—he put the thought resolutely aside and prepared to enjoy his stroll and his lunch. Today he was holding court with the writers, artists, and musicians in his circle—people of no importance whatsoever in the modern world, except to him; he was their patron. (*Patroon*, he corrected himself, with a nod toward the towers of Peter Stuyvesant's water-girdled village.) One, whom he might even consider making the next of his wives if she continued to shape up, he had even licensed to keep cats, creatures as useless as aesthetes in this hardening civilization, though a good deal less productive of solid wastes.

Nevertheless, he could not prevent himself—he was, after all, first and foremost a professional—from wondering how the masked men with the jackhammers were going to dispose of the asphalt they were cutting up. The project itself made sense: asphalt paving in a town where the noontime temperature rarely ran below eighty degrees ranged narrowly between being a nuisance and a trap. The dancers' shoes were already being slowed down by plaques and gobbets of the stuff. Nevertheless, it was virtually indigestible; once the men had dug it up and taken it away, where were they going to drop it? There was an underground tar pool in Riverdale in which such wastes were slowly—far too slowly—metabolized into carbon dioxide and water by an organism called *Bacillus aliphaticus*, but it was almost overflowing now and the sludge was being pushed up toward the top of the reservoir by the gastrapping stickiness of the medium, like a beer with its head on the bottom. The time wasn't far off when the sewers of Riverdale would begin to ooze into its valleyed avenues not ordinary sewage, but stinking condensates so tacky and . . . indisposable . . . as to make hot asphalt seem as harmless as cold concrete. Nor was carbon dioxide a desirable end product any more. . . .

But never mind all that now. Alex knocked at the door of the *Brackette de Poisson*, was recognized, and was admitted. At his table his coterie was waiting, and hands were lifted solemnly to him. His glance had only just sought out Juliette Bronck in the dimness when Fantasia ad Parnassum rose ceremonially and said:

"*Ave*, garbage-man."

Alex was deeply offended—nobody used that word any more—
and worse, he was afraid it showed. People ought to understand that
it is difficult to be friends with friends who won't respect one's sensi-
tivities. But there was worse to come.

"Listen," Fantasia said with quiet vehemence. "Sit down. Drop
your shovel. You won't need it any more."

"Why not, Fan?"

"Why not?" Fantasia made a production of being astonished. At
last he added, "God damn it, Alex, don't you know *yet* that the
world is coming to an end?"

So here we go again; Fan has a new hobby. It didn't look, after all,
like it was going to be a very pleasant lunch.

"All right," Alex said with a sudden accession of weariness. He
sat down and looked around the table, trying to beam benevolently.
It shouldn't have been difficult. After all, there was Juliette, a cameo-
like, 26-year-old, bikini-sized brunette who, in fact, at the moment
was dressed in very little else; Will Emshredder, a tall, cadaverous,
gentle-voiced man who had once produced a twelve-hour-long Experience called *The Junkpot Philosophy;* Rosasharn Ellisam, who
was a cultural heroine of Alex's, since she made welded sculpture
out of old bones which otherwise would have had to have been
disposed of in some other way; Goldfarb Z, a white Muslim who for
years had been writing, in invisible ink, a subliminal epic called *thus
i marshal mcmoonahan;* Strynge Tighe, a desperate Irishman clad
entirely in beads made of blue-dyed corn, who specialized in an
unthinkably ancient Etruscan verse form called txckxrxsm; Beda
Grindford, famous as the last man to get out of Los Angeles before
the cyclone hit the Hyperion plant, but for nothing else; Arthur
Lloyd Merlyn, a genuine, hereditary drip who was spending his life
looking for somebody to put a plug in for him; Bang Jøhnsund, who
wrote an interminable 3V serial named *The T.H.I.N.G. from O.U.T.-
B.A.C.K.;* Girlie Stonacher, a blond model who had been a hostess
on the blimp limousine to the lunar orbital shuttle until all commercial lunar flights had been discontinued; Fantasia's wife, Gradus,
possibly the most beautiful woman since Eleanor of Aquitaine, who
went about totally naked and would cut you to ribbons if you gave
the faintest sign of noticing it; Polar Pons, who by virtue of being

nine feet tall was in great demand as a lecturer; and, of course, the usual youngsters, who didn't count.

And, also of course, the inevitable thorn in the side of any such group, in this case Fantasia himself; there was always one. He was a smallish but handsome man of about fifty who exacerbated Alex, first of all, by having the largest and most distinguished lineage of any man in America, so distinguished that a mere list of his names read like three pages of a hotel register from the heyday of the Austro-Hungarian Empire; secondly, by having become wealthy in a blamelessly social way by a number of useful inventions (for example, he had invented a container for beer which, when the bottle was empty, combined with smog and dissolved down to its base to leave behind a cup containing one more swallow of beer, after which the base itself turned into counter polish); third, by being willing to argue on any side of any question, without seeming to care which side he was on so long as he could make a case for it (that was, in this gathering of artists, his art); and last (or almost last), by turning out to be right nearly every time Alex had been sure he had caught him out in his facts.

Alex nevertheless rather loved him, and got along with him most of the time by refusing to believe that he took anything seriously. But this time, for the first time, Fantasia had genuinely insulted him; and—

"—the end of the world," Fantasia said grimly.

"Carry a sign," Alex said, picking up the menu with his very best indifference. He would have liked to have had Alaskan king crab, but it was extinct; the sea-level Guatemalan ship canal of 1980 had let the Atlantic's high tides flow rhythmically into the Pacific, with results similar to but much more drastic than the admission through the St. Lawrence canal of the lamprey eel into the Great Lakes. Today's Special was neon shrimp; knowing where they came from, Alex lost his appetite. He put the card down and looked at his sudden antagonist

"Listen, dammit."

"*Eri tu, Brute?*"

"Alex," Fan said with a sort of disturbing tenderness, "you won't get out of this with dub macaronics, even with garbage sauce. Don't

wince, it's time we called things by their right names. I've been
doing some figuring, and no matter how I look at it, I think we're
dead."

Juliette took Alex's elbow, in that gesture which said, *Don't listen,
don't let him hurt you, I'll make it all up to you later ;* but Alex had
no choice. He said, snake to mongoose, "Go ahead."

After the last gasp, and the last plea not to tumble off just yet,
Alex arranged his feet among the cats and was on the shimmering
verge of oblivion when Juliette said: "Alex, are you asleep?"

He sighed, kneed away a cat with the demeaning name of Hausmaus, and propped himself up on one elbow. Beside him, Juliette
exuded warmth and the mixed perfumes of spray deodorant and
love, but her expression was that of a woman who now, at last,
meant to get down to the real business of the evening. Thrusting a
big toe vindictively into the ribs of the fat Siamese called Splat!,
he said, "No, not lately. What is it?"

"Do you think Fan is right?"

"Of course not, he was just showing off. You know damned well
that if I'd agreed with him, he'd have switched sides on the spot.
Now let's get some sleep. School keeps tomorrow, for me at least."

"But Alex, he sounded so . . . *convinced*. He said, 'No matter how
I look at it.' "

"He always sounds convinced. Look, Juli, of course we've got
a junk problem. Everybody knows that. Who could know it better
than I do? But we're coping. We always have coped. People have
been predicting disaster for twenty years and there hasn't been any
disaster. And there won't be."

"He did seem to have all the figures."

"And it wouldn't surprise me if he'd got them right. They
sounded right, where I was familiar with them. But what Fan doesn't
take into account is the sheer mass of the Earth—including the sea
and the air, of which there's a hell of a lot. You can't create any
major changes in a body that big just by a little litter. Making changes
like that takes geological time."

"Are you sure?"

"Of course I'm sure. Go to sleep."

WE ALL DIE NAKED

Go to sleep . . .

Some kinds of wastes, weather, rust, decay, are metabolized, or otherwise returned to balance with the general order of nature. Others are not.

Among those which are not are aluminium cans, glass bottles, and jugs, and plastic containers of all kinds. The torrent began in 1938, when in the United States alone about 35 million tons of these indigestible, unreclaimable, nonburnable, or otherwise indefeasible objects were discarded. By 1969, the rate was three quarters of a ton per year for every man, woman, and child in the country, and was increasing by 4 per cent per year. That year, Americans threw away 48 billion aluminium cans, 28 billion glass bottles and jars, and uncountable billions of plastic containers of every conceivable size and shape . . . 140 million tons of indestructible garbage.

By 1989, the total for the year had reached 311 million tons. None of it had ever gone away. The accumulation—again, in the United States alone—was 7,141,950,000 tons.

Which is not to say that no attempts were made to cope with it. Cans that contained any iron at all were fished out by magnets. Some of the glass was pulverized to grains finer than sugar and fed into great cesspools like Lake Erie, where, since glass is slightly soluble in water, it would very slowly become a *dissolved* pollutant. But since glass had been being broken and thrown away since the Phoenicians invented it, the pulverising composters made no measurable difference in the world's rising burden of grit, slag, and ashes.

In the meantime, nylon "ghost nets" broke free from fishing vessels and were set floating as permanent fish destroyers. The composters tore up nylon stockings and socks into eight-inch fragments, which, however, refused to rot. Heavy concentrations of polyethylene continued to build in truck-garden soil, spread by compost plants which were supposed to be selling humus. Eventually, many of the polyethylene bags and plastic containers were screened out for burning, but almost nothing was known about what happens when plastics burn, and in fact most such polymerized substances simply evaporated, adding to the enormous load of air pollution, which by 1969 had reached the highest levels of the atmosphere from jet exhausts. By 1989, the air of the whole world—thanks to the law of the diffusion of gases, which no White House Office of Science and Technology had thought to repeal—was multiply ionized and loaded with poisons ranging from simple industrial gases like sulfur dioxide to constantly recomplexing hydrocarbons, and emphysema had become the principal cause of death, followed closely by lung cancer. Skin cancer, too, was rising in the actuarial tables, in incidence though not in mortality; the wide and beautiful sky had become a sea of carcinogens.

Masks were introduced, but of course nobody could stop breathing and emitting carbon dioxide. In 1980 there were 4,500 million human carbon dioxide emitters on the Earth—very few of other species—and so much of the world had been paved over, or turned into desert, that the green plants had long lost the battle to convert the gas into oxygen and water vapour. The burning of fossil fuels, begun in prehistory among the peat bogs, might have fallen off with the invention of nuclear power, but the discovery in 1968—when nuclear power was still expensive to exploit, and which produced wastes so long-lived and so poisonous that people had the rare good sense to be terrified of them while it was still early enough to cut down on their production—of the Alaskan oil field, the fourth largest in history, aborted the nuclear boom and produced a new spurt in burning. The breathers, in the meantime, continued to multiply; by 1989 nobody knew what the population of the world was—most of the statistics of the increase had been buried under the statistics for the increment of garbage.

Carbon dioxide is not a poisonous gas, but it is indefatigably heat-conservative, as are all the other heavy molecules that had been smoked into the air. In particular, all these gases and vapours conserved solar heat, like the roof of a greenhouse. In due course, the Arctic ice cap, which had been only a thin sheet over a small ocean, an ocean furthermore contained in a basin also heat-conservative, melted, followed by the Greenland cap. Now the much deeper Antarctic cap was dwindling, dumping great icebergs into the warming Antarctic Ocean. Great fog banks swept around the world, accelerating the process and chelating the heavier gas molecules as they moved, making them immune from attack by oxygen, ozone, or the activating effects of sunlight. The fogs stank richly of tars and arsenes, and were thicker and yellower than any London had seen in the worst years *before* the Clean Air Act had been passed.

And the ice continued to melt. Sea level in 1989 was twenty-one feet higher than it had been in 1938; every harbour in the world had been obliterated, every shoreline changed, and the brokers of lower Manhattan had been forced to learn to paddle. The worldwide temperature rose; more bergs fell into the Ross Sea; the last Ice Age was over.

Sleep, my child, and peace attend thee. . . .

For some reason, Alex woke just before dawn. Disgruntled, he went to the head, had a long drink of water, took a tranquilizer, roughed up Splat!'s fur along the back until he purred with contented indignation and bit him, peeked lubriciously at Juliette in her cocoon, constructed what replies he might have made to Fantasia at lunch had he not been taken so completely aback, and finally lay down again; but nothing served—he was completely alert.

Then he remembered: Today was the day of his appointment with Secretary de Tohil Vaca, and the beginning of their test of power. Suddenly Fan's irresponsible hypothesizing, and the poses, hobbies, crotchets, and vapours of the rest of the coterie, suddenly even Juliette herself, fell into perspective. He was back in the real world, where nothing ever changed unless you made it change, and never mind those who merely talked. Reality was what counted.

Swinging out of the warm bed with some reluctance, he sat on the edge until his hypotensive dizziness had passed, then washed, shaved, dressed, turned off the alarm—no point in having it wake Juli, since he had anticipated it—and kissed her on the end of the nose. She murmured disturbedly, "Lemonade," as though she were having some peculiarly private dream, and resettled herself. She still exuded that unpublic, compound, organic fragrance which was her gift to him, and for a moment he felt a desperate urgency to pull off all his clothes and other arrangements and lie beside her again; but at the same moment of the impulse, he happened to see the teddy bear on her dresser, which, though it made her seem more pathetic, and the room even tinier, also re-reminded him of the substantial world.

Well, but he would protect her. Part of protecting her was the matter of coping with the real world. He checked the contents of his briefcase carefully in the false dawn, and then left, closing the door very quietly.

Some forty-five seconds later he was fumbling with the key before her door and fuming with loveless indignation. He had forgotten to feed the goddam cats.

Juli's apartment was on the fifth and only habitable floor of what had once been a moderately expensive apartment building in the Chelsea district. Occasionally, the landlord managed to rent out a fourth-floor flat at reduced rates to some gullible and desperate family, on the showing that even high tide did not reach that far; but they seldom lasted a month, or until the first storm sent waves breaking over their windowsills.

Luckily, there was no wind today, nor even any rain. Alex put on his mask, settled his stretch homburg carefully atop it, and went down the hallway. Rats scurried and squeaked ahead of him. Juli let the cats roam free in the building after she got up, but the rats always came back; unlike the cats, they could swim.

The canoe was lashed to the balcony of the fire escape, swung on davits, an arrangement kindly rigged by Fantasia; Alex himself could not so much as tie a knot without getting his forefinger caught in it. The tide was down today, and after settling himself in the canoe, he took a full five minutes lowering it gingerly to the greasy surface of the water. Once he had cast loose, however, he paddled up Eighth Avenue with fair skill and speed, an ability which was a by-product— not achieved without many spills—of the affair with Juli.

Thanks to the earliness of his awakening, there was not much traffic yet. Even the few barges he passed were half empty, the identical masked faces peering out of them looking as disconsolate as he felt to be up at this hour. At Thirty-Second, a street-sweeper went by him going the other way, sucking into its frontal maw everything that floated except the traffic, and discharging from its almost as capacious anus anything that did not clink, clank or crunch. The theory behind the monster, which had been designed over a decade ago, was that anything that did not make a noise as it passed through its innards could safely be left in the water for the fish and bacteria.

Actually, of course, there were no fish anywhere near this close to shore any more. There were not many even in the high seas. The Guatemalan canal had resulted in the destruction of about 23,000 Pacific species, through evolutionary competition, but the destruction in the Atlantic had not been that selective. It had begun with the poisoning of the Atlantic phytoplankton, the very beginning of the chain of nutrition for all marine life, by land effluents loaded with insecticides and herbicides. The population of the Atlantic from pole to pole, from brit to whales, was now only 10 per cent of what it had been when the streetsweeper had been on the drawing boards. As for the bacteria, the number of species of molecules they could not digest now far outnumbered those that they could.

Nevertheless Alex waved to the monster as he went by. Obsolete or not, it belonged to his own working force. The men piloting it waved back. Though of course they did not recognize him in his mask, it was known that the boss often went to work this way: if somebody in a canoe waved to them, it was safer to wave back.

Slllrrrppp . . . Spprrrsttt, said the monster.

The city was waking up now. Outboard-powered car pools of men in wet-suits, painted to look tailored, were beginning to charge along the cross-streets, creating wakes and followed by the muffled obscenities of people in canoes. Most of these came across the Hudson from New Jersey, which had had a beautifully planned new city built north of Newark, on what had been the tidal swamp of the Meadows, only to have its expensively filled and tended lawns become swamps again and then go totally under water. Few of the commuters paid any attention to the traffic semaphores, having learned from experience that the rare police launches were reluctant to chase them—the wakes of the launches upset more canoes and rowboats than the speeding outboards did. Lately, some of the paddlers and rowers had taken to chucking sash weights over the gunwales of speeders when possible. The police were prone to ignore this, too, though they frowned at outright shooting.

Alex observed all the semaphores scrupulously and reached Forty-Second Street without incident. There, before turning starboard, he took off the homburg, stowed it in its plastic bag, and put on his crash helmet.

Again, thanks to the relative earliness of the hour, he had been able to thread his way through the jam of barges shipping produce into and out of what had once been Penn Station with considerable speed, but Times Square was another matter. There was no time after dawn when it was not a mass of boats of all sizes, many of them equipped with completely illegal rams and spikes, many locked together willy-nilly in raftlike complexes, the occupants swearing and flailing at each other with oars, paddles, barge poles, whips, boarding hooks, and specialized assegai-like weapons developed by the more ingenious. There was no alternate route to where Alex was going that was any better.

The police concentrated here as a matter of course, which prevented individual acts of mayhem from fulminating into outright riot, and often managing to keep some sort of narrow canal open in one direction or another. Alex watched for these canals, and those that opened accidentally now and then, with the intensity of a mariner trying to pass through the mythical mazes of the Sargasso. He had learned long ago that picking fights with other boats was a waste of time. The only weapon that he carried was a table-tennis racquet sided with coarse sandpaper, with which he banged the knuckles of people in the water who tried to climb into his canoe. He did this completely impersonally and without malice; he knew, as the strugglers should have known, that it is impossible to get into a canoe from the water without upsetting it.

He took only two paddle blows elsewhere than directly on the helmet, which he thought must be a record for the course. Past Sixth Avenue, the furtive canals got wider and tempers tended to have cooled a little. By the time he reached the Public Library—whose books were now no more inaccessible to the public than they had been fifty years ago, though the reason had changed—he felt justified in removing the helmet and resuming the homburg. There was remarkably little water in the scuppers and he himself was only moderately splashed—the latter of no moment at all, since his clothing was entirely by Burberry and all he needed to do once he arrived was step into one of the Bell System's booths, deposit a quarter, and have the random garbage showered off with salt water.

All in all, he thought as he turned the canoe over to an Avis docker,

it was a good thing that he hadn't been able to sleep. The trip had
been an out-and-out snap.

Secretary de Tohil Vaca was a tall, fair, bearded man of almost
insufferable elegance of manner. Ringed and ringleted, perfumed
and pomaded, fringed and furbelowed, beaded and brocaded, he
combined nature and nurture so overpoweringly, in fact in such an
absolute assonance of synesthetic alliteration, that it became a
positive pleasure to remind one's self that the underlying essence
of his official cachet, like the musk of sex and the ambergris of
the most ancient perfumes, was—Alex bit silently but savagely
down on the word—garbage.

His office was on the top floor—in fact, *was* the top floor—of the
old Pan Am building, which was itself one of the principal monu-
ments to the ways junk had been piled up willy-nilly in the heyday
of the Age of Waste. The building itself still sat over the vast septic
tank which had once been Grand Central Station, a tank over which
the tides gurgled semidaily without in any way slowing the
accumulation of filth in those deep caverns and subway tubes.
Most of the immense, ugly structure, which had always looked
like the box some other building had been shipped in, was
now occupied only by tax accountants, 3V producers, whores,
mosquitoes, anthologists, brokers, blimp-race betting agencies,
public-relations firms, travel agents, and other telephone-booth
Indians, plus hordes and torrents of plague-bearing brown rats
and their starving fleas.

Secretary de Tohil Vaca, however, reached his office, when he did,
by private blimp, much accompanied by hostesses and secretaries
rather like Girlie Stonacher; and he had been known, when he was
in a rare hurry, to settle down upon the top of it by air-polluting
helicopter. Rank had, as it is written, its privileges.

The office was flooded with sunlight from all sides when the smog
let it through, and was hung alternately with Aztec tapestries and
with modern collages of what was called the Reconstituted Findings
school. The air was cool and almost odourless, and usually carried,
as now, a discreet purring of music. In apparent—but only apparent
—deference to Alex, the system was now playing a version for four

exhaust-flutes of *Hector, the Garbage Collector*, the eighty-year-old anthem of Local 802.

It was all very well prepared, but Alex was not going to be seduced. He not only knew what he wanted, but knew that he had to get it; he was, after all, as much a creature of his constituency as de Tohil Vaca was of the administration.

"Sir down, Alex," he said affably. "I'm sorry this meeting has been postponed so frequently, but, you'll understand, I'm sure, there have been other pressing matters. . . ."

The Secretary waved vaguely and allowed the sentence to trail off. Alex thought he understood well enough: the Secretary had sought to convey the impression that the Administration did not regard the matter as serious and could, if it had to, get along very well without the services of Local 802. They both knew this to be nonsense, but the forms had to be gone through.

Now that he was actually in the presence, however, Alex found this diagnosis weakening a little. The Secretary's expression was that of a man rather grimly amused by some private piece of information, like that of a wife accepting flowers from a husband she knows is having an affair with the computer girl. Of course, de Tohil Vaca was a superb actor, but nevertheless Alex found the expression rather disquieting. He tried not to show it.

"Quite all right," he said automatically. "Of course you realize that having left so little time for negotiation means that you'll have to accept our terms as stated."

"Not at all, not at all. In the first place, my dear Alex, you know as well as I do that a strike by your men would be illegal. In our present society we could no more allow it than a wooden city could allow a fireman's strike."

"I'm quite prepared to go to jail if I have to. You can't jail the whole union." He did not go on to add that winning this strike would also win him de Tohil Vaca's office in the next administration. The Secretary knew well enough what the stakes were, which was the real reason why no negotiation would have been fruitful; the strike was absolutely inevitable.

"I'm not threatening you, I assure you. No, really, that issue has in reality become quite irrelevant. You see, Alex, there have been new developments of which you're not aware. They are of sufficient importance so that we no longer care if your men quit work and never go back."

"That," Alex said, "is pure nonsense. The only justification you could have for such a statement would be the development of machinery which made all my men obsolete. I know the technology at least as well as you do, and no such advance has occurred. And if such machines exist in theory, you can't possibly get them into production and on the job fast enough to prevent a disaster if we strike— not even if in theory they're capable of solving the entire problem."

"I imply no such thing," de Tohil Vaca said, with a calmness that seemed to conceal a certain relish. "We have not solved the problem. Quite the opposite. The problem has solved us."

"All right," Alex said. "You've produced your effect. Now, just what *are* we talking about?"

The Secretary leaned back in his chair and put his fingertips together. "Just this," he said. "We cannot 'dispose' of our wastes any longer. They have tipped the geological scales against us. The planet is breaking up. The process has already started, and the world will be effectively unhabitable before the next ten years have passed."

The Secretary was watching Alex narrowly, and actor or no actor, could not prevent a faint shadow of disappointment from flitting over his face; Alex had only smiled.

"Good heavens, man," the Secretary said. "Do you hear an announcement like that every day? Or are you utterly without imagination?"

"Neither," Alex said. "But as it happens, I did hear a very similar stetement less than twenty-four hours ago. It didn't come from quite so august a source, but I didn't believe it then, and I don't believe it now."

"What," de Tohil Vaca said, "would you think I stood to gain by making it?"

"I can't imagine. If you were another man, you might be hoping I'd carry this story back to the union and get the strike called off. Then, when the end of the world didn't come through on schedule, I'd be destroyed politically. But you know I'm not that credulous, and I know that you know you wouldn't dare to use such means; it'd destroy you, too."

"Well, at least we are now out in the open," de Tohil Vaca said. "But the fact is that I mean every word I say, and furthermore, I'm prepared to offer you a proposition, though not at all of the kind you thought you came here to discuss. To begin with, though, I had better offer you my documentation. You have, no doubt, noticed the Brooklyn earthquakes."

"Yes, and I know what caused them," Alex said, feeling suddenly, unexpectedly grateful for Fan's passionate lecture of the preceding day. "It's a residium of deep-well disposal."

The Secretary looked openly astonished. "What on earth is that?" he said. "I've never heard of it."

"I'm not surprised. It hasn't been widely used in a long time. But back around 1950, some private firms began disposing of liquid wastes by injection into deep wells—mostly chemical companies and refineries. Most of the wells didn't go down more than six thousand feet and the drillers went to a lot of trouble not to get them involved with the water table. Everybody liked the idea at the time because it was an alternative to dumping into rivers and so on.

"But then the Army drilled one *twelve* thousand feet down, near Denver. They started pumping in 1962 and a month later, after only about four million gallons had gone down, Denver had its first earthquake in eighty years. After that, the tremors increased or decreased exactly in phase with the pumping volume. There's even a geological principal to explain it, called the Hubbert-Rubey Effect."

"My word," de Tohil Vaca said, taking notes rapidly. "What happened?"

"Well, nothing for a while. More than a hundred such wells were in operation by 1970, mostly in Louisiana and Texas. But by 1966 somebody had noticed the correlation—which was pretty sharp because the Denver area had never been subject to quakes before, and the quake zone was right underneath the Army's arsenal—so the Army stopped pumping. The quakes went on for another eighteen months—in fact, the biggest one of all was in 1970—but then they began to die back.

"And that's my point. The injection system was outlawed in most states, but there are still eight of them in operation in Pennsylvania, pumping into a strata system only marginally suited for them, and another right out here in Brookhaven, which is totally *unsuited* for it. That brackets Brooklyn neatly—and unlike Denver, Brooklyn always has been subject to slight temblors. So there's your answer: cap those wells, and as soon as they get back into equilibrium again— which will take as long as it takes, eighteen months only applied to Denver—then, no earthquakes.''

The Secretary dropped his stylus and stared at Alex in frank admiration.

"My word," he said again. "That's the most ingenious theory I've heard in years. I do seem to have underestimated you, after all.''

"Well, it isn't entirely mine," Alex admitted. "The man I talked to yesterday thinks that once you trigger an earthquake, you can't untrigger it. But the Colorado experience shows you can.''

"Even if you can," said de Tohil Vaca, "I regret to say that the theory, while elegant, is also irrelevant. The real process is something quite different, and absolutely irreversible. It's the greenhouse effect that's responsible—and I hope you'll pardon me if I read from notes here and there; I am no scientist.''

"Go ahead.''

The Secretary opened a folder. "You know the Arctic ice cap is gone. But that's minor; it was only pack ice. The real problem is down south. There are unthinkable billions of tons of ice over the Antarctic continent—which is volcanic, as Mount Erebus shows. Now the first effect of letting up the pressure of all that ice is that it changes the isostatic balance of the Earth's crust, which would be bad enough, but there's worse to follow.

"There's a thing called precession of the equinoxes, which means that not only does the Earth rotate on its axis, but the axis of rotation also moves around its own centre, like the secondary motion of a top when it's slowing down.''

"I know about that. It means the poles describe a small circle, so we don't always have the same pole star. But I also know just one of those circles takes twenty-five thousand years.''

"Yes, but that's geologically a pretty short time. And bear in mind that swinging all that concentrated ice around and around represents an enormous amount of energy—of momentum. If you melt the ice and distribute its mass as water evenly all over the globe, where does the energy go?"

"I'm not a scientist either," Alex said. "But as an engineer, I'd predict that it'd show up as heat."

"And so some of it will—in *lots* of heat. Good-bye, fish, just for a starter. And the sea-level rise will total thirty-three feet when all the ice is gone. But there's still more, Alex. Besides the precession, the top wobbles. It used to be called the Drayson Effect, but I gather that everybody sneered so hard at poor old Drayson, whoever he was, for proposing it, that when they discovered the wobble was real, they gave it another name; it's called Chalmer's Wobble now. It shows up in a cyclical disturbance of the polar path, the equinoctial path."

"And how long is the cycle?"

"Fourteen months."

"Fourteen months! Are you sure you've got that right?" "That's what it says here," de Tohil Vaca said grimly. "And it's been known for twenty years that any major variation in the cycle is a signal that a *very* large strain release is about to occur somewhere in the crust. Lately, my dear fellow, the polar path has been wobbling irregularly all over northern Canada.

"The outcome is going to be vulcanism on a scale never seen before in the lifetime of man. I'm told that we are in for a new era of mountain-building, the first since the Rockies were thrust up. *That* will bury all our old cans and bottles and junked cars very nicely—but there'll be nobody left around to rejoice."

"My God," Alex said slowly. "And obviously it's irreversible— we can't take the carbon dioxide and the other heavy gases out of the air. We've changed the climate, and that's that. The ice is going to go right on melting. Faster and faster, in fact, as more energy's released."

"Precisely."

Irrationally, Alex felt a momentary flash of pleasure at being now able to tell Fan of a disaster that made Fan's hypothesis look like a mild attack of hiccups. The moment's elation vanished in a horrible nightmarish sinking of every recognizable human emotion except

terror. He could not doubt his erstwhile antagonist; the whole
sequence, even he could see, flowed inevitably from as fundamental
a law as the conservation of energy. Trying to keep his voice from
shaking, he said,

"And yet you said you had a proposition."

"I do. We are going to evacuate some people to the Moon. We
still have the old commercial ships, as well as military vehicles, and
we've been maintaining the bases, mostly because the Soviets have
been maintaining theirs. Of course there's no hope of mankind's thriv-
ing on the moon, but it's at least a tenable way-station until we can
organize a further jump to Mars, which we just *might* make livable."

"And what about the Soviets themselves?"

"They'll just have to think of the idea for themselves," the
Secretary said. "We certainly aren't going to propose it to them.
Personally, I'd a lot rather outnumber them when it's all over;
lunar bases are terribly vulnerable."

"Hmmm. How are you going to choose our people?"

"Partly by need, partly at random. We want people of proven
ability and necessary skills; but we also want to minimize genetic
drift, which I'm told will be a real danger in so small a population.
Myself, I'm not even sure that it is. So we're picking out a small
group of technicians and known leaders, and we're issuing each of
them ten tickets, which they can hand out to anyone they please."

"Without restrictions?"

"There are several restrictions. Secrecy is one, though of course
we know we can't maintain it for long. Another is baggage: twenty
pounds per person, which has to pack into five cubic feet. But the
most important one is that in every group of ten there must be six
women. Under the circumstances, men are almost unimportant. If
they weren't our main repository of technology, and of creative
energy—and of course there's the high possibility of accident—
we'd make the ratio nine to one, and still think it too high."

"No children, I suppose?"

"No children. We want skills plus genes. And potency. We'll
generate children later, when we're sure we can take care of them.
We can't ship them. So if any of your friends want to give up their
seats for the bairns, you will have to tell them No."

"I can see myself doing that," Alex said.

"I hope you can. I'm sorry, Alex. It's ghastly, to be sure. But it's the way it's going to have to go."

An easy policy for an obvious homosexual like de Tohil Vaca to adapt to—or a childless man like Alex. But de Tohil Vaca was not going to have to tell anybody No; he had passed that obligation on. To, among other people, Alex.

"The system distributes the moral problem nicely, too," Alex said bitterly. "Every may a god to his friends."

"Would you rather have the Administration choose everybody?" The answer to that was obvious. "What about livestock?"

"Oh, these vessels will be arks—animals, seeds, everything. Why? Have you got pets?"

"Two cats."

"We're taking ten. If your cats are of opposite sexes and haven't been altered, I'll issue you a ticket for your two; you're the first to ask, and with cats we don't care about breeds—they all reduce to alley cats in one crossing anyhow. Naturally they'll have to pass a medical exam, and so will your friends. These tickets, by the way, are being issued by commercial agencies with no connection—no *visible* connection—to the government. That cover won't last long, so don't fail to apply for yours *instanter*."

"I won't. But there must be a price for all this. There always is."

"My dear fellow," de Tohil Vaca said, "I told you we valued you. I do hope you'll call off the strike, as an obvious and complete irrelevancy now; just help us keep the garbage down to a dull roar until we get the ships off, and don't, if you'll pardon me the pun, rock the boat. No other price, except for the tickets, which are the same price the old spacelines used to sell them for to the Moon: a thousand dollars—ostensibly, round trip. That's a part of the cover."

"I see. Well, many thanks." Alex arose, hardly seeing his surroundings. The audio system was still playing that damned tune, which he had always hated. At the door, he turned and looked back.

"Mr. Secretary—you're going, of course."

"No, I am not," de Tohil Vaca said, his pleasantly vapid face suddenly turning to stone. "I am the man who failed to prevent this horror, as I was charged by my office to do. My presence on the Moon would dissolve the last chance of man in the bitterest kind of political strife. Under no circumstances would I introduce such a serpent into this rock garden." Then, suddenly, he smiled. "Besides, I want to see the end. When Ragnarök comes, there ought to be somebody on the spot who is capable of appreciating the spectacle."

When the door closed behind Alex, he felt, aside from all his other burdens, somewhat less than three inches high.

On the way back to his own office, Alex found himself wondering how Fan would take it. He had almost automatically decided that Fan would have to be one of "his" three men. There was nobody of his own sex that Alex loved better, and besides, the man was omni-competent—almost as much so as he made himself out to be. (Hmmm . . . John Hilary, Alex's assistant, had better go, too. He was an expert on pressure systems, a good electronicist on the side, easy to get along with, and a vigorous forty *ae*.)

There was more than a little irony in Fan's being an obligatory survivor. He had lived an astonishingly full life, starting from the utmost poverty, leaving home at fourteen without a penny in his pocket, turning all kinds of odd jobs in a world where such jobs hardly existed any more, devouring the public library in every town he visited, eventually becoming a highly successful journalist until he got bored with the hours the job required him to keep, cranking out small but socially useful inventions at odd moments, and en-joying himself hugely every step of the way. The lives of most men, even when looked back at from the vantage point of half a century, by comparison resembled nothing so much as the slow growth of a forgotten turnip. Anything Fan accomplished from here on out would have to be regarded as a bonus.

And there was another side to the matter which might be even more important. Though Alex was nobody's adventurer, he had once faced death himself, but in retrospect it now seemed to have been very nearly a false alarm—an undifferentiated tumour of the mastoid process, of the same general class that struck many people these days, which had scared hell out of everybody concerned . . . and then turned out to be as easily operable as a hangnail, or almost.

Fan's experience had been quite different: he had been attacked by a mutated leukemia virus which had nearly cleaned out his bone marrow as thoroughly as if it had been sucked by a dog, leaving him virtually without any of the tissues necessary for generating blood cells. This had been followed, with utter inevitability, by a whole series of secondary infections for which it had been impossible to give him antibiotics—or, for that matter, even aspirin—because his natural immunity to any such foreign substances had been knocked out as well. And there was no treatment for the virus itself.

That siege had frightened nobody, for there was no doubt whatsoever that Fan was going to die. Fan's response was simply, "No thank you; not yet."

And so he hadn't. There was no explanation for that but Fan's own, which was preposterous: he claimed that he had directed his remaining blood-forming tissues to regenerate and get busy making antibodies against the virus, on pain of his extreme displeasure, and so of course they had. If you did not believe this analysis, Fan politely invited you to come up with one of your own.

It had become a moderately famous case history, and there were a good many medical research people who yearned for a few drops of Fan's blood to analyze for the antibodies. They had to go right on yearning, for any fooling around with Fan's blood was *verboten*. For nearly a year after his recovery, his attending physician had almost literally hovered over him night and day, waiting to slap a patch on him if he so much as cut himself shaving, until Fan tired of that too and told him to get out and go treat somebody who was *sick*, for God's sake.

That had all happened some years ago, but as a result Alex knew that few people in the world were as well equipped by temperament and by intelligence as Fan was to face the coming slaughter. If it had turned out that he had to stay behind, he would have watched the process with grave interest, and very likely some aesthetic pleasure. Rather like de Tohil Vaca, Alex thought; except that he had more confidence in Fan's ability to maintain his detachment to the end.

Maybe Fan ought to be left off the ship and asked to command the rock-tides to turn back. He would enjoy it so hugely if they did.

Now, who else? Juli, certainly; he would exercise that choice only because he had been given the power to do so and for no other reason, like an attorney's privilege for arbitrary challenge of a juror after all his challenges-for-cause had been used up. But the women were not the heart of the problem yet, for even with Juli ruled in, he had five more he could choose.

But since Fan had to go, and Hilary, he was left with only *one* more man. And very few of his male friends, he realized grimly, were really good for anything but amusing him . . . or, to put the matter more bluntly, flattering him and eating on his credit. Merlyn could be ruled out at once; he had no talents whatsoever, not even little ones, and besides had a vicious streak which would be dangerous in a small community. Grindford was a somewhat pleasanter person, with a demonstrated talent for survival; but what else could he do besides duck when he saw the egg approaching the fan? Not a damn thing, except brag about how irresistible he was to women. Even if the brags were true, which Alex gravely doubted, a great seducer would be nothing but a living fossil on the Moon, under the conditions de Tohil Vaca had specified.

Those two eliminations were easy, but from there on out the pain set in. All of the remaining men in the luncheon circle were creative in some slight degree—apparently equally slight, and all utterly negligible, until you examined them each on their merits under the new situation. Take Bang Jøhnsund, for instance: who on the moon could use a talent for writing the most moronic and endless kind of 3V serial? The answer might well be, *everybody;* surely, under such confined and near-hopeless conditions, a talent for taking people's minds off their troubles might turn out to be of tremendous value. Much of the same kind of value might inhere in Polar Pons; he entertained people, no, more, he told them things about their world that they needed to know in such a way that they thought they were being entertained while in fact they were learning. The fact that he had to simplify the information he imparted so well beyond the point of caricature—without knowing that he was doing so—counted against him, but he might shape up under pressure; almost everyone did.

Goldfarb Z and Tighe were only superficially easier cases. To be sure, the subject of Goldfarb Z's Cantos was unknown to everyone, including himself, since he had sworn not to develop the invisible ink he had been writing it in until he had finished the work. After that, he would read it, and probably change the title in the light of what he found; the present title was only a sort of running head or slug. But he *was* a poet, with a fair record of production behind him before he had undertaken the completely hermetic opus. The same could be said of Will Emshredder, though he worked in multimedia and thus—if one could judge from Goldfarb Z's working title— was of a completely opposite school. Obviously the lunar colony could not afford to be without a poet, but did Alex have to choose between schools as well, or was it only the genes for creativity that mattered? And Tighe was a scholar, and there again a propensity for scholarship might be more important than the fact that Tighe's particular field of study had no social utility on Earth even now, and would completely cease to exist on the Moon.

Although he had never given the matter any thought before, Alex had the feeling that poets were scarce commodities, whereas almost any other ten-man cadre might come up—literally—with a scholar. Which poet, then? Goldfarb Z, though gregarious, was also a man of almost impenetrable reserve; but even after all these years, Alex could not say he knew Emshredder any better, because the man was almost fumblingly inarticulate except when he was in front of his consoles. He thought he did not know which of the two he liked better, which was some small advantage, in that it made for at least a little impartiality. And sheerly on instinct, he felt that Will Emshredder had the larger talent. Very well; he should be the third man.

And promptly upon this decision, Alex found out what he had never known before: that it was in fact Goldfarb Z whom he liked better. It was astonishing how acutely painful the discovery was.

The pain became worse when he came to consider the women. Rosasharn had a limited talent—how limited, he had no way of assessing—but she was somewhat beyond her child-bearing years, and decidedly ugly to boot; taking her along would be a betrayal of one of the essential premises of the escape, if Alex had understood de Tohil Vaca on that point. By the same token, Girlie Stonacher was young, pretty, promiscuous and provenly fertile; she would fit into the proposed colonial society like a key into a slot, and furthermore enjoy it hugely. Count her in. The same terms, with some minor

reservations as to what era one was thinking about, had been said—
Alex did not know with how much truth—of Irene Pons; but how,
how, how could he give Irene a ticket and refuse one to Polar? And
would Irene go without him? And if she did, would she not feel the
guilt of her husband's death all the rest of her life, regardless of the
fact that it would be in no way her fault, and hate Alex for forcing
the choice upon her?

Worse was to come. He realized that he had been assuming all
along that Fan's wife Gradus would also be among the Chosen, not
specifically because she was Fan's wife but because she was the
quickest intelligence among all the woman, as well as being the most
beautiful. But in both these departments, Goldfarb Y was not far
behind and should surely be included; and the one emotion Goldfarb
Z had ever shown in public was a passionate devotion to her. Alex
was therefore in the position of having to part them forever, while at
the same time arbitrarily taking along his own Juli, who, though
pretty and sweet and good in bed, had a brain about the size of a
truffle, and no talent he had ever been able to discover.

This was a more painful case than that of Polar and Irene Pons—
not to them, but to Alex. The numbers simply and inexorably ruled
Polar out; Alex was entitled to only one man out of the group, and
he was morally certain that, having included one administrator and
one engineer, that third man should be a poet. But suddenly he
thought he saw a way out. It was genes that counted, wasn't it?
Wasn't it? And Will Emshredder had a daughter. . . .

Slowly, feeling as though he were dividing his own soul in two,
he drew a line through Will Emshredder's name and wrote down
that of Goldfarb Z.

It had never occurred to him before that the reason God demands
love of everyone is that He must feel overwhelmingly guilty.

The basement warehouse was huge, but there were not many
echoes in it; the Chosen were very subdued about their baggage-
checking. Juli examined her two cartons for the umpteenth time.
Twenty pounds and five cubic feet had not turned out to be much,
and in the end she had decided on taking almost nothing but keepsakes—and, of course, Splat! and Hausmaus, currently crouched in

a carrier on the labelling table, from which occasionally issued low, hoarse cat-howls of protest. Presumably Alex's cartons, which had already gone out, had been more practical.

Of course her cartons were not *all* keepsakes, really. She had also put together the best approximation she could think of to a survival kit, consisting of small tools, a medicine chest, blankets, and a few other such items, including a nest of plastic containers—no matter where a woman went, she would find some use for those. She hoped the teddy bear wouldn't be discovered; it probably wouldn't show up on the fluoroscope, except for its eyes, and there were several dozen other buttons, all loose, in that box. She knew the stuffed animals had no business being in there at all, but it had been the only toy she had ever had.

Well, if she had forgotten anything important, it was too late to include it now. Reluctantly she shoved the cartons onto the moving belt, which would carry them to the blimp for Rockland Spaceport. The cats ought to go now, too, but suddenly, seeing nobody else around her that she knew, she decided not to part with them just yet.

Where, above all, was Alex? Juli already had her reservation, but Alex had to confirm his own, and it was getting close to the time for the helicopter shuttle for today's flight (only the baggage went by blimp), on which they were both booked. He and the other people he had chosen, not without much agony, had been holding some kind of farewell party to the Earth, which she had chosen not to attend as likely to be entirely too painful. Had they all gotten drunk and lost track of the time?

She did not dare to go looking for him; suppose he should show up at the last minute and find her gone? But time passed on the big warehouse clock, and passed, and passed. . . .

The elevator doors to the shuttle closed for the last time today. The endless belt stopped moving. There was nobody human left in the warehouse but herself.

They had missed the flight.

Halfway between panic and fury, she picked up the cat carrier, the contents of which had fallen asleep but now resumed its moans and squalls of despair, and marched off to a telephone booth, where she phoned, first of all, the ticket agent. For more than half an hour she got nothing but a recording telling her all the lines were busy, which she had fully expected. The secret was not yet out, at last reports, but all the same that office must be a madhouse; just the rumour (there had been no announcement) that commercial lunar flights were being resumed had generated a tidal wave of would-be tourists.

At last she got through to a clerk. No, Dr. Stewart had not picked up his reservation. No, neither had Mr. ad Parnassum. Neither had any of the others.

Next, by citing the code formula which stood for (though the clerk did not know this) the real intent of the exodus, she reached the agent himself and made her plea.

"I'm-sorry-moddom, but you must understand that we have many standbys for each flight. Your seats were doubtless filled long ago."

"You don't understand. I know we've missed *this* flight. What I want to do is transfer our reservations to the next flight."

"I'm-sorry-moddom, but our instructions are strict. We cannot under any circumstances issue alternative tickets to no-shows."

"Now that's just silly. We weren't entirely no-shows. After all, our baggage is already *on* today's flight. What's the point of shipping all that baggage and then not sending the people it belongs to?"

"I'm-sorry-moddom, but I'm sure the people who took your seats will find some use for it."

"No, they won't." Juli began to cry, and at least half the tears were real. "No, they won't; it's almost all just keepsakes. Things that w-won't be valuable to anybody b-but us."

The agent had doubtless had to slosh his way through gallons of previous tears. "I'm-sorry-moddom, but regulations do not permit us to issue a second set of tickets."

"Oh, damn your regulations! Now listen, my . . . husband is the head of one of these groups of ten people, a, a cadre leader."

"There are hundreds of those, moddom. We are not allowed to treat them any differently than anybody else."

"But he's not just an ordinary cadre leader. He's somebody that Secretary de Tohil Vaca *particularly* wanted to go. The Secretary told him so, personally."

"I'm-sorry-moddom, but surely any faceless person could claim that over the telephone." In the background, people were shouting at him to answer another phone.

"If I were just anybody, how would I know the project code?"

"These things leak, moddom. Now if you'll excuse me—"

"Wait a minute," Juli said desperately. "Why would just anybody be asking for tickets under these particular names? You should have some sort of list with the names on them."

"Yes, moddom, we do, but for today's flight only. We cannot issue second chances."

"If you called the Secretary—" And then, right in the middle of this sentence, which in fact she did not know how she was going to end, she remembered that Alex's priority number was different from the secret project code number. She said: "My husband has priority number FHGR-One."

There was a long silence, except for the dim pandemonium in the background. She could only pray that the agent was looking the number up.

At last he was back. "I have confirmed the priority, moddom. I am therefore issuing you two reservations for tomorrow's flight."

"Oh . . . thank God. And thank you, too."

"Please bear in mind, moddom, that this is the last chance. The last, the final, the ultimate chance. Are you sure you understand that?"

"Yes, I do," she said gratefully. Her relief was so great that instead of flipping the hang-up toggle, she hit the shower toggle instead, and was promptly drenched with salt water. She hardly noticed.

The panic ebbed, but she was still worried. There might, after all, have been an accident. They might have all been killed, or anyhow hospitalized, on the very eve of escape. Oh God. She called the *Brackette de Poisson*.

And God damn them, they were there. They were *all* there.

Now free to feel completely unadulterated rage, she left a message for them with the management, put on her gas mask, snatched up the cats, and stamped out to flag down a water scooter.

The eight were still there when she arrived (after parking the grumbling cat carrier in the expensive supermarket next door, by polite but firm request of the restaurant's manager)—the eight who had survived Alex's playing God: three males (Fan, Goldfarb Z, and a man she placed vaguely as an engineer from Alex's office) and five females (Gradus, Girlie, Goldfarb Z's wife Y, Polar Pons' wife Irene, and Will Emshredder's divorced daughter Evadne).

Scanning this much constricted remnant of the old crew, and registering just exactly who remained of it here, Juli realized that more than the pains of choice and of partings had been involved here. There has also been a considerable spectrum of selfless sacrifice. With the realization, her righteous indignation began to simmer down toward the slightly more manageable level of simple resentment.

They all had indeed been drinking, but they did not look drunk. On the contrary, they were steady, quiet, and sombre. As for Alex, he did not look guilty, or even contrite; only inexplicably sad.

"Why are you all just *sitting* here?" she demanded, but with much less vehemence than she would have believed possible only a few minutes ago. "Alex, I got us another reservation, I fought like mad for it, but you have to pick it up right *now*—we won't be able to get another!"

"I'm sorry, sweetheart," he said in a low voice. "You pick yours up if you want to. I wish you would. But we're leaving ours for the standbys."

"What?" she said, feeling dizzy. "Standbys? You're—you're *not going?*"

"No," he said, lower still. "We're staying here."

Juli felt as though she had been gored by two icicles. Then she at long last let the hysteria sweep through her. Blindly, she let them lead her to a chair. They all tried to comfort her, more or less clumsily—only the women thought to produce handkerchiefs—but the clouds had been gathering far too long to be checked now.

"And I, I p-packed everything so carefully—all the, all the things I loved—the things you g-gave me—"

"Ssshh, dear," a woman's voice said. "It's all right."

"It's not all right, it's not all right! Now we'll not only die—we'll die without our things! Oh, Alex, I p-picked out a b-book for each of us—our toothbrushes—my t-t-t-t—"

The rest came in a howl, about which she could do absolutely nothing. Pats rained gently on her from various angles, making her cringe and want to fight at the same time. She knew defiantly that that last word was going to have been "teddy bear" and waited for them to laugh; but nobody did.

The woman's voice said:

"Juli, love, it doesn't matter . . . really it doesn't. No matter how else we die, we all die naked."

Perhaps—she would never know—this truism would have done Juli no good at all had it come from any other source; but she just at this point recognized the voice as that of Girlie Stonacher, the last person in the dying world from whom she would have expected the consolations of philosophy, even of the tritest sort. She got herself under partial control with a humiliatingly juicy sniffle, and allowed the women to finish mopping her face.

Only then could she manage to look again around the circle, out of eyes she was sure were as red as her nose. After a pioneering hiccup, she said:

"Alex, why didn't you tell me? Instead of leaving me alone in that awful warehouse, getting scareder and scareder—while you sat here with all the friends we—"

"I did tell you, Juli," he said. "I remember telling you very distinctly. I even remember when, and where."

Juli still felt so frustrated and confused that under any ordinary circumstances she would have believed him gladly. After long suspicion of men in general, she had come to believe that Alex really did have an odd sort of trick memory, especially after drinking; where some of her previous lovers had had convenient blackouts, or at least blank spots where their promises had been lodged, he instead quite convincingly—to both of them—remembered things that hadn't happened at all, in particular things he hadn't told her but knew he should have, and hence readily admitted to. It has been a source of trust, though not one she would have felt comfortable explaining to anyone else, even a woman.

But these were not ordinary circumstances. "Alex," she said, "I don't believe you."

Clearly, this didn't surprise him. Instead, at last, he did look shamefaced.

"Well," he said, "Juli, the fact is, I *didn't* tell you. You see, I wanted you to have the chance, whatever I'd decided about myself. After all, we could still be wrong."

That did it. Juli's sorrow and hurt vanished; she was right back to being furious again.

"Wrong about what?" she fumed, clenching her fists until the nails bit into her palms. "Won't *somebody* in this high-and-mighty crew tell me *why* we're all committing suicide? I'd kind of like the chance to make up my own mind!"

"I told you so," Gradus said to Alex. "But you wouldn't listen to me."

"Juli," Alex said. "I can't explain it myself. I don't have the training or the terms. And I couldn't quite face up to asking you to listen to hearing your life being explained away by Fan, with my consent. He's been wrong before."

"Do you believe him, Alex? Enough to stay behind?"

"Yes."

"Then I don't resent anything but your thinking that I'd want to go without you. Fan, explain it, will you? I'd really like to know. And somehow I'm not surprised to find you pronouncing our funeral oration. It seems sort of comfortable. Please speak, Fan, please."

"Thank you," Fan said. "I rise to the occasion."

But in fact he did not rise; he sat where he was, and spoke very quietly.

The only thing that puzzled me at first (*Fan said*) about our fairy friend de Tohil Vaca's theory—which made perfect sense otherwise —was the fact that *he* wasn't going to the Moon. That didn't seem to be in character with what I knew about the man. I talked to Alex about it, since after all I only know the Secretary by reputation, and Alex seemed surprised by it, too.

Alex gave the Secretary the benefit of being a more complex man than he had seemed. I never give any man such credit until he's proved it by a lifetime of complex reactions. The Secretary's history didn't deserve it; his public history, it seemed to me, accurately reflected what little depths he had. He certainly had never struck me as a natural martyr.

So I looked at the theory again. The Secretary had also told Alex that he wasn't a scientist, and by God, on that second look, I found out why he'd said so.

The theory *is* right, mind you. *But the Moon Project is wrong.* The Moon is no safer now than the Earth is. As the ice melts and the two precessional movements of the Earth's axis get more and more out of synch, the Earth's centre of gravity also is shifting. That will make the earthquakes even more violent, but we don't have to worry about that now; enough is enough; *es ist vollbracht.*

But in addition, the Earth-Moon system is a binary system—a pair of twin planets, or at least close enough to being one dynamically. Other planets have satellites bigger than the Moon: for instance, there's Saturn's satellite Titan, which is actually bigger than Mercury. But nowhere else in the solar system can you find a satellite which is a quarter the size of its primary.

One result of this is something we've known about ever since Herschel's time. The Moon raises very large tides on the Earth—that is, it exerts a significant amount of gravitational energy on the sea, the atmosphere, and even on the crust. Now, every action has an equal and opposite reaction, as poor old Newton told us, and the reaction has to show up somewhere. And it does. It shows up in the Moon's angular momentum, so that the Moon has been gradually drawing away from the Earth for millennia. I forget the rate—something in the nature of a few hundred feet per year, but I could be wrong by several orders of magnitude.

Suddenly—very suddenly—there's going to be a lot more mobile water on the Earth for the Moon to affect. Result: the Moon's velocity in its orbit is going to increase, equally suddenly. Viewed on a geological time scale, it will be one hell of a lurch.

At the same time, something *still* more drastic will be happening. Because the Moon is so big in proportion to the Earth, the Moon never has revolved around the exact centre of the Earth. Instead, the two bodies revolved around a common centre, which was inside the Earth, but not at the Earth's centre.

Both these centres—the centre of revolution of the twin planets, and the Earth's centre of gravity—are now shifting, both independently and in relation to each other. This change will feed back to

the Moon, too. And there is still some vulcanism on the Moon—
enough to shake it up drastically, since compared to the Earth, the
Moon is a low-density, rather fragile world. While new mountains
are being built here at home, all the sheer escarpments of the Moon
will be tumbling down on our colonies—those that great fissures in
the surface haven't swallowed in advance.

I suspect that this process has already started, and that it's why
the commercial flights to the Moon were cancelled so arbitrarily
five years or so ago. Or maybe not; I'm just guessing. If it hasn't
started, it will surely start soon.

I wish with all my heart that we'd had the sense to seed one of our
planets—or the stars, it could have been done—a long time in the
past. Did you know there was a starship in the planning stage in
1965? Well, there was. Even then it was clear to some people that
the Earth was too small and too vulnerable for us to risk the whole
future of our race on it alone. But instead, we killed off space-flight
almost entirely—and that's that.

And so (*Fan continued*) in the end I agree with Juli. If I have to
die, I too want to die with my *things*—under which I mean to sub-
sume my world, my history, my heritage, my race. Not in some
warren underneath a desert world that's fit for nothing but a quarry
for tombstones. Naked we come into the world, but we do *not* all die
naked; we have a choice. We can die naked on the Moon—or we can
go to Hell with Shakespeare.

I don't find the choice very difficult.

There was a small colour 3V in operation over the bar at the rear
of the restaurant, which Juli had ignored from the beginning. If she
had noticed it at all, she supposed she had assumed that it was tuned
to a baseball game, the only channel 3V sets in bars ever seemed able
to receive; and the audio volume was gratefully low.

But in the silence following Fan's peroration, she realized that
the announcer was talking about the resumption of traffic to the
Moon, and the imminent launching. Glancing up at the little holo-
gram tank, she saw the ship that she and Alex were supposed to be
on. It looked exactly like two raw onions, one white, one red, joined
by a mutual sprout. It occurred to her that they would probably

work better if they were boiled. The red sphere, the 3V announcer was overexplaining, was the power sphere, which had to be kept separated from the people, because of the radiation.

The vessel's immense size showed, however, by comparison with the crowd of spectators. There did seem to be a lot of them, held back only with difficulty by armed guards. The background murmur from them did not sound festive.

She felt tears beginning to come again.

"It seems so cruel," she said, almost to herself. "Luring all those people on such a hopeless journey. And so wasteful. Do you suppose the government really doesn't know? About the Moon?"

"Sure they know," Fan said. He reached for his beer bottle, but ten seconds earlier it had turned into counter polish. "They just don't care. Or maybe it's just that they've been lying to us for so long, they couldn't tell us the truth if they wanted to." Morosely, he mopped up his invention with his sleeve.

"Fan, that's a guess," Alex said. "And let me remind you, I do know de Tohil Vaca, and you don't, except by reputation, just as you said. I still don't think he's the villain you make him out to be. He knows there's a risk, and he told me—I think he told all the potential trippers —that there's a risk. He didn't say exactly what it was, but if he had, nobody would have wanted to go at all."

"And maybe," Goldfarb Z said, "he hopes that at least a few of the bases will survive, after all. That would explain the effort, the expense, the deception, and so on. Otherwise, why bother?"

Fan snorted. "Impossible . . . *Herr Ober*, another beer here! . . . And even supposing that . . . no, damn it, I want a *glass* bottle, not one of those dissolving ones . . . even supposing a few bases do survive, they won't have the resources, or the population, or the spirit to put together a second jump to Mars. If there are any survivors on the Moon—and I insist, it's impossible that there will be—they'll just die a little later of attrition. People can't hope if there aren't enough of them to keep each other hoping."

"Fan, as a psychologist you're a pain in the ass," Irene Pons said. "There's one thing you have to give de Tohil Vaca. He's given his passengers the chance to roll the dice. Which is more than we've got the courage to do. And I'll bet he knew exactly how many of us would chicken out, too."

"I do not play," Fan said stiffly, "with loaded dice. But since you insist, I'll give de Tohil Vaca one gold star: He did say, more or less vaguely, that the dice were loaded. It's a limited form of honesty, but honesty it is."

"And decency," Juli said. "Even pity."

"Pity? Juli, I love you, but sometimes you're rather hard to follow."

"I mean, here *I* am, with Alex, and people I love around me— and I've even still got Splat! and Hausmaus. So—I mean, oh well, that's not so bad, after all. But for most of the people who're going on the trip . . . do you think they'd be going if they had anyone to love? Someone to help them look death in the eye? And for them, isn't it better to have a little hope? Better than just to stand around, waiting for the end, like so many snowmen waiting for a thaw?"

"By God, Juli," Goldfarb Z said softly, "I love you too."

"It's a nice notion," Fan said, "but it's Juli's alone, I'm afraid. That kind of motive doesn't ordinarily move governments into spending billions of dollars on a foredoomed project."

"What good is a dollar now?" Alex demanded. "And what else would be worth spending it on instead? Now? Not sewage, I can tell you that, and the Secretary knows it. He told me so, and damn bluntly, too."

Fan shrugged. "I can't quite see them breaking the thinking habits of a century," he said. "But on the other hand, it doesn't cost *me* a cent to give them credit for compassion. Blessed be thee, de Tohil Vaca."

There was another silence, underlined by the rumbling of the crowd at the spaceport, now sounding somehow ominous. By un-spoken assent, they turned their chairs to watch the tank.

Juli found herself calm, resigned, washed out. She was even interested in seeing the take-off, though such things had never interested her before; and not entirely because her "things" were on board. Goldfarb Z ordered another round of drinks.

A moment later, the floor twitched under them, like the hide of a horse trying to dislodge persistent flies. Bottles fell from the bar. The 3V image flickered, and the crowd roar from it swelled suddenly.

Most of the customers at the bar made for the door, at speed, and almost everyone around the table sprang up. Chairs fell over.

Fan shot out one hand and grabbed Gradus by a wrist. "Sit down," he said. "Where are you running to?"

"That was an earthquake," she said glacially, "in case you hadn't noticed."

From the 3V the roar grew louder. Juli saw that the crowd was rushing the ship. Evidently, the secret was finally out. Then there was a dull sound of sneeze-gas grenades going off.

"Really, Fan," Goldfarb Y said, "it's better to be out of doors in an earthquake. Everybody knows that."

"If that was ever true," Fan said, "it doesn't apply any more."

There was a second shock, and the 3V gave up entirely.

"Damn," Fan said. "I wanted to watch that. Alex, how tall is this building?"

"Seventeen stories, but the elevators only go up to the fifteenth. If they're still running at all."

"The lights are still on."

"But supposing the elevators quit on us while we're up there?" Girlie said.

"Suppose they do?" Fan said. There was silence. He went on:

"Girlie, do you really care what floor you die on? Wouldn't you rather see the first survival ship leave—or whether or not the quakes and the mob even let it leave—than run around in the street like a mouse? Let's be human beings to the end, goddam it. I'm going up. The rest of you can suit yourselves."

"Me too," Juli said. But she took Alex's hand with great determination.

And there below them was the Earth, and its wide sky of islands; and the towers of the city to the south. It was a bright day; they could see the fugitive highlights of the sun glancing off the canals of lower Manhattan. It was all quite beautiful. Juli thought her heart ought to be breaking, but in fact she felt only a vast, free exhilaration. Soon it would all be gone; but she had never expected to outlive it. What filled her heart, instead, was something oddly like gratitude.

"There she goes!" Fan cried out suddenly, almost with joy. She felt his hand on her shoulder, turning her around to face towards the northwest. A thin, towering plume of pure white steam was rising slowly on the western horizon, rising, rising. . . . For an instant, just above its tip, there was a splintery flash of metal. Then the plume began to twist and drift.

There was a strange sound from the little party on the roof, a little like a sob, a little like a cheer.

"They made it," Goldfarb Y said, like a prayer.

Then the building jerked like a whip under their feet, and the sound turned to screams and hoarse yells. Asphalt and gravel ripped into Juli's knees and palms. A roar floated up from the city, laced with still fainter screams, like the glints of sunshine on the water.

"My God," the nameless engineer was saying mechanically. "My God. My God."

Alex's hands grasped her, helped her to her feet, steadied her. The building was still swaying a little. Once more, they were all looking south.

Not far away—perhaps ten or fifteen blocks—a few small, old buildings were toppling and sliding down into rubble and dust, unheard in the general uproar. Juli scarcely noticed them, nor did the others seem to be watching that. Much farther downtown, perhaps in what had once been the financial district, or else from the waters of Red Hook or Park Slope, a thick, dense column of black fumes was rising toward the risen half-Moon, like a Satanic mockery of the trail of the vanished ship. It made a sound like the full diapason of some gigantic organ.

"Fissure," Fan shouted, in an otherwise perfectly neutral voice. "I do hate to see my predictions jump the gun like that. It might make people think I lack influence in the proper quarters."

"*Your* predictions, Fan?" Alex said ironically.

"Certainly. That break's in Brooklyn Heights or thereabouts. That's where I said it would open if the injection wells were responsible. So you see the Secretary and I were both right."

"How nice for you both," Gradus said, but for once there was no malice in her voice. Of course she was all ready to die naked, having been dressing the part for many years; but no one else seemed at all alarmed any more. Irene and Evadne were weeping silently, but without even seeming to notice it.

The black fumes rose in the bright sky. Gradually, they parted at the top, and began to spread gently, parallel to the horizon, as if along some low air stratum. The striations fanned out a little to the west as they drifted; the hinge of that fan did seem to be focused somewhere over the near shore of Brooklyn.

"Temperature inversion," Fan said. "New York's last smog attack."

"Omniscient to the last," Gradus said.

"It's funny," Juli said. "I mean, it's odd. I never thought of it before."

"Of what?" Alex said, taking her hand.

"That everything means something special, no matter what it is, if you know it'll never happen again. Even smog."

The dark striations floated toward them, their shadows making broader stripes over the groaning city in the brilliant sunshine. Were they just parts of widening circles? Or had the prevailing winds also changed? Or—

The roof lurched again. Evadne, who had been standing closest to the parapet, would have gone over it had the unnamed engineer not grabbed her. A cornice fell off and went smashing down the setbacks toward the street.

"There won't be," Fan said gently, "any flight tomorrow. Good-bye, all."

The cats!

With a cry, Juli raced for the stairwell. Alex called after her, something about the danger and the power being off, but she did not care.

She was almost fainting with exhaustion by the time she reached the dust-choking, bombarded street, and another temblor threw her to her knees just in front of the smashed glass display windows of the expensive supermarket. Shaking her dirty hair out of her face, she got up again and staggered inside.

"Hausmaus! Splat!"

There was a dim cry. Inside, the cement and plaster dust was almost impenetrable, but she could see vaguely that the place had been looted before the last panic had struck. Not only were there cans, bottles, and packages lying where the shocks had thrown them, but there were also a number of half-filled string bags and two-wheeled pushcarts abandoned near the door.

"Here, kitty! Kitty, kitty!"

Three or four meows responded. Through her watering, gritty, gas-inflamed eyes she seemed to be seeing thousands of cats. And indeed there were a great many. The carrier was where she had left it, half buried under a pile of loose cornflakes, diet cookies, and other things that had burst out of fallen pasteboard packages; but the door had fallen open and it was empty.

Through the haze and the tears, she was able finally to make out that all those thousands of cats were actually only a store cat and four squealing, barely ambulatory kittens. Then she saw Splat!, who somehow had managed to scramble to the top tier of a display rack which still held a few canned goods. He was too fat to get back down by himself, or at least that seemed to be his theory, and Juli decided to leave him there for the moment. He would be no safer anywhere else, and as long as he was treed like that, she would at least know where to find him.

"Hausmaus? Hausmaus?"

There was another violent earth shock. The entire front of the store crunched down to about half its previous height, and masonry roared into the street in front of it. Overhead, parallel to the street, a beam burst through the plaster of the ceiling, one end hanging free. Instantly changing her mind, Juli grabbed Splat! and stuffed him back in the carrier, followed by a kitten who happened to be in reach, and latched the door.

Was there another way out of the store? Yes, a door that evidently gave into the lobby of the building. It was wooden and had split at the top; its frame was twisted.

"Hausmaus! Here, puss!"

Another shock.

"Juli!"

It was Alex. He was pounding on the door, which evidently was locked, jammed, or both. "Juli, Juli, where are you?"

There was the sound of a heavier blow, as if he had kicked the door. Juli tugged frantically at the knob. It would not give.

He kicked the door again, and almost at the same time, there was another tremor. Part of the bottom panel fell out of the door. Juli dropped to her hands and knees, and found Alex facing her on the other side in the same position. He could not see her, however, for blood was streaming into his eyes from a slash which ran diagonally across his forehead and up over his scalp.

"Alex, here I am!"

She heard Splat!'s hoarse Siamese cry behind her, and then he was clambering clumsily over her calves. Evidently the door to the carrier had come open again.

"Juli—"

She reached out for Alex. As her hand touched his cheek, there was still another shock, and the free end of the ceiling beam began to fall, slowly at first. Juli felt the soft, familiar thump of Hausmaus landing on his frequent perch between her shoulder blades, and